D.A. Dwinell

# *The Bloom's Cradle*

## Guardian of the Stone
BOOK TWO

D.A. Dwinell
The Bloom's Cradle
This book is a work of fiction, and the events, incidents, locations, and characters are products of the author's imagination or are used fictitiously. Any resemblance to actual persons, living or dead, businesses, companies, organizations, events, or locales is entirely coincidental.
Copyright © 2021, D.A. Dwinell
Self-published

This book is dedicated to my three children, Austin, Samantha, and Jacob. You have brought such joy to my life.

Special thanks go to Audrey, Bill, Maryanne, Mark, Stephanie, Tammy, and Tim. You have helped me make my dreams come true.

# One

I'm sitting at the desk in the library trying to find additional details about the case of Picasso's "Le pigeon aux petits pois" or as we called it "Pigeon with Pea". The news had a surveillance video showing the stolen painting being returned to the Paris Museum. Interviews with illusionists were being blown up on social media. Each one had their theory on how two mysterious masked people could suddenly appear on the surveillance cameras, drop off the stolen Picasso painting, and suddenly vanish. They had some interesting theories. It was my understanding the detectives were also interviewing illusionists, but they were being closed-lipped about the case with the press. I had become obsessed to the point I was neglecting my studies.

I needed a break and decided to go for a run before starting my homework. I neglected to check the weather, so I immediately regretted my decision. It was 46 degrees and damp. The cold air filled my lungs as I inhaled. Very few people were out. I usually passed people walking their dogs and mother's taking their toddlers for a stroll.

I thought about my mother not understanding the obsession I had with the case. I could not share with her the reasons behind it. That was something that must remain between Greg, Phyllis, and myself. My boyfriend, Greg, and I had discussed a quick trip to Paris to see if we could discover what they knew about the two people. Extraordinarily little was being released to the public. We decided we should stay far away from there out of fear they might discover it was us that returned the painting.

As I dried my hair, the warmth of the hot air was soothing. I thought about the few times Greg, and I went to the Granaldi's house in Italy. We listened to the recording pen we hid in Anthony's room and watched the surveillance cameras we set up. For our safety, we stayed away for a while. The few times we checked in on them, we remained invisible, and eavesdropped on their conversations.

I continued my thoughts as I applied my makeup. During one conversation, they were fuming about us taking the painting and the ring from Anthony's hand. However, they seemed most angry about us returning the Picasso to the museum. The last few times we went to their home they were gone.

My thoughts were interrupted by Greg.

**GREG:**          Guess what…I love you.

He was a sweetheart. I sent him an emoji blowing a kiss.

I continued applying my makeup. *Perhaps they were hiding out to prevent their arrests.* We had not seen them. *Perhaps they think their fingerprints were still on the painting.* They did not know, we had to wipe the painting clean of prints before we returned it to the museum. I had touched it without gloves. *I won't make that mistake again.*

I finished getting ready for class and headed downstairs to grab something to eat. Phyllis left a note on the counter. She had gone grocery shopping. I scanned the items in the refrigerator. There was leftover chicken soup. I heated up a bowl and sat at the counter to eat.

My thoughts returned to the Granaldis. My guard was up. I was certain they would retaliate. Greg and I were still training to develop our spy skills. Not just in karate and parkour, but other skills needed for spying. We had even begun going places and pretending we were different people to blend into a variety of crowds while working on our observation skills. As I thought about the various things we had done, I smiled. It was fun pretending to be someone else.

I was reminded about us practicing our surveillance skills with some people at the mall; thinking I was far enough out of the walkway when my arm moved forward awkwardly because a woman ran right into it. She looked around with a look of confusion. The woman proceeded in the direction she was headed. I was grateful we were invisible, but it still made me nervous.

I blew on my soup. This reminded me of the soup I had in Italy. The villa was amazing. I was free to go there and stay in my reserved room whenever I liked. I would not have that luxury everywhere I traveled. Greg and I had ordered our passports, but they had not arrived yet. We were still working on the details about how we would get them stamped. Since we do not use the normal means of transportation, we would need to study the procedures. Using the Bloom of Dreams to travel was better than dealing with the long lines and frustrations of traveling by plane, train, or bus. It had its disadvantages though. It was difficult to arrive and make sure no one knew of our teleportation abilities.

the time. I rinsed my dishes and put them in the dishwasher. I grabbed a bottle of water and my lunch from the refrigerator.

During the drive, I thought about what a blessing the Bloom of Dreams and its powers were to me. It was a lot of responsibility. It bothered me Mom still did not know the power this stone carries. I wondered what other powers it might possess now that it is in its cradle. The only new power we had discovered since placing it in the cradle was the power to heal a person I touched. I did not know if it would heal me if I was injured. For now, the mysteries it held would remain a secret. My focus needed to be on my classes.

I pulled into the parking lot and circled it several times as I looked for a spot. A couple of students were headed to the lot. I watched them to ensure I got one of their spots. This semester was nearly over. Greg and I would see if we could discover other secrets it might hold.

I was early and had a few minutes before class. It was too cold to sit outside. I sat on the floor across from my classroom. I looked down at the stone. I only knew the stone allowed me or anyone touching me to transport to a familiar place. The stone also warned me of danger. It must be used with a mirror or something allowing me to see my reflection. If it was large enough, I could walk into the reflection. Of course, the small compact mirror my grandmother gave me with the necklace was not big enough to walk into, but it sucked me in and pushed me out to the destination I pictured. I chuckled as I thought about how I would flop all over the floor when I first began teleporting. Now I could easily land in whatever way I needed to.

During class, I tried to stay focused on my professor, but Phillip popped into my mind. We had not heard from my cousin Phillip, which I was glad about. Knowing he was working with the Granaldi family to get the stone made him dangerous. My mother and he talked on the phone about when he would visit again. No word when he was planning his next visit. Perhaps he was lying low as well. As a relative, Phillip was the black sheep of the family. Surely there were nicer relatives to get close to.

The instructor began walking around the class as she talked. I started taking notes on everything she was saying. Once class was over, I headed to my next class. I saw Jacob and Juliet talking as they walked to their next class. It occurred to me that nearly every time I saw Juliet walking around on the campus, she was with him. I thought about talking to them, but they seemed to be enjoying their time together. *They would make a cute couple.* I walked quickly to the next building to get out the cold. I was still not used to this weather. It was days like this I missed Florida.

I was sitting at my desk waiting for class to begin when my phone vibrated.

**MOM:**           Lance and I have a dinner date tonight.

Mom and Lance had been seeing a lot of one another. She had not brought him by the house yet or introduced me to him. I think she was afraid he would see the house and realize she had money. My mother was not letting the money she inherited from grandma get to her head though. Mom rarely spoils herself. She had a lady come in and help Phyllis, our housekeeper and cook, twice a week because we were messier than my grandmother Lillie ever was. I could tell Phyllis appreciated it. It allowed her to spend more time with her sister and occasionally I took her to Italy to see Leonardo and Isabella.

As I sat in my last class before Thanksgiving break, I thought about my career. Currently, I was a Journalism major, but not sure that was the direction I should go. As the guardian of the Bloom of Dreams, I was developing new skills. This had caused me to rethink my major.

I needed a career with a flexible schedule. A better understanding of the law and access to information was important to help me protect the Bloom of Dreams and its cradle. Therefore, I considered changing my major to Criminal Justice or Law Enforcement. At eighteen, I had already broken so many laws trying to stop the Granaldi family and protect the stone. They say police must think like a criminal and I believe attorneys should too.

At least everything I had done was not for criminal activity. It was to protect the stone at all costs. I had broken into a home, stolen, and helped install surveillance cameras and listening devices in the home I broke into. Whatever I decided, I needed to figure it out soon. I needed to register for my spring classes before all the slots were filled.

After leaving class, I headed straight to my car. *Who's standing near my car?* I was too far away to tell. As I was approaching the vehicle, I noticed he was a tall man. The silhouette told me it was not one of the Granaldi brothers. As I got closer, I noticed the person appeared to be reading a book. When I was close enough, I realized it was Juliet's friend Jacob. I called out to him. The man seemed to be about 6'3". When I was nearly at my car door. I realized it was Jacob.

"I'm glad I caught ya before my class," he said as I unlocked my car.

I opened the door and tossed my backpack into the passenger's seat. "Is everything okay?"

He told me about Juliet. They had become rather close. Jacob wanted my opinion of him inviting her over for Thanksgiving to meet his family. As I thought about my answer, I realized Juliet had not told me they were dating. I knew she was interested in him. Jacob and I had spoken a little, but I was glad he came to me. Juliet and Jacob were seemed to like one another but did not seem to have the courage to do anything about it. I felt I could give him the advice he needed.

I asked him some questions to find out where they were in their relationship. It turned out it was nothing more than a friendship at this point. "Perhaps it's a little early for that. Being too eager might scare her. Take her out on a few dates first," I advised.

Jacob agreed. We had begun discussing what type of date he should take her on. Juliet was from Hawaii and was missing her friends and family, so I suggested the restaurant Pokehana because it served authentic Hawaiian food. Jacob could bring a little of Hawaii to her.

He expressed his nervousness about asking her out and how to move their relationship to more than friends. Jacob had little experience in dating. Jacob was a tall, thin, and attractive guy. Focused on his studies, he had a passion for computer work. When his walls were down, his sense of humor emerged. Jacob led a rather sheltered life. He explained he had never let girls distract him until now. Juliet had caught his eye. She was smart and beautiful with her tan skin coloring and dark hair and eyes. After some discussion, we agreed we would double date, if Juliet agreed to it. The location of the date would be a surprise. We said our goodbyes, and I headed home.

As I drove up to our new home, I looked at the large three-story brick house. *Wow, my life had changed.* Mom and I lived in a small apartment in Florida. Now we live in this grand house. I pulled toward the back of the house by the garage and remembered all the fun times my grandmother and I had while she was alive. She loved this house. Despite the massive size of the home, it had always felt cozy and warm.

My grandmother had a wonderful love of antiques and decorated every room herself. As I entered the house, I expected to find Phyllis in the kitchen whipping up one of her scrumptious dinners. As the door swung open, the aroma of her cooking did not greet me. With my backpack slung over my shoulder, I sprinted up the stairs toward my room on the second floor. As I approached the library, my eye glimpsed at Phyllis sitting at the desk. She was focused on a picture of my grandmother. The picture was from one of their many adventures together. I knew the loss of my grandmother had been hard on Phyllis because she lost her best friend.

Phyllis had done a good job hiding her emotions about her loss. This made me think about losing Greg or Mechelle. It would be awful. I attempted to sneak by, but Phyllis looked up and inquired about my day. Quickly summarizing, I began telling her about my conversation with Jacob. Phyllis had not met Juliet yet because we hung out after class, or we meet somewhere. She listened until I concluded the details of my day.

It was then Phyllis let me in on her latest discovery. "Your mother told me Lance will be coming to Thanksgiving dinner. Not knowing how you would feel, I wanted to give you a heads up. It's been just you and your mother for so long now. She really seems to like him and wants this to go well."

Thankful she had given me a heads up, I planted a kiss on her left cheek before heading to my room. It had begun to feel like someone had placed a brick on my chest. Not sure I wanted to speak with anyone, I closed my door for privacy. I dropped my backpack and plopped myself on my bed and tried to compose the emotions I was feeling from the news about my mother and Lance.

*Is my mother serious about him?* She had never introduced me to anyone before because she always wanted to make sure it would last, and they never did. *Is it possible I could have a stepfather soon?* They had not been seeing each other very long. My mind was racing about how much my life would change if she remarried. Deep in thought about my future, I jumped when Mechelle's text came in.

**MECHELLE:** Can you chat?

Mechelle and I had not seen each other since she flew up from Florida and surprised me on my birthday at the beginning of the summer. We caught each other up on everything. It had been hard not telling her about the Bloom of Dreams and its cradle, but for her own safety, she should not know.

I grabbed my computer to figure out what I should change my major to and what classes to register for. Criminal Justice might be a good fit. Criminal Behavior classes could help me with understanding the Granaldis along with more prerequisites. I set up an appointment with my advisor the following week to discuss my change in major. I could not tell her about the genuine reasons for the change. I had to limit those who know about the Bloom of Dreams. If I went to law school, I could open a law practice. It would allow me to make my own hours. From what I gathered; I would not need to worry about money. I needed a suitable career as a cover.

Everyone knew my grandmother's family had money. She did not need a cover story. Everyone, including myself, just thought she was seeing the world like other rich people. Phyllis and she described their travels that way, too. It was not until I became the protector of the stone; I realized why she really traveled so much.

I heard my phone vibrate and noticed a text from Juliet asking me to call her. I bet Jacob asked her to dinner. Curious, I called her back.

She was excited he was interested in her. Juliet seemed surprised I was aware of the date. I assured her she needed to hear it from him. We talked about what she would wear. Despite her persistence, the restaurant was still a secret. I wanted to suggest a Hawaiian dress, but it was too cold.

After my call, I noticed the time. I went to see if Phyllis needed help with dinner. Before my foot hit the last stair, the aroma of garlic filled the air. I entered the kitchen and found Phyllis removing the side muscle from the scallops. This was a skill she taught me many years ago. I offered my help. Phyllis put me on salad duty. I washed the spinach for the spinach, pear, and pomegranate salad. While the spinach dried, I chopped toasted walnuts and collected the pomegranate arils. Phyllis and I discussed the double date.

As I removed the arils from the skin of the pomegranate, it reminded me of when my friends and I would sit out in the yard and eat these during the summer. I collected three quarters of a cup as per Phyllis's instructions and then moved on to the pears, which I cored and sliced. Meanwhile, Phyllis was making the salad dressing. She asked me how I felt about Lance coming to dinner.

I turned to her, with a bemused look, "I'm not sure."

She pulled the brussel sprouts out of the oven and began stirring them. They looked amazing, as did the au gratin potatoes. Phyllis said, "My suggestion, give him a chance. You might find you like him." She began making a lemon sauce for the vegetables.

I placed the baby spinach in the bowl. On the outer rim of the bowl, I lined pear slices making sure they were all facing the same direction. I nestled the crumbled feta in the center of the salad. I took a quick scan of the counter to see what I should place next. Phyllis handed me a half cup of dried cranberries. I sprinkled them over the entire salad and grabbed the pomegranate arils repeating the process. It looked beautiful. As I admired my work, Phyllis began cleaning up the dishes we used to prepare dinner. I heard mom's car coming down the driveway. I took the salad to the table and headed back to the kitchen. Through the glass in the back door, I saw mom heading up the stairs. I opened the door. Mom appeared tired. I asked, "How was your day?"

"Busy. My boss got back into town today. He gave me a lot to do before a 10:00 am meeting tomorrow. I should be able to finish everything up, but I'll need to go in early tomorrow." She turned to Phyllis. "Everything smells amazing."

Mom headed out of the kitchen. Every night she placed her things at the desk in the foyer. She returned without her purse and jacket and began making herself a glass of sweet tea.

Phyllis had scallops searing. She began pulling the other items from the oven.

Earlier Phyllis had set the table. I made everyone a drink. Mom placed the potatoes and the brussel sprouts on the table. We waited in the dining room for Phyllis to bring the scallops and herself to join us for dinner.

As she entered, I noted the caramelization on the top of the scallops. Phyllis settled herself into her chair before mom began saying the grace. Dinners were casual around the house when it was just the three of us. Mom did not expect Phyllis to plate everything. We served the food right out of the pans she cooked in to allow Phyllis less work. At first, she had a hard time with it. I think she had accepted it because it gives her more free time for herself.

We were about halfway through the meal when mom brought up Thanksgiving. "I'd like to invite Lance over for dinner for Thanksgiving. How'd you feel about that?"

I had mixed emotions. On one hand, I want her to be happy. On the other hand, I do not want to share her. The thought of them getting married scared me. I knew it was selfish of me, but I needed to give him a chance. I told her, "I'd like to meet him." This was true. I was not sure about sharing my Thanksgiving with him. She looked pleased with my answer. I then asked, "With him coming, Phyllis will still be able to eat with us, won't she?"

Phyllis jumped into the conversation, "I'll only be serving the meal. I'm celebrating with my family. Your mother wants to eat at 1:30 pm, which would allow me time to get everything cleaned up and be with my family for dinner. The leftovers will be your dinner."

"You could still eat lunch with us," I informed her.

"That'd be nice, but I've got family coming from out of town. I want some quality time with them. I'll be staying there through the weekend," she notified me.

After we had finished dinner, we worked together, cleaning the kitchen before we headed to our rooms for the evening.

# Two

It was nearly time for Lance to arrive. I finished my makeup and headed down to see if mom needed me to do anything. She was nowhere to be found. Phyllis was in the dining room fussing with the flower arrangement. "Where's mom?"

"She has not come back down yet," Phyllis informed me. She then looked me over and told me how nice I looked. I chose my burgundy lace skater dress. From the waist up was lace. The lace on the sleeves revealed my skin. The bottom of the dress flared out much like an ice skater's outfit but was not as short. It hit me mid-thigh. My hair was curled, which created long, light brown ringlets that complimented my face. I used my hair wand, and it looked beautiful. The sound of footsteps coming down the stair's signaled mom was coming down, so I headed toward the foyer to see what she was wearing.

Mom looked fantastic in her long-sleeved collared floral dress. It was taupe with orange and rust-colored flowers, perfect for Thanksgiving. The dress hit her mid-calf, and she had on cute boots with it. She looked nervous, so I complimented her on her dress. Mom and I went into the sitting room to wait for Lance to arrive.

As I sat there looking around the room, I wondered what Lance would think about our home. *Would the grandeur of the antiques and the massive pocket doors in nearly every room on the first floor intimidate him? Then there's the grand staircase and the woodwork. Will he want to explore the home? Would mom even take him upstairs? I pray he is a good man, but I have my guard up.*

When we heard the doorbell, my heart skipped a beat. Mom shot me a look as though she did not know what to do. I told her I would get the door.

As I started to get up, she stopped me. "No, it should be me." Before heading to the door, she took one last look at herself in the mirror behind the bar.

I stood up and waited in the sitting room for her to return with him.

I could hear them chatting for a moment, and then she escorted Lance into the drawing room. He was a little overweight man, about 5'10", with grey hair and a goatee, wearing a blue-collared button-up shirt and black slacks. Lance smiled and said, "Brooke, it's nice to meet you."

He had a friendly smile and seemed nice, but my nerves were getting to me. I wished Greg were here with me, but he went hunting every Thanksgiving with his dad and uncle. He would not be back until about 4:30 pm.

We sat down. Phyllis gave Mom and Lance wine and me a sweet tea. Phyllis put out wild mushroom tartlets and a platter of baked brie with slices of a baguette for us to enjoy before dinner. Lance seemed to enjoy them both. Mom and I just picked a little. I think mom and I were both nervous. She did not even look at the tartlets, and they were her favorite. I barely ate because my nerves about meeting Lance were getting to me. I felt a little short of breath. *Calm down, Brooke. You knew this day would come.*

Lance asked me some questions about school and how I liked it in Kentucky. Providing only brief answers, I realized I was being rude. *What could I ask him? What do I know about him? Nothing, that is what I know.*

Lance began looking around the room. "This is a beautiful home. You were modest in your description of it, Sandra."

Mom told him about the history of the home and how she came to own it. It seemed like forever before Phyllis announced dinner was being served. I glanced at the clock and realized it had not been long. The conversation bored me.

We grabbed our glasses and headed into the dining room. Mom sat at the end of the table. I sat to her left, and he sat to her right, which gave him a view into the sitting room. Phyllis brought us our first course, which was butternut squash soup. I was not a fan of squash, but they seemed to enjoy it. Not being rude, I ate half the bowl.

To be polite, I inquired about his family. I wanted to know why he was not with his own family on a major holiday.

He explained it was just him. He had no siblings, and his parents had died. Phyllis served us a walnut and apple salad with raspberry vinaigrette. This I enjoyed. The dressing was amazing. I thought about licking my plate, but I refrained. The entrée was turkey breast

12

roulade, cornbread stuffing, Yukon gold mashed potatoes, asparagus, and cranberry relish. For dessert, we had pumpkin cheesecake.

Everyone agreed the meal was fantastic. We discussed Phyllis being an artist in the kitchen. The food was the only thing interesting during dinner. Lance and my mother had a great deal to talk about. They started comparing Phyllis's food to the food at the restaurant they met at. He appeared to be impressed with her cooking skills.

"She could open a restaurant of her own. She's so talented," he suggested.

After dinner, I excused myself and headed to the kitchen to help Phyllis so she could leave to enjoy time with her family. When we finished, I helped her load some food she had made for her Thanksgiving dinner and her suitcase into her car before saying goodbye. I headed back into the house and found mom and Lance seated in the sitting room chatting about their lives.

I sat down with them, knowing I had not really given Lance a chance, and started talking to him again. When I let my guard down a little, I discovered he had a great sense of humor. Mom seemed pleased by my change in behavior. I discovered it was not possible for Lance and his wife to have children. This affected their marriage, which resulted in divorce. His ex-wife was now living in Indiana, and they had not talked in over ten years. He was an Insurance Sales Agent that enjoyed fishing and loved to grill. Lance promised us a barbeque when the weather warmed up in the spring.

In the middle of the discussion on what to barbeque, I got a text from Greg inviting us over for dinner. I did not want to be rude and mention it while Lance was here, so I waited to respond until I could find out if mom wanted to go. We continued chatting for a while, and then mom went to get them some coffee and I followed her to fill my drink and tell her about the text.

She said she would go if Lance went home but told me I could go either way. I texted Greg to let him know what was going on. We returned to the sitting room and began discussing his love for fishing.

I decided to give them some privacy, I told Lance it was nice to meet him before I excused myself and headed to my room. Feeling stuffed from the delicious meal, I laid down on my bed and began texting my friends to wish them the best. I then moved on to scanning social media.

Bored. I decided I should spy on Mom and Lance. I stood in front of my full-length mirror and struggled with the idea. *This is the only way I am going to know where they are in their relationship.* After convincing myself I had a logical reason, I confirmed I had the compact mirror my grandmother gave me. I looked into my full-length mirror and pictured myself invisible in the foyer. I could see they were still sitting on the sofa, but they were sitting closer together and were holding hands. Quietly and slowly, I made my way through the mirror to the pocket door at the opening of the room.

Mom was telling him about Greg, "He impressed me the day I met him, and he continually impresses me. Greg treats my daughter well and has even taught her karate. He said she's exceptionally good, but I haven't seen her doing it. Before coming here, she was not athletic at all. Now she's in great shape and seems so happy."

"It sounds like they spend a lot of time together," he commented.

"Yes, I think they're getting serious. It's hard to believe she's grown up so fast," she stroked her free hand up his arm.

Lance leaned in to kiss my mother. I was not expecting that. *Ya, nope. That is enough for me.* I quickly made my way to the comfort of my bed. Trying to recover from what I just witnessed. I do not remember mom and dad being affectionate like that. Initially, my stomach felt uneasy, but it eased up the more I thought about how happy mom seemed.

Trying to take my mind off what I had seen, I thought about my landing. I was so proud of myself for not being tossed like a fish flopping all over the ground. No more of that nonsense. I had the ability to land firmly on my feet.

It was nearly 5:00 pm, so I touched up my makeup and checked my hair before heading downstairs. Mom was in the sitting room reading a book entitled, One Amazing Moment. I knocked on the wood paneling on the side of the room entryway and asked, "Is Lance gone?"

She placed her bookmark in her book. "Yes. He has been gone for about an hour now. Is it time to head over to Greg's?"

"Yes."

She looked at her watch, put her book down, and then got up. "Guess, I best go freshen up."

I decided to check out the book mom was reading and found myself reading it until Mom returned. "This is interesting. Let me know when you are done with it," I said placing it back where I found it.

Mom asked me to help her find something to bring to dinner. We headed to the kitchen to see if Phyllis had made anything that would be acceptable to bring. Everything we found was either not cooked or was our leftovers. Searching the pantry, I noticed a mini wine refrigerator built into the shelving. "There's wine in here," I informed my mother.

Mom looked through the wine to see which one she would bring. She took one out. "Good find Brooke. Let's grab our coats."

Mom had not spent a lot of time with Greg's family, they had met a few times when they would see each other coming and going from their homes. Karen, Greg's younger sister, answered the door and cheerfully invited us in. I noticed mom looking around their home, which had a lot of character with the rustic farmhouse style. Mom loved this style, but it would not fit in our home. Karen led us to the kitchen and introduced mom and me to everyone; her parents Joann and Andrew, her Uncle Gary, which was her mother's brother, and the young girl was Debbie her cousin, who had the most adorable black poodle at her side. I asked as I reached out to say hello, "Who's this cutie?"

Debbie tried to keep him from jumping on me, "This is Jet."

I petted him a little before Karen and Debbie went toward Karen's room. Joann and Andrew thanked mom for coming. My mom had not made many friends since we moved here. It was nice seeing her socializing. Gary seemed to be giving her a lot of attention too. I knew mom was older than him, but she looks great for her age.

Greg and I went into the living room to hangout until dinner. Once out of view of everyone, Greg pulled my body up against his and placed his perfect lips on mine. My body began tingling all over. His kiss made me forget there were other people around. I wrapped my arms around him and could smell his cologne as he started to pull away. I held him tighter to let him know I was not ready for this moment to end. Suddenly knocked off balance, I looked down to see Jet running out of the room, followed by Karen and Debbie.

Once the coast was clear, Greg hugged me and kissed me on my forehead. "Happy Thanksgiving."

My lips longed for another kiss. I gently placed my lips on his and my body began tingling again. Knowing we might get caught, I gently

15

pulled my lips away from his and found myself staring into his beautiful green eyes. They had the power of pulling me closer to him. *Brooke, you need to stop this.* I pulled myself away only leaving my hands touching his. As I looked at Greg, I noticed the tan he had acquired during the summer was fading.

We made our way to the sofa before he told me about the hunt which was uneventful. Before long, we were called to dinner. Everyone was so welcoming to us. I had really enjoyed myself. Mom seemed too also. It was getting late when we eventually made our way back home.

# Three

Juliet and I had gone shopping for our outfits for tonight's double date. This cold weather had made me aware of how few winter clothes I had in my closet. There was no need for them in South Florida. The meteorologist stated the temperature would be in the low 30s tonight. I picked out beige jeans, dark brown knee-high boots, a crème-colored sweater, and my brown double-breasted knee-length coat to wear. After dressing, I headed downstairs to wait for Greg but found him and Mom in the sitting room, chatting. My music had drowned out the doorbell because I did not know he was already here. As I entered the room, Greg stood up. "Stunning, there's no other word to describe how amazing ya look."

His compliment flattered me. I could feel the embarrassment of not knowing how to accept it. I knew my cheeks must be turning red.

We said our goodbyes to mom and headed to his truck. Greg did not know Juliet or Jacob well. He had only met them a few times when we would eat in the courtyard at the University of Louisville between classes. Jacob was a quiet guy. I was not sure how much Greg and Jacob would have in common.

Greg opened the truck door. Once I was in, he closed the door. I noticed the middle console was up, allowing me to sit next to him. I slid over before he opened the door to get inside, but barely made it before his door swung open. He looked over and he seemed to notice because he smiled, jumped in the car, and wrapped his arm around me, and placed his lips to mine. "I love ya."

*Music to my ears.* I pushed my lips against his with more passion than ever before. My body did not notice the chill of the air. A warmth flowed over me. I wanted more. I pulled him closer.

Greg pulled away. *What did I do? Did I upset him? What am I doing wrong?*

"Brooke, we need to slow down," he said as he placed his hand on mine.

I knew he was right. Embarrassed by my behavior, I pulled myself away from him. I moved to the passenger side seat when he grabbed my hand. "I didn't mean to upset ya," he said in a loving way.

17

I assured him, "I'm not upset, just embarrassed."

"There's nothing to be embarrassed about. We love each other. I respect ya, Brooke, and I don't want to mess this up. There's no rush. I just want us to take our time. There's no need to rush into anything. A person's first time should be with the person they're spending the rest of their life with. It's a memory they'll share. There should be no regrets."

*Did he think I wanted to have sex? Oh no, not ready for that. Did I hear him say he was a virgin, too?* "I love you, but I was not thinking about having sex with you. I'm not ready for that either. It's nice to know we're on the same page regarding that."

"Someday, I can see us moving to that step. I can see us spending our entire lives together. Don't think for a second, I don't desire ya in that way. I do, but I think we could easily get lost in the passion and do something we might regret," he said as he leaned over and kissed me again. With our lips locked, we began feeling the heat buildup between us again.

I longed for his touch and, just like that, we both pulled away from one another and buckled up. I stayed in the seat next to him and placed my head on his shoulder. He just had me fall more in love with him. He was not like any boy I had ever met. There were very few not trying to get into a girl's pants. God had truly blessed me with him.

We arrived before them at the restaurant and got a table for four. As I looked around, I noticed this was a very casual restaurant, but I heard the food was delicious. I was so hot and bothered by the make-out session; I found it hard to keep my mind focused on anything else. To get my mind off of it, I began chatting about our workouts once I had figured out what I wanted to eat. It was tough working out when it was so cold, but I did not want to join a gym. I liked it being just us, with an occasional visitor. As I was talking, Greg leaned in for another kiss, but I pulled away because out of the corner of my eye, I noticed Jacob and Juliet coming in. As they approached the table, Greg stood up to shake hands with Jacob, "Hey man." Jacob shook his hand before pulling out a chair for Juliet. Juliet sat in front of me, and Jacob sat in front of Greg.

Greg and I informed them we knew what we wanted. So, they looked at the menu; while we sat quietly, holding hands while they decided what to get. We created our custom bowls. Mine had shrimp, and he chose octopus. I guess he wanted to be adventurous. My eyes began scanning the room for potential danger. I noticed Greg seemed to do the same.

"This place is great. I love Poke bowls. We've got these all over Hawaii," she said excitedly and placed her hand on top of Jacob's forearm. Jacob looked down and then made eye contact with me and tried not to smile. Juliet got the Ahi Poke Bowl, which was tuna with cucumber, onions, and avocado. Jacob ordered the Bulgogi Bowl, which contained steak with grilled onions and sesame seeds with white rice. It had a Korean chili sauce.

The conversation was going well. Jacob opened up some, and we noticed he was quite intelligent. We discovered he and Greg were both from Mount Washington. They talked about the town for a while and found out they had a few friends in common. Our food came, and we discovered Jacob enjoyed his meal, but the Korean chili sauce was too spicy. I think he was a little embarrassed by his sudden need for lots of water, but Juliet comforted him by being sympathetic and telling him many people cannot handle the spiciness. We continued eating and enjoying our conversation when the stone started heating. I glanced around the room for the Granaldi brothers, but they were nowhere in sight. A couple of groups had come in together and were finding their way to their seats. It had to be one of them. The stone only warned me of danger when danger was close. I excused myself to go to the restroom because I needed to text Greg to let him know we were in danger.

I locked myself in a stall and texted him about the stone warning me. I waited for his text to see if he had any suggestions. He finally texted back, telling me he would watch the people to see if anyone was paying attention to me. There was a pause before his next text. He informed me a woman was heading into the restroom. I heard the bathroom door open. It did not sound like she was going to a stall, but the stone got hotter. I could not see who it was.

**BROOKE:**      It's her! The stone is hot.

I could not stay in this stall all night. She had not left, and I needed to get back to the table before Juliet and Jacob started worrying about me. I headed out. I flushed the toilet to give the impression I was using it and hoped she would head back to her table. She did not leave.

I hid my necklace under the sweater and headed out of the stall. The woman was standing in front of the mirror, acting like she was fixing her hair. As I got closer, the stone got hotter. This woman, although attractive, did not seem to be the type of person who spent a lot of time primping herself. She was about 5'5", thin with black curly hair with hints of gray. She was not carrying a purse and appeared to be carrying a wallet in her back pocket. I used the sink to her left and washed my hands while I watched her in the mirror. She appeared to check me out.

I grabbed some towels and dried my hands, but before I left, I said, "Have a good night." Making sure I looked directly into her brown eyes and got a good look at her face. The further I got from her; the stone temperature cooled down. It was still warm, though. I sat back down and watched her exit the bathroom. She appeared to look at someone in the restaurant and motioned toward the door before she exited the building. I could not tell who she was motioning to because there was a large crowd waiting to be seated obscuring my view. I watched her walk away from the building and was hoping the stone would cool down, but it remained warm.

I had a hard time getting back into the conversation because the strangers distracted me. *Had the Granaldi's hired someone to follow me or, even worse, to steal the stone from me?* Whatever the reason, my guard, which had been down, was now up and alert.

Once everyone finished eating, Jacob suggested we go ice skating. That was something I had never done. Under normal circumstances, I would have liked to try it. But I was leery of the danger that was lurking nearby.

Greg said, "Sounds like fun."

Jacobs suggested we all ride together rather than take two vehicles. I think he was not sure what to say or do if he were alone with Juliet. Greg said, "Sounds good. I'll drive."

*What is he thinking?* As we exited the restaurant, I pulled Greg aside. "Why did you agree to this? We'll be putting them in danger," I said, as I could feel my concern for their safety growing. As we walked, a cool breeze drifted across my face from the chilly night air, piercing its way through my jacket.

"It'll be fine," he informed me. Greg wrapped his arm around me. "The woman could've attacked ya in the restroom, and she did nothing. Perhaps they're just hired to watch us."

I hoped he was right. We made it to his vehicle, and I told Jacob to sit behind me. I thought about letting him sit in the front seat for more legroom, but I wanted him to be next to Juliet, which I know would make her happy. I pulled my chair up to give him plenty of room and then looked around to see if I could find the woman from the restroom. She had walked out of view when she left. I forgot to pay attention to her when she left the restaurant. Nor did I notice what she was driving. My focus was on Greg and his lack of concern about the situation.

We started making our way to the ice-skating rink, conscious that Greg and I were both looking to see if anyone was following us. He was constantly checking his mirrors. I noticed Juliet and Jacob whispering in the back seat, but I could not understand what they were saying. Greg reached over and gently squeezed my hand. I think he was trying to tell me everything would be okay. It was then that I noticed the stone was no longer warm. I wondered if we were out of danger for the night.

After parking, we exited the vehicle. The cold air hit me in the face. Greg pulled me closer, and we wrapped our arms around each other's waists. Jacob and Juliet lagged. Greg paid for us, and we headed over to get our skates. Jacob paid for himself and Juliet. They met up with us after they picked up their skates. Juliet and I had white skates, and the guys got skates like the one's hockey players would wear. Once my skates were on, Greg came over and helped me get up. I felt so unstable. My feet wobbled when I tried to move. It was awkward walking over to the ice. Juliet had never been skating either. She seemed to be having as hard of a time as me.

Once Juliet and Jacob caught up with us, Greg helped me out onto the ice. I could feel my heart racing. I was afraid to step onto the ice. *Come on, Brooke. You can do this.* I nearly fell when my skate hit the slick ice, but I could grab the wall. However, I nearly knocked a small child over. I pulled myself along the wall to move out of Juliet's way as she made her way onto the ice. Jacob helped her get on the ice, which appeared as graceful as my maneuver.

"We're off to a good start, Juliet," I said as I began laughing at how badly she and I were at this.

Jacob gave her some instructions. She was able to move away from the wall. Juliet slowly passed Greg and me with a smile of pure joy. I was so glad she was enjoying this. It was now my turn to leave this wall. I lacked courage. The wall was my security blanket. Greg was there encouraging me. I conquered a great deal since moving to Kentucky. *You got this.* I reluctantly released my grip on the wall. Before I knew it, I was skating. With the excitement of this, I had forgotten about the potential dangers that lingered in our near future.

# Four

We made it around the rink several times. I was finally feeling more comfortable on the ice. Jacob and Juliet were in front of us, holding hands as they slowly made their way around the ice. Jacob was a talented skater. It surprised me how much better he was than Greg, who was doing great. A slow song came on. They announced it was time for the couples to hit the ice. Many people, including the young kids, found themselves in line for hot cocoa. Greg never made a move toward leaving the ice. I was at his mercy. Jacob swung in front of Juliet and was skating backward as he held both of her hands. It was so sweet to watch them.

Just as Greg was leaning over for a quick peck from my lips, the stone warmed. I wobbled back and forth, trying to catch myself, and landed on my butt. I could feel the cold from the coldness of the ice going through my pants to my skin. It was freezing. My bare hands were also on the ice and in desperate need of gloves, which I had put in my pocket because it was a little warm with them on before I found myself in this position. In a gentlemanly way, Greg leaned over as bow. He extended his arm and said, "Falling for me?"

I smiled and grabbed his hand to help me get up. My skates were not cooperating with me. I was sliding all over the place. Eventually, I found myself an upright position. I made my way to the wall and looked for the mysterious stranger, but she was nowhere in sight. I told Greg someone was here. He looked around as well. We decided we needed to get out of the skates, so we made our way around to the rink exit. Greg motioned for Jacob and Juliet to join us. I quickly took my skates off and put my boots on. By the time Juliet and Jacob made their way to us, Greg had left to return the skates. "I can't explain, but we need to leave right now," I said with worry in my voice.

Juliet looked concerned and confused. Jacob quickly took his skates off and retrieved his and Juliet's shoes.

Greg came back a little short of breath and said, "Found nothing."

I looked up at him with concern. *It could be anyone. How many people were after us?*

Juliet pulled me aside and asked, "Is everything okay? Are you and Greg fighting or something?"

I looked her in the eye, trying to find the right words to explain without letting her know the danger I had placed her in. "I really can't explain, but you need to trust us, and do exactly as we say," I said with a sense of urgency.

Juliet seemed more puzzled than ever. She nodded her head and seemed to await instructions.

"Let's get out of here. Stay close," Greg instructed. He looked at Jacob, who then looked at Juliet. Jacob appeared confused, too.

Juliet looked over at him and shrugged her shoulders with a confused expression.

We threw on our jackets and rushed out to the vehicle. The closer we got to Greg's truck, the warmer the stone became. "Greg, it's getting worse," I informed him. I knew Greg would know I was referring to the stone's warning.

We had parked far away from the entrance door. When the truck finally came into view, we could tell that another vehicle was blocking the car from being moved. Greg and I stopped immediately. *What do we do now? If it were just Greg and me, we could easily escape, but Juliet and Jacob do not have the skills or even understand what was going on. We have put them in danger.* "What should we do, Greg?" I asked because I had zero ideas on how to get us out of this one.

"Let's go back in and exit out of a back door," Greg suggested.

Juliet grabbed my arm and said in an angry tone, "What is going on?"

"Look, I don't have time to explain now, but I'll tell you when we're safe," I pulled her in the entrance's direction to the rink.

With fear in her voice, Juliet said, "We're not safe?"

"No. Now both of you follow us," Greg said with a sense of urgency.

We all quickly made our way back to the rink. At first, they were going to charge us again, but Greg and Jacob showed their receipts to the cashier. We made our way to the back of the rink, into the storage room where they kept the Zamboni.

While we took a break to warm up before exiting the building, Jacob asked, "Where are we headed?"

"Yes, and why are we in danger, Brooke?" Juliet added.

Ignoring Juliet, Greg suggested, "We can make our way to that liquor store down the road. An Uber can take us back to Jacob's car."

I nodded in agreement.

"We need to get going before they figure out what we are doing," Greg said as he pushed open the door only to find a large blonde man at the back entrance.

The man looked like we surprised him. It looked as if he was going for a gun or something. Greg and Jacob quickly pulled the door shut. We could hear the man talking to someone and telling them where we were. We went back to the door where we had entered the storage room from and peeked out. It was only a matter of seconds before the mystery woman from the bathroom appeared.

Greg said sternly, "Brooke, we need to get out of here!"

I knew he was right. I was trying to work it out in my head. *Would they keep my secret?* I was just getting to know Juliet. *How would she react when she found out? Would she keep it a secret? And what about Jacob? I really don't know Jacob at all.* Not knowing what to do, I prayed, "Lord, what should I do?"

Greg told me she was nearly at the door, and it did not have a lock. He and Jacob pushed their weight against it to prevent her from entering.

That was when I knew I needed to get them to a safe place. *Lord, I hope I'm doing the right thing.* I looked at Juliet and then Jacob and said, "You need to trust me, and you mustn't tell a soul what's about to happen." Grabbing my mirror from my bra, I instructed, "Hold on to me tightly."

Juliet and Jacob looked at me like I was crazy until they saw Greg remove one of his arms from the door and take my left hand. Juliet grabbed my left arm and Jacob my right. The mysterious woman started pushing on the door.

I pictured myself in my garage. We were sucked into the mirror and spat out onto the floor of the garage.

*Now the tough part. How would I explain to them what happened?* When they looked around, they realized they were in a strange place. I turned to them and said with a smile, "We're not in Kansas anymore?" They seemed less than thrilled with my comment. I turned the lights on. "Your safe. We're in my garage."

"Are you a witch or something?" Juliet asked with more than a hint of fear in her voice.

Surprised, I answered, "No, I'm no witch. If you truly want to know, I'll tell you. This must be our secret and you must protect this secret at all costs. You must take the information you learn to your grave with you." They looked at me puzzled. "Seriously, you must promise with your life because your life could depend on it," I insisted.

Greg then chimed in, "Brooke's right. If anyone finds out you know her secret, it could put you and others in danger, just as it did with you tonight."

Jacob, being a curious person, seemed intrigued by what had just happened. He commented, "I'm trying to work this out in my mind. I know I'm not dreaming, but we just got sucked into a mirror and transported to a garage." He opened his arms as if to say, wow. He continued, "This is amazing. There's no logical explanation for this, Brooke, unless... Are you an alien?"

I chuckled and replied, "No, I'm not an alien. This is a family secret. Very few people are aware we have this ability." I began doubting my decision to use the stone to protect them.

There was a long pause before Jacob cleared his throat. "I'll keep your secret, Brooke. I promise."

Juliet seemed genuinely scared. "Brooke are you sure this is not some wicked type of sorcery?"

"No. My family is on the side of good, not evil," I said, hoping to reassure her.

"I'm not sure I want to know Brooke," she said with fear in her voice.

I turned to Juliet and said, "I know this is scary. It was scary when I found out. This secret comes with great responsibility. Like many other ancestors of mine, I'm tasked with its protection. I'm not a witch; I'm the person you've gotten to know. My family has been protecting a powerful thing few people know about. Some evil people are aware of its existence and are trying to take it. I must do all I can to prevent them from getting it."

"I do trust you. If it's that important, I want to help," Juliet said firmly.

Feeling relieved, I took a deep breath. "My family was entrusted with protecting the Bloom of Dreams," I said as I pointed to the

26

pendant on my necklace. "Not everyone in my family is aware of the powers of this stone. Not even my mother. My grandmother was its protector for most of her life and when she passed, she entrusted it to me. I'm responsible for it," I said. I noticed Juliet looked like she needed to sit down. I pulled a chair from the corner of the garage and motioned for her to sit.

I continued, "The stone has certain powers, one of which is teleportation. That's how I got us here. I only revealed my secret to you because your lives were in danger. I don't know who the people were that showed up today, but they're dangerous. The stone warns me of danger. It warned me at the restaurant, but it only appeared to Greg and me they were observing us. It wasn't until the rink when we saw Greg's car blocked, we realized we were in danger."

Jacob inquired, "I've so many questions. Where does this power come from? What other powers does it contain?"

I had to interrupt him. "These questions aren't important. We need to get you both back to Jacob's car. After that, Greg and I will get his truck. This is going to be embarrassing but move in as close to me as possible and hold on," I instructed. We could not go to Jacob's car because I had not seen inside of it. I opened my mirror and pictured us in the handicap stall of the woman's restroom at the restaurant. No one was in the restroom when we arrived.

With a puzzled look, Greg asked, "Are we in the ladies room?"

"Yes, so be quiet while I see if the coast is clear," I whispered as I exited the stall. I looked out the ladies' room door and saw the restaurant only had customers at two tables. The staff appeared to be getting ready to close. I told them to hurry and get out of the restaurant as quickly as possible with their heads down in case there were cameras.

Once we made it back to Jacob's vehicle, we all got in. Jacob started driving to Juliet's house.

"I don't want to alarm you, but Greg and I are going to check on his truck. If the coast isn't clear, we're coming back. If we're able to get out of there, we'll be heading home ourselves," I said as I pulled out my mirror.

"Wait, Brooke. Text me when you get home, so I know you are okay," Juliet said with concern in her voice.

I nodded and realized she cared. She could be trusted.

When Greg and I arrived inside his truck, we looked to see if they still had it blocked in. It was not, so we headed home. He kept checking the mirrors to ensure we were not being followed. We discussed who these people might be. Other than suspecting they were working with Phillip or the Granaldis, we had nothing. The stress of the evening left me exhausted. We pulled into Greg's driveway, and he walked me to my door.

"If we take the mysterious stranger incident out of the equation, I had a great time with ya tonight," Greg said before leaning over to kiss me goodnight.

I texted Juliet as soon as I was in the door about making it home safely.

# Five

Mom and I took separate cars to church because she was meeting up with Lance and his friends for lunch. I invited Juliet and Jacob over to discuss what had happened at the Ice-Skating Rink. I needed them to understand the importance of keeping my secret.

Upon arriving home, I quickly changed into casual clothes and grabbed some leftovers from the refrigerator to heat for lunch. While the food heated, I contemplated what I should say to them. It occurred to me Jacob had skills we could use, but how would I get him to help us. Although, I think he would be easier than Juliet. Jacob seemed inquisitive and fascinated by the stone, but what we might ask him to do could be illegal. What if he was not willing to help? He could teach us about computers. Juliet was harder. I was not sure how we could use her, and she might not even be interested. The more I thought about it, I think Jacob would be easy to sway if we needed his skills.

The microwave dinged, and moments later I was quickly scarfing down my lunch. As I finished, the doorbell chimed. Gently tossing my plate in the sink, I headed to the door. It was Greg. He had his back to the door. Unknowingly, I felt a smile appear on my face just thinking about him. I found him to be an amazing person. As I opened the door, I closed my eyes and had my lips waiting for a kiss. He did not disappoint me. The cold air was blowing in, so I quickly shut the door.

"What do I smell?" he asked.

I replied, "Leftovers. Do you want some?"

"Did Phyllis cook it?" he inquired as we strolled toward the kitchen.

"Of course," I assured him. Greg opened the refrigerator and started making himself a plate. I started cleaning up my plate before they arrived. Greg had just sat down to eat when I handed him a glass of sweet tea. He leaned over with a kiss to thank me. The doorbell interrupted our kiss.

As I walked down the hall to the foyer, I could see Jacob and Juliet trying to look in through the glass of the door. I opened the door and welcomed them in. "Brooke, this house is gorgeous!" Juliet announced as she slowly rotated her body around looking in every direction to try and make sure she did not miss anything.

Closing the door before responding, "Thank you. My mother inherited it when my grandmother passed. I assure you I didn't grow up in anything like this."

"Well, I want to see it all," she said, clasping her hands together as she moved away from the door.

"How are you today, Jacob?" I asked.

"I'm still in shock. I've been trying to figure out a scientific way to do what we did, and I've got nothing. I'm awestruck by this and want to learn more."

I took them to the kitchen, where we found Greg placing his plate in the dishwasher. Greg and I gathered some drinks and snacks before we walked to the library on the second floor to hang out. I showed them the first floor prior to us going up and Juliet insisted on a quick tour of the second floor. When the tour concluded, we made ourselves comfortable in the library.

I started the conversation, "I know last night was a lot, but before I share anything more with you, I must confirm with you again you will keep my secret." They both looked at each other and said they would.

I continued, "Greg found out about my secret the same way you did. We were being chased. Only they were shooting at us. The Granaldis have been trying to get the Bloom of Dreams from my family for centuries. They've earned their money doing illegal things. Unfortunately, Greg and I had to do some illegal things to stop them."

Juliet's eyes widened when she heard that. Jacob did not seem phased by it.

"The people last night, well, we don't know who they are, but we suspect they want the Bloom of Dreams and by the weapons they were carrying, they mean business," I said.

"Is this why you had Greg teach you Karate and do all that Parkour stuff?" Juliet asked.

Jacob leaned forward and seemed captivated by what I was saying. "Yes, Greg has been great at teaching me how to defend myself. The Parkour hasn't only helped me get into shape; it has helped me get out of a few sticky situations. Now I have a question for you, but before you answer, know that anything you do to help me or to protect the Bloom of Dreams comes with risks. Would either of you be interested in helping us if you had the skills we needed?"

Without hesitation, Jacob said, "I'm in."

"I want to help you, but I must admit, I'm a little scared. I should also share with you I know Kapu Ku'ialue. It is an ancient Hawaiian martial art. I haven't used it since I moved here because my father has been so busy with his new job, but I can try to teach it to you," Juliet informed us.

"That's awesome. I definitely wanna try it," Greg said excitedly. Jacob's face showed his shock at her statement.

"Perhaps we could be like super spies and have a secret name for our group." Juliet suggested.

"That's not a bad idea. What do ya guys think?" Greg said, as he looked over at Jacob and me.

"It can't be anything girly. It must be a powerful name." Jacob advised us and leaned back in his chair.

"I'll tell you what, let's all think of a name, before our next meeting." I instructed them. *That would mean that this is an official meeting. Wow, it is nice to have people I can share this with who can help me along the way. I wonder if Grandma had a team. She had Phyllis, Isabella, and Leonardo, but did she have anyone else?*

Greg took a gulp of his drink, and said, "Perhaps we should try to figure out who those two people that came after us last night are."

Finding myself half-listening to the conversation because I kept thinking about who might have been helping Lillie. "Yah, we should try to figure that out," I answered before I realized what he had really said. "I agree Greg. If you see them, let me know immediately. I'll get there as quickly as I can. They have no boundaries. The Granaldi family has showed up at our school, broke into my home, chased us in my neighborhood, and even followed us around town. Oh, and they even broke into my grandmother's attorney's office to get a copy of her will. They'll let nothing stop them from getting this stone." Lifting the pendant from my chest. "We suspect it has powers we haven't discovered yet, but we know it'll allow me to transport, making me invisible, and it allows me to understand different languages. It doesn't let me speak in those languages, but we should try itwill it? We recently found out it can heal. I don't know if it'll heal me, but it can heal a person I touch."

31

Jacob asked, "Why can it heal now and not before?"

"Good question." I looked over at Greg before answering, "Anthony Granaldi III had a ring that held the Bloom's Cradle. The cradle provides more power to the stone. We broke into his house, drugged him, and stole the ring. Now, before you say anything, we did it to keep the Bloom of Dreams safe. The Bloom's Cradle and the Bloom of Dreams were meant to work together. The Granaldi family stole it from my family in the 1800s. We're just taking back what rightfully belongs to the protectors of the Bloom of Dreams."

Saying it out loud made me feel more guilty than I had before. I started questioning how much I should really share with them. "They don't know who you are yet, but they're going to try and find you. We need to figure out a way for us to meet with one another without others knowing. Arriving at the same place at the same time is not an option. We also need a place to meet that is discreet," I stated. It was just then I thought about my attic. I suggested, "We can meet in my attic. No one will see us or be able to hear what we are saying. We just need to figure out how to get us there undetected." I put my head down in my hands as my arms rested on my knees to think.

"You could pick us up at our houses and teleport everyone here," Jacob suggested.

"That's a great idea, Jacob! Is everyone okay with that?" I said, looking around the room to see if we were all in agreement. We were.

"Finals are coming up; can we meet after that? Unless, of course, something else comes up," Juliet suggested.

"I agree. We all need to concentrate on our exams, but if anyone sees them, we need to meet to find out our next step," Jacob added.

"I nearly forgot. Before our next meeting, I need to come to both of your houses. I can only teleport to places I've seen," I said. We worked out the details of when I would see their homes.

Jacob called me when his parents were not home. I drove over there to look at his house. He said he spent a lot of time in his room. We agreed I would pop into his closet to ensure I did not walk in on him changing or anything. He would need to figure out how to explain to his parents his car being there and him not if it ever came up.

Juliet was more difficult because her mother was a stay-at-home mom. Juliet said her mother was always dropping in on her. She may need to leave her house. I went over to check it out in the event she needed me to get her from there.

# Six

I had not seen the mystery man and woman since the Ice-Skating Rink, but I knew they were out there somewhere waiting for an opportunity to pounce. We were all in class, taking our final exams for the semester but despite trying to stay focused on my exam, my mind kept drifting off. I thought about who they might be. My thoughts faded as the sound of a pen clicking echoed in my head from the person two seats over from me.

Greg's last class let out about an hour after mine. I did not know when Juliet and Jacob's classes would be over. Greg and I agreed to meet at the Derby City Pizza. I texted Jacob and Juliet to see if they could join us. I had not heard from either of them when I arrived. The amazing aroma of pizza comforted me as I entered the pizzeria. I got us a table for four. I noticed two guys eating a loaf of hot cheese bread with marinara at a nearby table. It looked delicious. I sat in the back near the restrooms to stay away from most of the customers.

As I waited, I worked on being more aware of my surroundings. The two guys eating the bread appeared to be college students. One was wearing a U of L shirt, and the other had on a black Grateful Dead shirt. They studied as they ate.

There was only one server who focused on her duties. Her skills showed experience. She had an average look that would allow her to easily blend into a crowd. She was darting back and forth from her tables to the kitchen.

The chef looked like he hated his job. He was an overweight man in his fifties. He seemed unkept. His black and gray beard did not look like he had shaved in a few days. He just leaned up against the counter until the next order came in.

The server came by and asked me what I would like to drink. I ordered water with lemon and asked for a couple of menus. I continued with my observations. A lady in her late twenties had come in and was in the corner looking at a paper. She appeared to be looking at ads. Perhaps she was looking for an apartment or a job.

I moved my attention to the exit doors. There was one at the front of the restaurant, and there should be another in the back. It must be past the bathrooms or through the kitchen. I could not see it from where I sat.

The windows and the floors were impressively clean. I looked out the windows to see if there was anything of importance to observe. As I looked at the surrounding area, I saw an older lady trying to jaywalk to the other side of the street. I saw a black Toyota Corolla parked a few spots away from my car. I sat up in my chair to get a better view of the driver. *Could it be them? Are the Granaldis here?* The car door opened. I held my breath. As the man exited, I realized he was unfamiliar. He was heading to the restaurant. As he opened the door, I could feel a burst of cool air come in. The man appeared to be in a hurry as he picked up his order.

As a truck passed the window, it caught my attention. Greg was here, and Jacob's car was just behind him. They came in together. Jacob sat on the other side of the booth with Greg and I. Greg sat next to me, and immediately gave me a kiss. The server returned with my drink and took their drink orders. Greg also told her we wanted a large sausage pie, which he knew was my favorite.

I turned to Jacob and asked, "I'm so glad you could come, Jacob. How are your exams going?"

"I'm nearly done. I've one more tomorrow," he said as he took off his jacket. "Juliet can't make it. She has another exam today. She said she wanted to review her notes before taking the test." He placed his jacket on the seat and took a deep breath before telling us what was on his mind, "Juliet's great. Thanks for helping me with the double date."

I told him I was glad to help. There seemed to be something else on his mind. I waited another minute before asking, "Is there something else you wanted to say?"

"Yes, I'd like help from you both," Jacob informed us. He took a deep breath and exhaled before continuing, "Juliet knowing the ancient Hawaiian martial art is very intimidating. I've not seen her use it yet, but I've zero skills in knowing how to defend myself. Would you mind teaching me some things?"

Greg said with a smile, "We know Karate, and yes, I'll teach ya."

Greg paused for the server to put their sodas down. I could hear the fizzing of their cokes from across the table. Not knowing much about Jacob, I asked, "We noticed you're rather good on the ice. Are you good at any other sports?"

"No. I played a little hockey when I was younger, but I got into computers, and that ended my sports career," Jacob stated with a smirk.

"No, worries. We'll get ya in shape, and we'll need to do it quickly for ya safety," Greg encouraged. The server came by and placed the large steaming hot pizza on a stand in the middle of the table, along with three plates, before leaving.

Greg grabbed a slice for me, but it was so hot the cheese just kept stretching. After a friendly laugh, I pulled on the cheese to break it from the rest of the pie. Greg worked out times they could meet with and without me to work on his skills. He also informed him he needed to run daily. I was finishing my first slice when I noticed Jacob was finishing his second slice. I grabbed another slice and continued listening to Greg explain to Jacob what he needed to accomplish in a week.

Jacob asked, "Juliet told me you both do, Parkour. That's intense. Do you think I could try that?"

"Let's start with the basics first. The last thing we want is for ya to get hurt." Greg quickly flipped his head in my direction with an eye wide.

Remembering my error in judgment, I said, "That's right. I broke my hand doing it. It's important you know your strengths and weaknesses before attempting something that dangerous."

Jacob finished the pizza before we all headed out.

With nothing to go on, we had learned nothing about the two mysterious strangers that attacked us at the Ice-Skating Rink. We spent winter break training Jacob, the basics of Karate. He asked us not to tell Juliet. He wanted to surprise her when he was better. Juliet's parents insisted she spend time with them over the break. As a result, we saw little of her. It had been a while since we had been back to the Granaldi's home. We decided we would take Jacob with us to see if he could find out anything on Anthony Granaldi III's computer. We practiced transporting invisibly with Jacob to various places to see how he would do. At first, he said he felt sick to his stomach, but he was eventually able to overcome the nausea.

I retrieved the map of the Granaldi's home from the safe room at the Villa Dianella. I did not see Leonardo and Isabella while I was there. Even though I would have loved to see them. They were like family to my grandmother, and they knew our family secret and had kept it quiet for many years. My grandmother provided them funds for the use of protecting the Bloom of Dreams. Leonardo had many connections to assist us with our unique needs.

Jacob's skills were getting better. However, he could not defend himself yet. We decided Jacob would be fine if we did not get into a confrontation with anyone. I instructed him to stay near me.

We made sure we were all wearing rubber gloves and ski hats to avoid leaving fingerprints or hair as evidence at their home. I still beat myself up over not wearing them when I took the painting out of the Granaldi's car. They would be in jail now if I had.

We were prepared to go. Before leaving, Jacob said, "You're not to tell a soul I know how to hack computers."

*Was he really asking me this?* I responded, "Jacob, do you really think I'd tell your secret when I've entrusted you with mine?"

"Sorry, I'm just nervous. Hacking into someone's computer from the safety of my home is one thing. This is a whole different level of espionage," he said as he fiddled with his hat before putting his gloves on.

I turned to Jacob and said, "Greg and I'll keep watch while you try to see if there's anything on the computer that would help us know what they're up to next. Jacob, did you hear me?"

"Sorry, yes," he said. He took a deep breath and grabbed my arm.

We arrived just outside Anthony's closet door in the secret spiral stairwell that led down to a room by the indoor pool. Greg listened to see if he heard anyone and motioned the coast was clear before slowly opening the door to Anthony's closet.

As we entered, I noticed Jacob seemed nervous. I told him, "You can do this. We'll keep you safe." We moved through the closet. I could feel the clothes brush against my arms. When we got to the bathroom, I realized I had forgotten how big this room was. Greg peeked into the other room to see if anyone was in sight. We followed. Greg moved on to check the two doors in the room that lead to the rest of the home. One led to a hallway on the first floor and the other to their ballroom.

I whispered to Jacob, "The computer's over here." I pointed.

Jacob moved toward it. I grabbed his arm and whispered, "Don't start working until Greg gives us a thumbs up."

After checking both doors, Greg told us he did not hear anyone in the house. This was odd because the maids and butler were almost always here. Jacob worked trying to get into the computer. I quietly made my way to the hall door to see if I would hear anyone, but it was quiet. Greg told me he was going to grab the recording pen and replace it with a new one.

Jacob was clicking away on the computer. Greg moved on to downloading the data from the camera in the closet, which was aimed at the safe.

"We need to get the footage from the other safe," he instructed.

"We can't leave him," I advised.

Greg moved toward the bathroom. "I will go down and check it," he said before he slipped out of view. I could not stop him.

*What was he thinking! We should stay together.* Jacob continued working for what seemed like an eternity before he said, "I think we're done here."

*He thinks. I hope he knows what he's doing.* I grabbed his arm and transported him to the bottom of the spiral stairs. We entered the guest bedroom and quietly made our way to the room with the indoor pool. I peered out the door, making sure there was no one near before heading to the sauna. Jacob grabbed my arm. *That poor boy is so nervous.* In silence, we made our way to the sauna, where I expected to find Greg retrieving the data from the second camera, he had installed to capture the combination to the safe. It was well hidden in the wall.

I quietly opened the sauna door… *Where is Greg? Lord, please tell me he's okay.* I felt a tap on my shoulder. Startled, I jumped and turned around. In my panic about Greg, I forgot Jacob was with me.

"Where's Greg?" he softly asked.

*Yes, where is he?* I was confused too. I was not sure if I should tell him I was freaking out, but I was sure he could see it on my face. I said, "I'm not sure, but we need to find him. Would you like me to take you back to the attic before I look for him?" Secretly, I was hoping he would want to go back because he was not ready to take on anyone.

"No, I'm not leaving you here by yourself," he said sternly. Jacob pulled a pepper spray bottle out of his pocket to show me he had come prepared. I smiled. This made me feel better.

We made our way out of the pool area toward the back of the house. The moon had crept in through the windows. *Where would you have gone, Greg?* With Jacob on my arm, we made our way down a small hallway to the exercise room. The bathroom doors in the exercise room were open. I could see he was not there. On to the recreation room. We were on the basement level. I whispered to Jacob, "Stay alert."

It was so scary not knowing if or when someone might pop out at us. Greg had never left me alone before. My heart was pounding, I was perspiring, and to top it off, I had someone even more scared attached to my arm. *Would Jacob be able to handle himself if something were to occur?* We made our way through to the hallway near the maid quarters. The door to the first room was locked. My nerves were rattled. *Panic. Yes, that's what I'm feeling right now. Where are you, Gregory? If he's not in trouble, I'm going to kill him for this!* We got to the door of the room that was always locked. A noise came from the room. I instructed Jacob to hide behind the spiral stairs behind us. I looked back to make sure he was hidden. He was peaking over the railing. His right hand was on the railing with the pepper spray ready for action.

I slowly turned the door handle to the unsearched room. As I opened the door, a bed and a nightstand came into view. I listened again and heard nothing. Wanting to call out for Greg. *What if it's not him in the room?* I made my way into the room when something from behind the door caught my eye. A lamp! I ducked and prepared to defend myself when I noticed Greg holding a lamp.

In a loud whisper, he said, "I nearly hit you!"

Greg seemed shocked I was there. I snapped at him, "That's what you're worried about. You scared me to death. I thought you could've been kidnapped or even killed. Why are you here and not where you told us you would be?" Feeling as though lasers could come out of my eyes at any moment. I could feel the blood in my veins had begun to boil because I was so mad.

"I'm sorry. Jacob was busy, so I thought I would see if this room was unlocked, and it was. Let me show you what I found," he pulled a book out of his backpack and handed it to me.

I glanced at the book. It was a journal, and it surprised me it was in English. I read a few paragraphs and told Greg, "This is the butler's journal. Let's take it with us." I turned to leave the room. Greg followed me. We met up with Jacob.

"We've been here too long. Let's go." I said forcefully. I had already had enough for the night.

When we returned to the attic to discuss the evening, Jacob let out an enormous sigh of relief. I quickly turned to Greg and snapped at him, "That can never happen again. We're a team and you let us down tonight!"

Jacob seemed like he did not know what to do with himself. He had never heard us talk this way, which was because we had never fought. I was so worried; it seemed like my emotions were out of control.

"Again, I'm sorry," he said in a gentle voice. "Ya we're taking so long to come down, I thought I would just sneak over and see if I could get into the room. It surprised me to find it unlocked. I thought I'd only be gone a few minutes, but I must've lost track of time."

"Look, I love you and it terrified me something had happened to you," I said, as I could feel the tears filling up my eyes.

Greg wrapped his arms around me and said, "I never meant to scare ya. I love ya, too."

He continued holding me, and my tears turned into sobs.

"Sweetie, I'm sorry. It won't happen again," he said, pushing me away from his chest to wipe my tears.

I caught Jacob in my peripheral vision. I wiped another tear from my eye and said, "Jacob, you did well tonight. Were you able to find anything?"

"I was able to set his computer up to notify me when he gets on. I've access to his camera and everything. I'll search the computer to see if I can find anything. In the short time, we were there, I saw nothing of importance. Looking at his computer, he is not very computer savvy. Perhaps one of his sons has a computer. Would you mind taking me home? I need to get into his computer while no one's home."

I quickly took him back home and returned to Greg in the attic to look at the journal again. Greg handed it to me and said, "About that." He paused and pointed to the journal before continuing, "You can read that?" He sounded puzzled.

"Of course, it's in English," I said, as I turned to show him the words in the book.

"Brooke, that's not English. It's Italian," he informed me.

A quick glance at the book again and my first thought, he was wrong. *What if he was not wrong and I am?* I pulled the stone away from my skin and the words in the book changed before my eyes to Italian. Placing it back on my skin, showed it in English. I turned to Greg and said with excitement in my voice, "You're right! Hey, I can read Italian now."

Greg smiled and said, "Would ya say that again?"

"What? Oh, the part about you being right," I said, giggling.

Greg widened his eyes as if to say, "I'm waiting."

"Okay, you were right. I can read foreign languages. This is crazy," I said excitedly. I pulled out my phone and looked up Spanish songs. I could read everything.

When we finally got over the excitement of our new discovery, Greg went home.

# Seven

We caught Juliet up on what had happened at the Granaldis, and Jacob said he had nothing new to report. The four of us headed downtown for dinner for a second double date. We were hoping it would be less eventful than our night at the Ice-Skating Rink. Greg and I decided, for now, to keep our new discovery a secret. They did not need to know everything.

We decided on the Old Spaghetti Factory in downtown Louisville. Jacob offered to drive us, which was nice of him, but Greg liked to be in control of the car. He seemed a little distracted when Jacob drove. We dined early and tried to figure out something else to do after our meal. It was apparent Jacob had been here before because he instructed Greg on the best place to park. The parking garage was next to the restaurant.

As we walked out of the parking garage and headed toward the restaurant entrance, I felt the chilly wind blowing between the tall buildings chilling my face. Even with the scarf around my face, it did little to protect me from the bitter cold. Greg seemed to notice because he pulled me closer to him to help shield me from the wind. Fortunately, we did not need to walk far.

As we approached the restaurant, the crimson-colored awnings arched over the first floor of the building caught my eye. The second floor looked like black iron, which gave the building an aged look. The upper floors were a variety of colors that worked well together. Some areas were beige with rust trim, and others were a light beige with a dark mustard color. The entrance amazed me. It had beautiful gold doors that shimmered in the evening light.

Jacob held the door open for us. The warmth of the room was comforting. Jacob and Juliet talked to the hostess; I was admiring the décor of the restaurant. There was an old-fashioned trolley car in the middle of the room with tables inside for diners. The antique lighting provided a romantic atmosphere. There were large, colorful booths along the edge of the room. The walls and stair railings were a dark cherry color wood with a lot of ornate decoration on them to give

43

them a vintage look. Tiffany lamps hung above the bar, where once again the dark cherry wood adorned the ceilings.

I was so engrossed in admiring the décor; I did not hear Juliet call for me. Greg grabbed my hand, and we followed them to the table. We glanced over the menu before placing our order. I ordered minestrone soup, lasagna, and a hot tea. I was still trying to defrost and was looking forward to the tea and soup. The outdoors felt to me like the North Pole. South Florida was never this cold.

We discussed our plans for the holidays. Juliet and I started discussing things to do after dinner when Greg interrupted us, "We've a surprise for both of ya." He looked over at Jacob before adding, "We're going to the Actors Theatre to see A Christmas Carol."

Juliet and I looked at each other before hugging our dates. *What a sweet surprise.* We finished dinner before heading out the front door. I turned toward the garage and Greg said, "We need to walk a block in that direction." He pointed to South 3rd Street. I pulled my scarf up around my face as we headed around the corner and down South 3rd Street. The wind was not as bad on this road, but I was still freezing. I admired the Christmas lights and decorations along the way. As we turned on to US 31, the freezing wind greeted us again on West Main Street. Again, the arctic air resumed its attack on my face. It made its way inside the many layers of my clothing. *Special report: Brooke and her friends were found frozen on West Main Street.* As I looked up, I noticed the theatre was the next building.

The theater had an interesting ceiling. There was a large circle with ornate features. They decorated the entrance area for Christmas, the centerpiece being a very tall tree embellished in red and gold with thousands of tiny white lights threaded their way through its branhces. We sat down. Greg advised us to take this time to work on our observation skills. We decided we would compare our observations of those in the theater on the trip home.

When the play started, I glanced over to see if everyone was engaged in the performance. It seemed most of us were. Greg seemed distracted. Perhaps he was not into this kind of thing and was just trying to do something nice for me. I returned my attention to the show.

Once the show was over, we got up and Greg asked us to sit back down, which we did. Greg waited for the people in our area to be out of earshot to tell us what he had observed. He said, "During the show, I saw the two people from the rink. They came in and looked around before finding a seat, but just before the play ended, they left. They're here somewhere."

Juliet asked, "Brooke can get us out of here. Right?"

"It's not that simple. We can't just teleport whenever we want. We must be discrete about it," I responded.

"Brooke's right. We need to leave with the crowd. Some people should be parked in the same parking garage. Let's stay with another group of people," Greg advised.

We quickly made our way out of the theater and saw a small group in front of us moving toward the Old Spaghetti Factory. Our stride became longer as we tried to catch up with the group in front of us. I continually scanned the area looking for the couple from the rink, but I couldn't locate them. We passed the restaurant and entered the parking garage. We hurried back toward Greg's truck. As we turned into the row the vehicle was on, I could feel the stone heating. I leaned over to Greg and quietly informed him. He stopped walking, which caught our attention, and we stopped as well. Looking at Juliet and Jacob, Greg said, "I want both of you to walk as fast as you can back to the restaurant."

"We'll pick ya up in front of the restaurant once we get them off our tail. Don't leave the restaurant. You'll be safe there," Greg commanded.

They quickly left the area. Now we needed to figure out where they went. We started walking toward a different row away from the vehicle exit area, but the stone seemed to grow cooler. I told Greg they were not in that direction. We turned and started walking toward the vehicle exit. As we got closer to Greg's vehicle, the stone got hotter and hotter. Just near the exit ramp, I saw the woman with black curly hair and the blonde man in a black Dodge Charger. I made sure not to make eye contact with her as I told Greg where they were.

"We need them to follow us," Greg suggested.

Without even thinking. I looked right at the woman and said, "You want me, come and get me." I started using my Parkour moves, getting over the cars and the cement walls between levels to make my way toward the top of the parking garage. As soon as I took off, Greg started following me. There was no time for questions because they pulled out of the spot and tried to catch up with us at the top of the parking garage.

My adrenaline had been keeping me warm because I did not notice the chilly air. Once at the top, I noticed the building next to the garage was another story higher. I looked at Greg, wondering what we should do. He grabbed my hand, leading me away from the building with the restaurant and back toward the direction of the ramp they would come up. I could hear the tires from their vehicle screeching on the pavement. As we were nearing the edge of the structure, they headed right for us. I finally figured out where Greg was leading us. We both leaped onto the next building. I looked back and saw them staring at us. Greg said, "Follow me." We made it to the side of the building. I followed his lead, descending quickly. I looked up to see the mysterious woman looking down on us before leaving my view.

"Greg, I have seen the inside of their car. Make your way to the next roof and I will come to get you. I am going to get in their car," I said without waiting for a response.

I appeared invisible in the back seat of their Charger, making sure not to move and being incredibly quiet.

She shouted at her partner, "We're going to lose them. Hurry!"

"Nadine, stop yelling at me," he shouted back.

We traveled down the parking garage levels quickly. I had to hold my position to prevent myself from sliding as the vehicle swerved. With each turn, the tires squealed. We exited the garage; we turned left onto West Market Street.

"That's the building they jumped on. Turn left here," she ordered.

He immediately turned onto South 2nd Street. I do not think he was even looking for oncoming traffic.

"They've got to be around here somewhere," Nadine hollered.

They trickled down the street as they searched for us. I opened my mirror and went to rescue Greg from the roof. As I appeared, I could tell I startled him. I quickly grabbed his hand and took us to his truck. I called Juliet to tell her, we would be in front of the restaurant soon.

Greg drove us out of the garage. As we exited, we realized we could not turn right because it was a one-way road. Greg turned left, heading toward Nadine and her partner. We had to go around the block. We headed right on South 2nd Street in the opposite direction of them. I called Juliet to let her know when to exit the restaurant. "We had to go a lot further than we expected because of the one-way roads," I said. We finally made it to the restaurant, and I told Juliet to come out. They quickly jumped into the truck. As soon as they shut the door, Greg pulled away from the curb. We saw them as we passed the garage. They were about to turn in our direction.

"They must've returned to the garage to look for my truck and realized we left," Greg said.

As we passed in front of their vehicle, I made eye contact with Nadine. "At the next red light, I'm going to get out and try to get them to follow me. I'll return when I think you're far enough away from them," I informed everyone.

"I know that's probably the best idea, but I don't like ya being by yourself," Greg responded as we turned right onto South Brook Street.

The light at the intersection of South Brook Street and East Market Street turned red. When the vehicle came to a complete stop, I jumped out, and ran down East Market Street in the traffic's direction to make sure they could follow me. A scan of the area revealed a White Castle and another parking garage. I cut through the White Castle parking lot and sprinted toward the nearby parking garage. It was just north of the restaurant. I heard tires squealing and turned to see if it was them. They headed right toward me but had to stop because a vehicle was pulling out of a parking spot. I quickly made my way to the alley behind the garage. There was a low wall on the lower level of the garage. I pulled myself over it and headed toward the entrance of the garage. They drove down the alley and stopped to look for me.

Exiting the garage, I dashed back toward the White Castle, hoping they would see me as I ran down the road. I was nearly at the restaurant when the car pulled just past me, and Nadine got out and started running in my direction. I sprinted toward the entrance of the White Castle.

As I entered, I noticed several customers and felt trapped. *Think Brooke, think.* I looked around. *Ah, restroom.* I made my way toward the women's restroom and locked myself in the handicap stall. After a pat-down of myself for my mirror, I realized it was in my purse, which was in Jacob's car. I heard the door open and realized there was only a stall door between us. There was a mirror above the sink.

I looked at the mirror and focused. I could see the inside of Greg's truck. This would be my first attempt to use a mirror in a restroom, but I needed to jump into it. I quickly dove into it and found myself hurled headfirst into the passenger's seat of the vehicle. The vehicle swerved. I seemed to startle Greg with my entrance.

"We've lost them," Jacob informed me as I flipped myself over and buckled my seatbelt.

I told them what had happened and where I left them. We dropped them off and headed to my house. I popped Greg and I into the backseat of their Dodge Charger to see where they were.

"We'll start again in the morning," the man said, as he passed my house and continued down Fourth Street before making a right into a Bed & Breakfasts driveway. *Are they really staying just down the street from my house?* Greg and I looked at each other in shock. They got out of the car, and we quickly transported to the front porch of the three-story house.

"I'm still freezing. Next time I drive, and you can freeze your butt off," Nadine said as she entered the home.

I caught a glimpse of the foyer of the home. When I was sure they had moved out of that area, we teleported there. The sitting room just off the foyer contained many antiques, and many paintings and antique mirrors adorned the walls.

We followed the two up the stairs to their room. The door opened to reveal a lovely room with flowered wallpaper, a queen-size bed, a small table with sitting chairs on both sides of the table, and an armoire in the corner. Once the door was closed, we transported to the other side of the door, staying out of their way.

The man kicked his shoes off on the floor and put his jacket on the bed before plopping himself onto it. He put his hands under his head and closed his eyes.

She tossed her jacket on the bed and then sat in the sitting chair closest to the end of the bed and took her shoes off. "We'll get a fresh start in the morning," she said. Nadine grabbed their jackets and laid them over the other chair. "I can't figure out how I lost her. She's clever," she said as she grabbed a blanket from the end of the bed before snuggling up with it on the chair. She then looked up at the man and asked, "Eddie, go get us some hot chocolate?"

He responded, "Sure. Sounds good." He slowly stood up. We were pinned between him and the door. I quickly transported us to the end of the bed before he ran into us.

He headed out the door without his shoes. Once the door shut, she picked up her phone to call someone. The person on the other end answered, and she began telling them they were unsuccessful. She said, "Don't worry, we'll get it. Brooke is shrewd. I'm not sure how I lost her. She went to a restaurant. Well, I thought it was her. I followed this person into the bathroom but when I got there, there was no one in the restroom."

There was a pause as she listened to the person on the other end of the line. "Do you have any suggestions?" she asked. Another pause. "You never said you needed us to do anything like that," she said, surprised. Another pause. "Hey, I didn't say we wouldn't, but that's going to cost you. I'll get back to you on the cost because I need to discuss this with Eddie," she said before hanging up the phone and tossing it angrily on top of the bed.

We heard a knock at the door. We quickly pinned ourselves up against the wall, trying to avoid her. Fortunately, she did not run into either of us. She opened the door to let Eddie in. She grabbed one of the hot chocolates and headed back to the chair. He returned to the bed but was sitting up, drinking.

She took a sip and started blowing on it. She said, "He wants us to kidnap someone close to her. He believes she'll give us the necklace for that person."

Eddie responded, "Really? Do we do that?"

"I told him we'd discuss it, but it's going to cost him. The 10gs he's giving us will not be enough for us to do that. What do ya think we should charge him?" she asked.

"So, we're doing this? How's about fifty-grand?"

She seemed deep in thought. She blurted out, "I think we can get more. I am gonna ask for $100,000."

"If you think he'll go for it, I think you should. I don't think he's going to accept that offer. It's a lot of money," Eddie said before putting his hot chocolate down and adjusting his position.

Nadine picked up her phone. After a moment, she told someone on the line their fee, "It's gonna cost you an additional $100,000." There was a long pause. A smile came across her face, and she punched her fist up in the air. "We've got a deal then." There was another pause before she hung up the phone.

Nadine took another sip of her drink. She said, "Phillip told me he'd only pay us that amount if we got the necklace, but he'll pay us $30,000 for kidnapping someone. So, who do ya think we should kidnap?"

I could feel the anger growing inside me. I moved forward; Greg grabbed my arm to stop me. *This woman deserves what is coming to her.* As I turned toward him to shoot him a look, I bumped their suitcase, and it wobbled on the floor.

Nadine appeared startled. She asked, "Eddie, did ya see that?"

"Yes, the suitcase just moved," he sat up straighter.

Looking scared, she flew to the bed. With fear in her voice, she said, "Do ya think this place could be haunted?"

"They built it in 1884. It could have a lot of ghosts," Eddie commented.

"Well, I don't wanna stay in a haunted building," she snapped. Nadine attempted to squeeze herself between Eddie and the bed frame.

*This woman, possibly a killer, is afraid of ghosts?* She also did not seem to know the power of the stone she was trying to steal from me. A brilliant idea hit me. I needed to make her think the place was haunted. Surely, they would leave then. We were standing at the end of the bed, and they were both facing our direction. Gently grabbing the edge of the curtain behind me, I slowly moved it. Nadine jabbed her elbow into Eddie's side and tried to get more of her body behind Eddies. I tip-toed over to the Tiffany lamp on the table between the chairs and turned it off.

In a scared voice, Nadine said, "Eddie, do something!"

Eddie shot her a look and asked, "What am I supposed to do?"

I turned the light back on.

"Let's try to get some sleep. We can look for a new place in the morning," Eddie suggested. He got up and began removing his long sleeve black shirt, revealing a white thermal shirt.

She appeared shocked at his response. She snapped again, "How am I supposed to sleep here?"

I had been enjoying this. I pushed the pillow on the chair to the floor before deciding to leave for the night.

As soon as we returned to the driveway, Greg said, "Why did ya try to scare them? We don't know where they'll go, which would make it more difficult to find out what they're up to."

He was right. I had messed up. We still did not know who they plan on kidnapping or where they would stay when they left the Bed & Breakfast. There was nothing we could do about it now. We said our goodbyes for the evening.

The next morning, before I went over to Greg's house for our daily workout, I transported myself back to Nadine and Eddie's room, hoping to find out what their next move was. I made sure I was invisible. I placed myself in the corner of the room, to the left of the chair. Out of anyone's way. Nadine was ranting about the lack of sleep she had because of the ghost as she was tying her boots.

Eddie was sitting on the bed, ready to go, looking at his phone. He said, "Nay, this is the best spot to be for this job. Why don't we just ask for a room that's not haunted?"

Nadine looked like she was ready to pounce on him. She took a deep breath and slowly exhaled. With attitude, she said, "Fine, but I'm not staying in this room. I would rather sleep in the car than be in this room another minute."

Eddie got up and said, "Finish packing everything up and I'll go find out about another room." He left.

I transported to the foyer, making sure I would arrive in the corner invisible. I waited until Eddie made his way down the stairs and quietly followed him. "Excuse me, can we talk over here," he said to the manager, motioning him to move away from everyone in the sitting room.

The manager joined Eddie and said, "What can I do for you, sir?"

Eddie explained the situation. The manager seemed surprised by the events Eddie described. He let Eddie finish before he answered, "I'm so sorry for the problems you and your wife are having. We have another room available. Let me get you the keys. You may return the other keys when you have finished moving your things. Will you be needing help with moving your things?"

"No, we'll take care of that. Thanks," Eddie replied as he took the keys. He headed back upstairs.

I popped back to my location in the corner of the room and waited for Eddie. Nadine was zipping up a suitcase when I arrived. He told her they were moving to the room down the hall. Nadine appeared to be double checking the room. Perhaps to make sure they left nothing behind. She snatched her coat and followed Eddie.

The new room was a little different and only had one chair and a stool to sit on. The wallpaper was a checkered type of pattern. It had a fireplace, which the other room did not. The curtains were a pale pink color that matched the wallpaper and there were two pink round pillows on the bed. The antique furniture like the rest of the house was a dark wood. In this room, I could stand by the bathroom and see the room clearly without being in their way.

Nadine asked, "We need to figure out when the best time to grab her will be and where are we going to take her?"

"We could just hold her hostage in her house," Eddie suggested.

Nadine responded, "She knows the house better than us. It should be on our turf. That'll give us an upper hand. After breakfast, let's go look at renting a warehouse for a few weeks."

Eddie nodded and held the door for Nadine as they made their way down for breakfast.

I returned home and grabbed a water bottle and a towel before heading to Greg's garage for our workout.

Greg asked, "It's not like ya to be late. Is everything okay?"

I filled him in on everything. We stretched before heading out on our run. A bright sun hung in the sky, but there was still a cold day. As I ran, I remembered my first workout with Greg. It would be an understatement to say I was out of shape. I could barely make it around the block. Now I found running was a time to clear my head and de-stress. The cold did not bother me as much as it once did. However, on this day, I could not relax. I created a list of people Eddie and Nadine might kidnap. All I knew was it would be a woman. I don't think they knew about Mechelle in Florida. Kentucky was another story. They had plenty of people to choose from, my mom, Phyllis, Juliet, Greg's sister Karen, and Greg's mom Joann. They knew who Juliet and Jacob were. I was certain they knew about Phyllis and my mother. It was safe to say it would not be Karen and Joann. Unless, of course, they wanted to hurt Greg.

I went in circles with my thoughts until I heard a dog barking at us. I looked up. The cutest white Havanese was barking at another dog. He reminded me of a friend of mines dog. Her owner hollered, "Come on, Callie. It's not play time. We need to get inside." The owner appeared to be freezing as she stood there shaking in her robe and slippers.

We finished our run. I had come a long way with my Karate since the first day. My skills were improving daily. We still went to Parkour, but not as often as we would like because the cost added up. We practiced those skills running around town with parkour groups. Our Parkour skills had improved as well.

While we worked out, Greg and I discussed who they might try to grab and what we could do to protect the person. We agreed, my mother or Phyllis were the most likely targets. They might even think Phyllis was my grandmother unless they had information telling them differently. It was so hard having someone come after you and not knowing anything about them. Once we finished, we both got cleaned up and discussed with Phyllis how we could protect them.

Comforted by the warmth of the shower, I found myself not wanting to leave. I needed to deal with the situation. While putting on my makeup, I called Juliet and told her we needed to meet up and talk. She said her parents were at work and I could pop in whenever I wanted. We agreed I would arrive after my discussion with Phyllis. I liked how she referred to me teleporting as popping in.

My phone chimed.

**GREG:**          I'm on my way.

When I opened the door Greg greeted me with a lovely kiss. I pulled him inside and closed the door to prevent the cooler air from getting in. "Phyllis will be downstairs soon," I said.

We went to the kitchen and got some drinks while we waited for Phyllis. Just as Greg was leaning in to kiss me again, Phyllis walked in.

"I don't need to be seeing any of that now," she said with a smile.

I felt the heat in my cheeks from the embarrassing moment.

"Phyllis, please sit down," Greg said. He pulled out a stool from under the counter for her to sit down.

Phyllis looked confused and seemed concerned. She said, "What did you do and how hard is it to clean up?"

I smirked at her comment. I looked at Greg and back to Phyllis before telling her, "You and Mom are in danger."

Phyllis moved her eyes from me to Greg. She asked, "Why?"

"We discovered two people, Nadine, and Eddie, following us. At first, we thought they were harmless, but we've been following them. Phyllis, we heard them talking about kidnapping a woman close to me, hoping to get me to give them the necklace for the safe return of that person. You and Mom are the most likely candidates."

Greg asked, "Do ya know who they are?"

Phyllis shook her head.

Greg moved next to me and asked, "We've been trying to figure out the best way to protect ya. Do ya have any suggestions?"

With a puzzled look, Phyllis responded, "I've no idea who they are. Do you have a picture of them?"

"No, but we should be able to get one," Greg answered.

"I may have gone on many trips with Lillie, but I'm in no way qualified to help with this, other than to try and keep myself safe. I carry pepper spray. Perhaps we could talk your mom into doing that also," she said. This news seemed to alarm Phyllis.

"That should be a simple thing to convince her to do," I said. I took a moment to think about how I could help. "I can be with her on her way to and from work without her knowing. If they don't get one of you now, they'll have plenty of opportunities to do it once they know all of our schedules."

We thought more about it and in the meantime, Phyllis was going to be more aware of what was going on around her. "We need to try not to reveal anything to your mother," she advised. Everyone agreed on that.

Greg and I went to see Juliet. We told her the chances of them coming for her were less likely than my mother or Phyllis. She understood and said she had been working on her Kapu Ku'ialue. She also informed us she had taught Jacob a few things. Juliet assured us she had not forgotten about teaching us someday soon.

# Eight

I found out they got a warehouse. This meant they should strike soon. We were able to convince Mom to carry the mace, which she attached to her key chain. I could not find out who they planned to take or when.

Jacob, Juliet, Greg, and I went to Burger Boy for a late lunch and discuss what he found out about the Granaldis. We felt it was safe to venture out because Mom and Phyllis were at home wrapping Christmas presents. Mom wanted us out of the house so I would not see anything I would be getting. Burger Boy Diner was not too far from my home. It was a small burger joint decorated with Louisville Cardinal paraphernalia.

Jacob said, "I've not seen any activity from Anthony Granaldi III. I mean none. He's not been on his computer at all. Emails are coming in and not getting answered. Brooke's right, they must be in hiding."

"Yes, but once they figure out the cops are not suspecting them of having anything to do with the painting we returned, they'll come at us with full force," I said.

"Brooke is correct. They're not the type to let this go. Keep looking for something that says they are back. Brooke and I'll continue checking the house periodically to see if they've returned," Greg stated, as he squirted ketchup on his fries.

My phone rang. I noticed the caller blocked their number. Normally, I would ignore it, but something told me to answer it. It was then my worst fears came to light. I received a phone call from Nadine. She said, "We've got your mom and the maid. If you want them back alive, you'll give me that necklace your grandmother gave you. I'll be in contact." The phone went dead.

My heart started racing. I tried to speak, but the words were not coming out. *I can't breathe.*

Greg's face showed concern. He asked, "Brooke, what is it?" He grabbed the phone from my hand.

"Can't breathe," I muttered.

"You're having a panic attack. You need to calm down. Try inhaling and then exhaling slowly," Jacob advised.

I tried to calm myself by slowing my breathing down as Jacob suggested.

"That's it." He continued encouraging me.

"When you're ready, tell us what's going on," Juliet instructed.

I felt my breathing slow down some. I took a big gulp, followed by a deep breath. "They've got them both," I said as tears streamed down my face.

Greg asked, "Your mom and Phyllis?"

"Yes," I said as I tried to hold back the tears. *This is all my fault. I should've protected them.*

Jacob advised, "Stay calm. You need to focus. Did you hear anything on the call that might tell you where they are?"

I thought for a moment, and said, "No. Everything was silent in the background."

Greg told them to follow us to the house. When we arrived, they were no longer home. Other than a drink spilled on the floor, there was nothing that might suggest they had harmed them.

Juliet asked, "Shouldn't you call the police?"

"No. To protect the stone, we need to handle this ourselves," I informed her.

Greg and I checked out where they were, while Jacob and Juliet said they would remain in the area in case we needed them. I transported us to the backseat of Eddie and Nadine's vehicle. When Eddie parked the car, we found ourselves at the Bed & Breakfast. I teleported us to their room. They were not there, but their things were. We quickly went through their room but found nothing of importance.

We returned to their Dodge Charger and started searching for clues. Greg found a rental agreement for a warehouse. We immediately left their car and headed to Greg's truck because we needed to check out the warehouse. When we got to his house, Greg ran inside and came back with a pair of binoculars. He programmed the address of the warehouse into his GPS and we were on our way to rescue them. Juliet texted me and said they wanted to help. We told them where we were headed. They asked me to come and get them. They parked at the mall, away from anyone. I quickly popped in and got them both and brought them to Greg's truck. It was the first time I brought two people with me into a car. We were all piled up in the backseat. I crawled to the front seat and buckled up.

We found the address. It was a three-story red brick rundown warehouse on a dirt road. As we looked around, we realized they must not be there. If they just picked them up, there were too many people around here to bring them now. They would need to bring them in the dark because too many would notice them bringing in two hostages.

We went to get some food and drinks because it appeared we had a long night ahead of us. I waited in the truck while they got the food. I had one thing on my mind, and it was getting my mom and Phyllis back.

I tried to call their cell phones, but both went straight to voicemail. It was common for Phyllis not to answer, but Mom answered it 98% of the time. I started praying for their safety and for us to locate them quickly. I felt tears running down my face. I quickly sat up. *Pull yourself together. Stay focused on the mission. This is no time to become emotional.* I thought about how strong I had become since receiving the Bloom of Dreams. A total transformation had occurred. I was a new creation thanks to my faith, Greg's training, and my hard work. I was in deep thought because I did not notice them returning to the truck.

Once Greg settled back into his seat, he turned toward everyone and said, "We need a plan. I was thinking, Jacob and Juliet, can stay in the truck and let us know if we've anything to worry about. They'll be our eyes and ears out there."

"How're they going to do that? We can't use our phones." I told Greg.

"I don't know. They'll figure something out. We'll go in and rescue them. While Juliet protects Jacob," Greg added.

Jacob looked like he could sink into his chair before saying, "Was it really necessary to point out that Juliet's my protector." We all got a chuckle out of that, even Jacob.

Juliet commented, "I don't think he's going to need protecting."

We stationed ourselves off the main road. The building was within view when using the binoculars. Each of us took turns keeping an eye out for them. Once it appeared the workers in the area had left for the day, we moved closer to see better. We were still far enough away to be undetected.

The area had a fence, which made it difficult to get the vehicle too close. With the chilly temperature, we did not want to venture out into the cold until we were sure they were there. We were getting bored. We decided to each tell a story we had never told anyone. Juliet went first. Jacob was taking his turn with watching for Nadine and Eddie.

Juliet began, "When my father told me we were moving here and leaving Hawaii, it devastated me. My mother was excited because she went to college in Tennessee and knew she would be close to her friends that still live in that area. The new adventure excited my father. All I could think about was leaving my family and friends. We spent every Sunday with my grandparents."

She paused to take a sip of her water, "I went to school with the same kids my whole life. My friends were like family to me. We began packing and my parents informed me I could only take what I could fit in two suitcases because it was too expensive to move all our things."

Juliet looked down. Her eyes began to fill with tears, "I watched my mother in tears throw out my artwork from school. She didn't know I was watching her. I can't get the image of her tears streaming down her face out of my head. I felt the same way, trying to decide what I would pack. So many things I had held onto to remind me of special memories, were thrown in the trash, never to be seen again."

She wiped her tears that streamed down her face. "I stared at the few things that remained in my room. My walls, once covered with photos and drawings, were bare. Stripped of my memories. I decided I was going to run away. Leaving Hawaii was not an option for me."

I noticed Jacob was no longer doing his job. Juliet had his complete attention as he attentively listened to her story. "Jacob, I'll take over so you can focus on Juliet's story," I offered.

Without hesitation, he handed me the binoculars.

As Juliet continued her story, I adjusted the binoculars to see better.

"I packed a backpack full of a few cherished items and one outfit. I did not even pack a hairbrush or toothbrush. All I knew was I needed to leave and find somewhere to hide until they had moved," Juliet said before being interrupted by me.

"We must've missed them going in. There's a vehicle and a light on inside now," I said excitedly. I turned to Jacob and Juliet and said, "Remember to warn us if there's anything we need to worry about. Oh, and keep your phone on. We'll call you if we need you, but don't call us. Greg, silence your phone."

Greg and I put our coats and gloves on. I turned to Juliet and Jacob and said, "Say a prayer for us." I grabbed Greg's hand and transported us to the inside of the room I could see inside during the daylight hours. The room was on the second floor. The only lights on were on the first floor.

We arrived in a large, dark room with no furniture. It took a minute to let our eyes adjust to the light. I checked the mirror to ensure we were invisible before we headed toward the lower level.

Slowly and quietly, we made our way down a long hallway, looking for stairs to the first floor. I followed behind Greg to make sure he was in front if there was any danger. He halted and held his hand up to his ear to show me I needed to listen. I listened, but I drew my attention to whatever crawled across my boot. I was afraid to look, but something told me it was a rat.

Greg began moving again, heading down a different hallway. We finally made it to the metal stairs that led to the first floor. I tugged Greg's arm to let him know not to go down. The stairs would be very noisy. I looked at the bottom of the stairs to ensure the area was safe to transport to the first floor.

We continued toward the noise. When we were nearly outside the door, we could not see in, but we could hear them clearly.

"Sandra don't worry. Brooke will save us," Phyllis informed her.

Mom responded sarcastically, "Oh sure, my daughter's going to figure out a way to find us and take down these kidnappers. I think that drug they gave us must still be in your system because you're not thinking straight."

She sounded like her teeth were chattering. It was then we heard something coming down the hall. As they came into view, we could see two people wearing dark clothes, ski masks, and gloves, and one was carrying a bag. They entered the room they were being held in. We tiptoed to the doorway to get a better view of the room.

What I saw brought a tear to my eye. My mother and Phyllis were both tied to metal chairs. They were about five feet apart. Neither of them was wearing coats, and the building was freezing. The smaller one asked Mom if she wanted some water. As soon as I heard the voice, I was certain it was Nadine, which meant the taller one was Eddie.

The logical side of my brain wanted me to take Greg upstairs to plan our next move, but I did not listen to that side of me. I knew we had to be visible because we had to try to keep the stone a secret from them and my mom.

Making sure we would be visible, I teleported us into the room just behind Nadine but out of Eddie's sight line. I immediately hit Nadine with a leg sweep and brought her to the ground. She turned to me and looked me straight in the eye. She seemed incredibly surprised to see me. Greg was at this point in his own battle with Eddie. I stood, prepared to strike again. Nadine quickly got to her feet. She had begun her attack by attempting to use a jab punch on me, which I was able to block. Our battle continued with me getting a few punches and kicks in and her a few punches. Looking at her technique, it appeared she had boxing experience.

Nadine punched me so hard it knocked me to the ground. I shook it off and felt myself recover quickly. I rolled myself out of the way of her next punch and was able to get back up. Thankfully, Greg taught me how to defend myself. I was blocking more punches than I was throwing. As I watched the punches coming at me, I noticed her rhythm. I dodged one of her punches and could finally knock her down. We struggled for a while on the ground, each of us trying to get the upper hand on the other. I pinned her down. I glanced over at Greg and noticed he and Eddie still had their own battle going on.

Demanding to know the answer, I asked, "Who hired you?"

Nadine seemed determined not to tell me, but I had her arm locked and tightened my grip, which caused her more pain. I demanded, "Tell me now!"

I heard a large thud. I looked over and noticed Eddie had fallen to the ground and appeared to be out cold. Greg ran over to Phyllis and untied her. He took those ropes and tied up Eddie before returning to untie my mother.

"Nadine, it's just you and me now. Eddie is out of the game," I said as I moved her so she could see him but keeping my grip on her.

"Fine," she said in a hoarse voice. I released my grip some from her throat to allow her to articulate. "Phillip Davis," she muttered.

I looked over at Mom, who seemed shocked. Phyllis was trying to help Greg untie her. They were both shivering.

"We needed to get them out of here before they freeze," I hollered to Greg before returning my attention to Nadine. "If I let you live, I don't want to see you or Eddie again. You're going to tell Phillip you're done. You'll not work for him again, or I'll make sure my ancestors haunt you for the rest of your life no matter where you go."

"Okay. Okay, just let me check on Eddie," she said as she started crawling over to him.

"You're not to untie him until we're gone," Greg instructed Nadine.

I took my jacket off and gave it to my mom. Greg gave his to Phyllis. "Before we leave, I need to talk to Phyllis," I said as I walked her out to the hall. I whispered, "Do you think Mom knows anything?"

"She might, but I can try to blame anything she might have seen on the drugs they gave us to knock us out," Phyllis suggested.

I took out my phone and called Juliet. "Come to the front of the building and make sure the heat is on. We've got some very cold ladies here. I revealed nothing to my mother, so keep our secret," I said before hanging up the phone.

Greg asked Nadine, "How do we get out of here?" Nadine pointed in the direction they had come from before entering the room. Eddie started stirring.

As we walked toward the entrance of the building, my mom turned to me and said, "I've so many questions, but first I need to get warm."

I realized I needed to come up with a believable explanation. We squeezed all of us into the truck, and I made introductions before we headed back to my house. We were nearly home when Mom and Phyllis said they were warming up.

Greg and Jacob immediately started building a fire for them when we got home. Juliet and I went into the kitchen to get them something to eat. We looked around, trying to figure out what we would make quickly. We decided on making them scrambled eggs and toast. I made some decaf coffee for Mom and hot tea for Phyllis. When the meal was ready, we had them come into the dining room. They seemed to notice the temperature difference from the sitting room, so Mom asked Greg to make another fire in the dining room fireplace. Juliet and I brought their food and drink out to them while Greg worked on the fire.

I apologized, "I'm sorry about the food. We wanted to get you something warm and this was the quickest thing we could come up with."

Phyllis looked up after her first bite and said, "It is delicious. Thank you."

They both ate rather slowly, which concerned me. I needed a distraction, so I grabbed Juliet's arm and said, "We'll be right back." I took her into the kitchen pantry. "Do you want to do something fun?" I asked.

"Of course," she said.

I informed her of my plan, and we were off to Eddie and Nadine's room at the Bed & Breakfast.

When we arrived, they were fighting over putting ice on their wounds or staying warm. *Strange. I'm not hurting.* I picked up a wallet I found on the table and opened it up in front of them. Pulled the driver's license out and made a mental note of their home address. As I was doing this, they were both staring at the wallet. I was sure they thought I was a ghost as they watched the wallet float in the air.

"Eddie, she wasn't kidding. She sicked her ghosts on us," Nadine said, seeming to be frozen in place.

Juliet said, "This is a warning. Stay away or we'll haunt you forever."

I dropped the wallet and ID on the bed. I grabbed Juliet, and we returned to my house.

"That was so fun!" Juliet said excitedly.

I quickly jotted down the address from the ID on the kitchen notepad. "Quick, find something for dessert for them," I instructed.

Juliet found fruit salad. We made each of us a bowl before returning to the dining room. As we ate, Greg filled us in on what he had explained to my mother about how we found her.

I mouthed to him, "Thank you."

Mom said, "So, Phillip was behind this. I should have listened to you about him, Brooke. Why does he want Mom's necklace so badly?"

Jacob jumped into the conversation by saying, "Perhaps it is worth more than you think?"

Greg added, "I don't know anyone that has ever seen a stone like that. It seems rare."

"It could also have a special meaning to him. I mean it's a family heirloom," Juliet added.

I asked, "The question is, what are we going to do about it?"

Mom added, "Well, I think we should have the police track them down."

Phyllis interrupted her, "No, you don't need to get the police involved. Brooke can make sure he understands that we'll press charges if he anything like this happens again, but it's best to keep it in the family. This could have adverse side effects if the press finds out about it, and they will if you press charges. Not to mention, if the necklace is that valuable, it'll bring a lot of attention to it and could make things worse."

I appreciated her trying to discourage Mom from doing anything.

"Fine, but just so everyone knows. Phillip is not welcome here any longer," Mom announced. We all laughed.

Finding out Phillip was behind the kidnapping had made my blood boil. It was no wonder my grandmother had no contact with him or his family. I decided to pay my cousin Phillip a visit. To be more specific, Greg and I were going to go, but first we were going to see if we could find out more about him and his connection to the Granaldis. We decided to teleport to the west side of Central Park because his place was right next to it. I looked up images on Google maps using the street view to figure out where to go. There were large rocks covered with trees across the street from his place. We arrived by the rocks, making sure we were invisible. After moving out of anyone's view of us and becoming visible again, we climbed down the rocks onto the brick sidewalk.

I looked across the street at the grandness of his fifteen-story gray brick building. They made the lower two levels with large bricks, about the size of a cinder block, while all the other floors were normal size bricks in a variety of shades of grey. There was a large tannish gold revolving door with normal glass doors flanking both sides of it. We entered the building. A tall doorman with dark hair and a mustache greeted us. I told him, "I'm here to see my cousin Phillip Davis, he's in 80N."

The doorman looked down at me and then looked me over. He stood there for a minute, trying to decide what he should do. He took a deep breath before heading behind the marble counter to call my cousin.

While he waited for an answer, I spun around to locate the elevator and stairs. The elevator was opposite the revolving door, and it looked like the stairs were down the hall. As I waited, I took in the entryway's grandeur. They decorated it with white marble with gray streaks. There were modern furnishings throughout the entry.

The doorman cleared his throat. When he had my attention, he said, "I'm afraid the gentleman in question must not be at home. Whom, shall I say, was here?"

"We'll come back," I said, as I quickly made my way back through the revolving door. The chill from the winter hit me immediately. Greg and I needed to go back in, but we needed to find somewhere to teleport. It was freezing here. Much colder than home.

The many noises surprised me. The sounds of the city flooded my ears. I could hear people talking, cars honking, a siren, music playing, and someone slamming on their brakes. This was within just a few moments of exiting the building.

We walked around the block and found some stairs heading down to a lower level. Trash had blown down there from the street above. The walls blocked some of the wind, but I knew I wished I had a few more layers. Making sure we were not within view of anyone, we transported invisibly back into the building just to the left of the elevator.

The doorman was playing on his phone when we arrived. We waited for someone to exit the elevator and quickly jumped in when it was empty. We headed up to the eighth floor.

When the door opened, we headed down the typically unassuming hall, it's corporate styling making it indistinguishable from any other chain owned hotel. We finally found the door with 80N and waited until Phillip arrived. We stayed out of the way.

After waiting nearly 45 minutes, we sat down. I looked at the time on my phone and it was nearly 11:00 pm. I fought closing my eyes. Greg noticed because he moved closer to me and motioned for me to put my head on his shoulder. Once my head was comfortable, I closed my eyes, hoping to get a quick nap before he arrived. As I was falling asleep, I could feel Greg kiss the top of my head.

I do not know how long I was there, but Greg woke me when the elevator opened. In a quiet voice, Greg said, "He is here. You need to get up."

Phillip headed our way. Greg helped me up to prevent Phillip from tripping over me. He had made it about halfway down the hall when he dropped his keys. Greg and I hurried out of his way to be sure he would not run into us. I made sure I would be able to see inside his apartment when he opened the door.

Phillip slowly made his way past us and to his door. He began fussing with his keys and dropped them again. I noticed he appeared tired. He usually had good posture that enhanced his height of 6 feet. His brown hair, normally slicked back, had fallen some around his face. He dressed nicely in his dark gray fitted suit, light gray shirt, and navy blue, black, and gray striped tie. There was a dark overcoat tossed over his left arm. Today, he looked older than my mother even though they were about the same age. The lock seemed to be a bit of a challenge for him, but he finally opened the door.

I quickly attempted to create a memory of his foyer before he closed the door. I took a moment to recall what I saw and realized I had what I needed to return. There were various artworks hung about the walls and the floors were a light-colored wood.

"Aren't we going in?" Greg said, as he pulled himself away from the wall.

"Let's come back tomorrow when he's at work," I said, grabbing his arm. "Besides, I'm tired. I want my bed."

# Nine

Juliet came over to Greg's house to show us Kapu Ku'ialue. Greg had a small heater on in the corner of the garage to help keep us a little warmer. When Jacob and Juliet arrived, Juliet warned us that Kapu Ku'ialue or Lua was also known as the Hawaiian art of breaking bones. It incorporates throws, pressure point manipulation, strikes, and a variety of weapons. We were going to work on hand-to-hand combat. She had us first warm up with Hula. She explained Hula and Lua work together. You could tell that Greg and Jacob seemed embarrassed learning the Hula dance. I was enjoying it. As a bonus, it was warming me up some, but not entirely because of the physical activity. I found myself laughing from watching Jacob and Greg attempt the Hula.

She began showing us ways to defend ourselves and how to counter the moves with another move. Many of the moves she showed us reminded me of wrestling. Juliet demonstrated how to pin someone to the ground. She also explained a little about how she would use a weapon. She grabbed a broom from the corner of the garage. She spun around and went after Greg. It was impressive how much Juliet knew and how she could take him down. He put up a good fight. Greg wanted another shot but wanted to use a weapon against her. That was a much more interesting battle. Jacob and I had to dodge some of their attacks as well. Not that they were trying to swing at us, but because of the lack of space. *I think we should try this outdoors next time.*

When we finished, Greg pulled out some folding chairs and got each of us some water. We started discussing the four of us going to Phillips's house. I tasked Jacob with finding Phillip's computer and doing his thing with it. Juliet, Greg, and I looked for anything suspicious he might have been up to. We needed to find out what he knew about the stone. We all agreed we would wear spy attire, including rubber gloves.

"We must make sure we put everything back exactly where we found it," I reminded them before everyone went to get cleaned up. We agreed to meet at my house when everyone was ready.

I found Phyllis sitting at the kitchen counter drinking hot tea and reading a cooking magazine when I arrived. I filled her in on our plan. Phyllis and I had become much closer since I moved here. We talked a little about how she and Mom were doing after the kidnapping. She explained my mom was having a hard time. The trauma of the event was a lot, but Phillip being responsible was even worse. She explained my mother was considering taking a few days off and heading to Florida to see her old church friends.

I headed upstairs to get cleaned up before everyone came over. Once done, I headed back downstairs to see if anyone had arrived. I found Greg in the kitchen with Phyllis. They were discussing lunch plans. Phyllis planned on having lunch ready for us when we returned.

It was not long before Jacob showed up. "I thought Juliet was coming with you," I said, wondering where she was.

Jacob looked disappointed and said, "Her mom said she needed to do some chores, so she won't be coming."

"That stinks. I guess we should get going. Let me confirm he's not there before I bring both of you. I'll be right back," I informed them. When I arrived, the house was empty.

I scared them as soon as I returned by letting out a shriek, which caused them both to jump.

"So, ya think you're funny, do ya," Greg began tickling me.

Unable to hold back my laughter, I tried to get away. He finally released me.

"Enough of that. We need to get to work," I blurted out as I tried to catch my breath.

Greg spouted, "We are waiting on you, Brooke."

I grabbed their arms, but not before rolling my eyes at Greg. We arrived in the foyer with the paintings of abstract art in front of us. Greg was going to head toward the left, which looked like a den. I went to the right, down a small hallway. Jacob followed Greg and went left in search of Phillip's computer. The paintings continued into what appeared to be the living room. The furniture style was a modern art deco, and it complimented the artwork in the room. This room had little to search through. I looked under the sofa and chairs but found nothing. Directly opposite the doorway was another hallway. I followed the hallway until I came upon two bedrooms and a hall bathroom. I went to the left, to what appeared to be the master bedroom. There were several closets along the entrance to the room. Once past the closets, the room opened, revealing a bed on the right side of the room with a black and white bedspread adorned with several copper-colored pillows. Under the large window was a black loveseat with pillows which matched those on the bed. Just to the left of that was a full-length mirror. A wooden dresser ran along the same wall as the closets.

I began going through the drawers and turned up nothing. An inspection under the bed and sofa revealed nothing. *Why am I checking the sofa? He's not expecting us or anyone to be going through his things.* As I walked back to the closet, I noticed the modern bathroom. It was mainly black and white, with a colorful rug. *Move on, Brooke, there is nothing to see here.* After discovering several boxes in the closet, I pulled them down and made my way through them. One had what appeared to be mementos from his childhood. I checked the back of pictures for notes and then I paused. I found a picture of my mother and Phillip with what appeared to be their parents. They were young; my Great Grandmother...*Is that? It is!* My Great Grandmother had the Bloom of Dreams.

I wanted this picture, but I had leave it in its place. I could not even take a picture of it because we left our phones at home so no one could trace us here. Phillip had everything perfectly placed. I returned the box to its original location. My search continued. I made sure I checked each box. I placed the last box up on the shelf before moving on to the bottom of the closet. Phillip was like a woman with his organization and shoes, and more shoes. *Oh wait, there are more shoes.* The closet was nearly full of his boots, dress shoes for every occasion. There was a small bag stuffed in the back of the closet. I pulled it out and carefully went through it. It appeared to be a go-bag. There were even thousands of dollars in it and a couple of passports in other names, but they had his photo.

Once I completed my search, I headed to the room down the hall. This room was much more my style, with a navy-blue dresser with silver handles. The bedspread was cream with large navy-blue flowers. There were more beautiful abstract art pieces in this room. A small closet was on the other side of the room. I opened the dresser drawers, but there was nothing in them.

I went to the closet, and it appeared Phillip must store his summer clothes in this closet. Still nothing. I exited the room and headed down to the other end of the living room, toward the balcony.

The wall at the end of the room was mainly glass. The view was of the city. In front of the window, there were many potted plants on a small shelf between the two doors that led out onto the patio. At the other end, a round glass table with navy art deco chairs and a navy rug with some type of silver floral design on it looked as though it was rarely used. Just past that was the den, with a large L-shaped beige sofa. A cream round coffee table accompanied it with a sculpture on it. There was a large flat-screen television on the wall opposite the sofa. Behind the sofa was a large piece of art that had copper color along with shades of black, gray, and yellow. I searched every nook of this room and found nothing.

I headed to the room just off the dining room, where I found Jacob working at a glass desk with what must have been Phillip's computer. "Jacob, make sure you do not leave prints on the glass," I instructed.

"No problem. I'm nearly done setting this computer up," he muttered as he continued clicking away on the keyboard. His typing was almost like some strange musical sonata as he hit the keys.

The closet caught my eye as the next area that needed searching. Upon opening it, a filing cabinet greeted me. It seemed to be where he stored his real estate files. As I looked through the files with names like Escu, Glantzis, Greico, Moore, Schwartz, and Teitelbaum, I still found nothing. I continued looking until I heard what sounded like the front door. Jacob quickly got off the computer and put everything back as he found it, while I closed the filing cabinet and closet door. He ran his sleeve along the area to remove any prints before moving next to the wall. Thank God we were invisible.

I quickly popped over to check on Greg. He was quietly closing a closet. I motioned for him to come with me. We quickly transported back to Jacob, who looked as though he was becoming one with the wall behind the desk. Jacob shot me a look that told me he seemed annoyed I'd left him.

Phillip was sitting at his desk looking at the Multiple Listing Service. I grabbed Greg and Jacob's arms and took us back to my house out of fear one of us might make a sound. There was also a chance Phillip's keen sense of smell would detect us.

I had us reappear in the upstairs library. Jacob turned to us and said, "That was close."

Greg added, "Too close."

Grabbing a pad and pen from the desk, I began taking notes on what each of us had discovered. I asked, "Greg, did you find anything?"

Greg said with regret, "No, there were a lot of boxes in the bedroom that contained, serving dishes, holiday decorations, suitcases, and things, but nothing we could use. The room seemed to be used for storage and an occasional guest."

"I found nothing of significance," I added. "Jacob, did you find anything?"

"No. There was hardly anything on his laptop, but when he came in the room, he pulled a flash drive from his pocket. When he opened a folder from it, I saw there were a lot of files on it. I'm thinking he keeps everything there. I've no way of accessing it unless it's left on the computer and he's not there," Jacob said.

There was a long pause. Jacob continued, "I could check it in the middle of the night. Brooke will need to get it. Drop it off to me. Once I've made a copy, she'll returns it. The best part, this happens all while he's sleeping."

A smile came across Greg's face, flowed by, "I love it. That's a great idea, Jacob."

"I agree. How about I head over there tonight about 3:00 am. I'll find the flash drive and bring it to you. How long will it take you to copy it?" I asked.

"It won't take long," Jacob advised.

"Great!" I said excitedly. "We may find some information out about him soon."

We headed down to the dining room for lunch. The aroma of chili filled the entire first floor. Jacob seemed to enjoy it. He had two bowls. While we ate, we worked out the details about the retrieval of the flash drive.

After lunch, Jacob headed home, and Greg and his friend Austin were going to be shooting for the rest of the day. I hung out with Phyllis and helped her get some of her family's presents wrapped.

71

After dinner, I headed to my room and called my friend Mechelle in Florida. She was busy with our friend Amy. They were heading out to go Christmas shopping. *Christmas? How could I forget about Christmas?* Not one gift bought yet. Phillip had been occupying my mind so much I had completely forgotten Christmas was the following week. I spent the next couple of hours looking for gifts for everyone on Amazon and I had to pay extra for shipping to ensure they arrived on time for Christmas. I set my alarm for 2:50 am and went to bed early wearing my sweatpants and sweatshirt.

The annoying sound of my alarm woke me from a deep sleep. I nearly turned it off when I remembered Jacob and I had a mission to complete. An instant rush of adrenaline sprung me from my bed. I quickly fixed my hair in a ponytail and put a pair of gloves on before heading to Phillip's house.

Upon arriving, I took a moment for my eyes to adjust to the light. It was very dark in the apartment, but there was some light shining in through the curtains from the city lights. The computer was closed, and the flash drive was not there. I looked around the desk on the floor. It was then I felt my heart race. Knowing Phillip, he probably had it in his bedroom with him. I quietly made my way to the other side of the apartment.

Phillip's bedroom door was open. I tiptoed over to his nightstand, expecting to find his keys and phone, but only the phone was there sitting on a cordless charger. Phillip was sound asleep. As I looked around the room trying to figure out where he would put his wallet. I could barely see a thing. I headed to his bathroom, hoping it might be on the counter. There was nothing there. When I looked back at Phillip, he had not moved.

I noticed the nightstand drawer was not completely closed. Carefully moving over to the side of the bed. I pulled gently on the open drawer. The drawer was hard to open. It felt like there was a lot of weight in it. As I pulled, there was a thud. Something in the drawer shifted.

Phillip rolled over and was now facing me. My heart raced. *Please don't wake up.* Fortunately, I was invisible but if he woke up, he would notice the drawer. I was sure of it because everything in this house seemed to have its own place. It was even more difficult seeing into the drawer than it was in the room. I stuck my hand in and felt around. I felt what seemed like a watch, a bottle, and cologne. I moved a hand toward the center of the drawer. There was a large item. It felt smooth like a metal. It was difficult to tell with the gloves on, but as I moved my fingers along the edge, I realized it was a gun. Quickly pulling my hand away, I moved to the left side of the drawer and felt his wallet. Just next to the wallet was a flash drive.

I grabbed it and went directly to Jacob. When I arrived, I expected Jacob to be sound asleep, but he was playing a game on his computer and eating a bag of chocolate chip cookies. It amazed me he was as skinny as he was. He had not noticed I was in the room, so I cleared my throat to get his attention. Still nothing. I noticed he had a headset on. Tapping lightly on his shoulder got his attention, but I startled him. Once he composed himself, he told someone he had to go and took off his headset. He took the flash drive and started getting to work on copying it. I curled up in a black chair he had in the corner and before I knew it; I had dozed off.

I awoke to someone shaking my arm. As I looked up, I saw Jacob in front of me. He handed me back the flash drive. He told me he was going to head to bed and would look at it the next day. Trying to wake up, I got up from the chair and realized I really needed to wake up because I had to be focused on the mission of returning the flash drive. Once I knew I was ready, I returned to the nightstand and placed the flash drive back into the drawer. I slowly pushed the drawer back in and Phillip moved. I quickly got out of there and headed back to the safety and comfort of my bed.

# Ten

A text from Greg awakened me asking if I was okay. *Why wouldn't I be?* I glanced at the clock. *9:00 am!* I was late for our workout. I texted him back to let him know I would not be making it today and I would call him later. Exhausted, I went back to sleep until at 10:15 am, I got up and showered before heading downstairs for breakfast. Phyllis looked like she was getting ready to head out when I entered the kitchen.

"Good morning, sleepyhead," Phyllis said as she began fixing me a cup of coffee. "There are cinnamon rolls on the counter for you." She buttoned up her coat and grabbed her purse before turning to me. Phyllis told me about a letter and some Christmas cards that came for me. She placed them on the desk in the foyer. I grabbed a cinnamon roll and my coffee and placed them in front of the stool, but before sitting down, I retrieved my mail. As I sat down, the aroma of cinnamon brought back pleasant memories of Christmas morning. Mom always made cinnamon rolls on Christmas day, but they were not homemade like these. Shuffling through the mail, Amy, Jenniffer, and Mechelle's family sent me holiday cards. The letter only had my address on it. My curiosity got to me. *Who would have sent me a letter?* I opened it and the first thing I noticed was a picture of the inside of an apartment. *Why would anyone send me a picture of their apartment?* I looked to see who it was from. It was signed, Kevin. *Who is Kevin?* I returned my eyes to the top of the letter to find out.

Brooke,
    I know you don't know who I am, but I know a lot about you and your grandmother. You've been tasked with protecting a powerful secret. I'm here to help you protect it. I don't think it's safe for either of us if I came to your home, but you need to understand what Lillie has tasked you with protecting. We need to meet. I have enclosed a picture of my home for you to find me.
Kevin

*Yeah, that did not help.* I thought for a moment about people my grandmother had introduced me to named Kevin, but there were none I could recall. *Who is Kevin, and how does he know about the Bloom of Dreams?* I looked at the picture again. It was a picture of a small living room with a white modern sofa and a modern brown leather chair. The view was of a large city, perhaps New York City.

Kevin must want me to use the stone to go to his home. Thousands of things were running through my mind about how dangerous it would be to go. My curiosity got to me. I would arrive invisible, to check things out before revealing myself. I headed up to my room to get my compact mirror and to use my full-length mirror to see better into the room before I stepped into it.

I peered into the apartment, no one was there. I stepped in. Not revealed in the picture was a terrace just behind the back wall. I turned and looked at the other end of the apartment, which opened to a small kitchen with two stools at the counter. Upon a closer look out the window, it appeared to be New York City. I walked toward the kitchen and to the left was a small hallway that led to the bathroom and a bedroom. The bedroom had a queen-size bed with a dark brown suede headboard with cream-colored sheets and a light beige bedspread. There was a black dresser in front of the bed. This room also had two large windows, just like those in the living room. On the dresser was a picture of a man in his twenties with presumably his parents. The same man was in another picture on the windowsill with a woman with brown hair and brown eyes. I went through the closet and found he had nice, fashionable clothes. I headed to the kitchen where mail addressed to Kevin Davis was on the counter. *Why does that sound familiar?* I headed back home to see if Phyllis could be of any help to refresh my memory.

I looked all over for her before I realized she went out before I ate breakfast. I pulled out my phone to call her, but she rarely answered. She kept it in her purse and usually checked it when she returned home. No answer. I left a message for her to call me.

After an attempt to call Greg, he texted to inform me he was at the farm with Austin. They were working on Austin's truck and said he would not be back until late.

*Great, now what do I do?* Kevin was probably at work and would not be home till evening. I headed to our library to do some research while I waited for Phyllis. *Where is that photo album? I know it is here somewhere.* I looked through the many books my grandmother, or possibly my family, had collected. I remembered it having a leather cover, but so many of these books had a similar look. My grandmother had shown it to me once or twice, but I had not seen it in years. I was nearly done looking at the second bookshelf, when my phone rang. Phyllis called me back. I told her about the letter from Kevin Davis.

"I had forgotten about the Davis family," Phyllis said, not offering any additional information.

I asked, "What do you know about him?" There was no answer. I called out, "Phyllis?" There was some shuffling. I asked louder, "Phyllis! Are you okay?"

There was more shuffling. "Sorry, I didn't hear you. I had to put the phone down to get something off a tall shelf. I'm trying to finish my Christmas shopping," she said.

I felt so relieved she was okay.

Phyllis continued, "You asked about Kevin Davis. He's the son of William and Lainie Davis. They're your cousins. Your grandmother trusted them; beyond that, she shared nothing else with me. I need to go to the cashier. I'll be home soon." She hung up.

At least that was good news. *Darn it, I forgot to ask her about the album.* I continued looking.

It was not long before I found it. It was not as large as I had remembered. I took the album to my bed and made myself comfortable before opening it. I could tell this was an old album. I was delicate with it. The album had a lot of black and white pictures and next to the pictures were the names of the individuals, some pictures had dates, which must have been the dates they lived. Odd that the dates were not there for everyone. I continued flipping through the pages until I noticed symbols next to some pictures. *Why had I not noticed this before?* Some had doves near them, and others had ravens.

As I looked closer, I realized not all of them had symbols. I continued flipping until I found my great-grandmother. Her picture had a dove next to it. That led me to believe the dove must be a good thing. Next to her was a picture of a man named Paul Davis with a raven. He looked similar to Phillip. I wondered if this was Phillip's father. I flipped the page and found a picture of my grandmother

Lillie, Phillip, Kevin Davis, and myself. Each of us had a dove next to our picture except for Phillip, who had a raven. William and Lainie Davis were pictured with doves but no dates. Lillie had one date next to her picture. Kevin Davis and I had no date either.

I realized the date next to my grandmother's picture was not her birthday or her date of death. I flipped the page back and notice my great-grandmother had the same end date as the beginning date my grandmother had. My grandmother only had one date. *That's odd.* I looked at the other pictures with dates, and they were all connected. One date flowed from a person to the next person in the book.

Some of the people with a dove next to their name had a date. I wonder if the dates were when they were the protector of the Bloom of Dreams. My grandmother could not give me the necklace when I turned eighteen because she died before she could give it to me. *What does the raven mean?*

I pulled out my phone and looked it up. The raven was a symbol of death and doom, while the dove represents peace and love. I got a pen and wrote the date I received the necklace next to my picture. Next to my grandmother's photo, I wrote the day she passed away. I looked at the protectors, wondering what kinds of things they had to endure being the protector of the Bloom of Dreams.

Those names with doves next to them must also be protectors, so Kevin was trying to reach out to help me. When I finished with the album, I put it back in its place in the library. I headed downstairs to wait for Phyllis.

I had barely sat down when her car pulled down the driveway. I quickly grabbed my jacket and headed out to see if she needed help. Phyllis handed me a few bags and told me the rest could wait to be brought in when I was not around. She had bought my Christmas present. She had me put the packages in a closet just off the kitchen. As tempting as it was to peek inside the bags to see if there was a gift for me, I walked away from them. I wanted to be surprised.

Phyllis said she had some more Christmas decorating to do, which excited me. Every time we came here for Christmas, everything looked amazing. I could never help because my grandmother wanted to make sure it was perfect when we arrived. It was wonderful getting to help. Mom and I never decorated too much because we never had much. It was wonderful getting caught up with Phyllis as well. Before

I knew it, it was nearly 4:00 pm. Phyllis had to start dinner. It was time for me to head to New York.

Kevin was not home yet. It felt awkward waiting for him in his house when he did not know I was coming. Wanting to look casual on his sofa for his arrival, I tried a variety of poses but just felt uncomfortable. Even standing felt awkward. I nearly tried sitting on the arm of the sofa before realizing that would be rude. I looked up and saw the man from the photograph leaning against the kitchen counter watching me. *How long had he been there?* I could feel my cheeks getting warmer. *Great! Now he knows I am embarrassed. Why is he not saying anything?*

Kevin turned without a word and made himself a drink before saying, "It is nice to meet you, Brooke. Would you like something to drink?"

"No, thank you," I said, trying to recover from being humiliated.

"You're probably curious about why I reached out to you," he said. He placed a glass of water in front of me. "In case you change your mind," he said politely. Kevin planted himself in the brown leather chair. "They taught me about Lillie since I was little, and Lillie told my parents and I about you many years ago."

Puzzled, I asked, "My grandmother told you about me?" *Why would my grandmother not tell me about them?*

Kevin continued, "Our family, yours and mine, have been guardians of the Bloom of Dreams for centuries. The look on your face tells me you're surprised to hear this."

"I'm surprised everyone knows about this, but I just found out a few months ago when my grandmother died and willed it to me. Other than finding out you are my cousin and seeing you in a photo album today, I don't remember ever hearing about you or your family," I responded.

"Lillie intended on telling you about everything when you turned eighteen, but her death changed everything. With her sudden death, my family has been remarkably busy trying to find out about what our enemies know and what they are planning. You have an especially important job protecting the stone, and my family's job is to help keep you safe and to protect what we know about the stone. My family has something that is nearly as important as the stone, and we need to keep them apart to keep them both safe," he explained.

*What does he possess? What's he talking about?* Feeling more confused, I asked, "What's more important than the stone?"

"Good question. It's not more important, it's just as important," Kevin answered. He took another sip of his drink. "The secrets of the stone," He replied.

*What is that supposed to mean?* I was sure I knew more about the stone than he did. My grandmother was not aware of the additional power the stone had in its cradle.

Kevin's phone rang. He said, "Yes, the package is here." He listened for a moment before telling the person on the other end to hold. Kevin turned to me and asked, "My parents would like to come over and meet you. Would that be, okay?"

"That's fine." *I hope they could explain to me what Kevin was talking about.*

"She's fine with it," he said to the person on the other end of the phone.

He got up and filled his drink, while I finally took a sip of my water. It startled me when there was a sudden knock on the door. *How could they be here already?* Kevin headed toward the front door. I could hear them greeting one another.

William was a tall, attractive man of average build. Lainie was about four inches shorter with shoulder-length brown hair. I stood up and started walking toward them when Kevin's mother, Lainie reached out and grabbed me. She squeezed me lovingly. "It's an honor to meet you, Brooke. Lillie spoke so highly of you. She always told us how much you and she were alike," she said with a smile. Lainie released her hold on me and took a step back. "Let me get a good look at you," she said as she looked me over. "You look so much like her," she complimented.

William said, "Well, let me get a look." Lainie moved out of the way to let William see me. "You're a beautiful young lady that has made this family proud," he said. He gave me a hug too, which felt more like a nice cuddle from a dad.

After our greetings, we all sat down. Kevin filled his parents in on what little he had told me so far. William started explaining everything in greater detail how they fit into the puzzle, "My grandmother was your grandmother's aunt, which I think makes us second cousins once removed. The Bloom of Dreams has been in our family for centuries. Our family has been the protectors of the stone for as long as we've had it. No one knows where the stone came from or how it got its powers."

William cleared his throat, "Our ancestors have provided instructions to assist the protector with the stone. For the safety of the stone, the instructions have been and should always be apart. Lillie only saw the instructions once. You're the first in a very long time to have the Bloom of Dreams and its cradle. It is impressive you were able to get it. You were able to do in a short time what your grandmother attempted to do most of her life." He cleared his throat again and asked Kevin for a glass of water.

Kevin quickly jumped up and headed to the kitchen. William did not say another word until he took a few sips before continuing. "Not all of our family took their job seriously. A few bad eggs like Phillip and his father have tried to take the stone. Don't underestimate them. They're extremely dangerous. Phillip's father was able to get it once, but he didn't have it long before Lillie took it back. That's how the family discovered they couldn't be trusted. They, however, don't know about the secret we're going to share with you. We'd have more problems than we do now with Phillip if he knew what we possess. Very few people outside our family know anything about the stone. Occasionally, we find out about an ancestor who may have told someone about it when they came looking for it. It seems people hear about it and decided they want to become treasure hunters. None have been more persistent than the Granaldi family. The rumor is that their ancestor was like ours, one of the first to discover the power behind the stone. The bible says in Psalms 34:14, Turn away from evil and do good; seek peace and pursue it. This is what we must do," William explained.

William was filling in the blanks for me. I wanted and needed to know these things. I sat there listening intently to every word.

Kevin added, "We know about Phillip hiring those two thugs, but unfortunately, we found out after you took care of them. Now that you know about us, we can work together to make sure both the stone and the book remain protected."

I asked, "Book? May I see it?"

Lainie placed her hand on William's shoulder. She explained, "Yes, but it's not here. We must keep its location a secret from even you. It's the only way it'll be safe. We know it's important you get time to read it. When we are ready, we will let you know. We'll exchange numbers and when we are near the book, we'll send you a picture to allow you to join us. At that point, you will see it, but you must try to remember everything because we cannot let you see it frequently. Lillie only saw it once. We were only going to allow her to see it again if she obtained the cradle or discovered new powers. Do you understand?"

"Yes," I said, feeling disappointed. I felt like I had received an amazing gift, but I cannot get the instructions to get it to work.

Lainie showed me a small photo album. It had pictures of my grandmother and even my mother with them. It was a shame my mother could not know about me meeting them.

"I don't know about everyone else, but I am hungry," William said before he began rubbing his stomach in a circular motion.

*Food, oh no.* I had forgotten about dinner. "I don't mean to be rude. It was lovely meeting you, but I am late for dinner," I said. We exchanged numbers, and I headed home.

I ran downstairs to the dining room and found Mom helping Phyllis set the table. Mom asked, "How was your nap?"

At first, I was confused. I noticed Phyllis wink at me to let me know she covered for me. "Good, I'm sorry I'm late for dinner," I answered.

Mom advised, "You're just in time. Phyllis asked if it was okay to have a later dinner because you needed a nap. So, Phyllis is about to serve dinner. Our drinks are on the counter. Please bring them to the table?"

I headed into the kitchen and grabbed the drinks when Phyllis caught up with me. She asked, "How did it go?"

"Very well. They're so nice," I informed her. Trying not to disclose much, I headed back to the dining room. Keeping secrets from Phyllis did not make me happy, but it was apparent that my grandmother did not tell her about the book. The less she knew about it, the better. I even planned to keep Greg in the dark about the book and the Davis family.

During dinner, I tried to find out if my mother remembered William and Lainie, but she did not seem to remember them. Perhaps that was for the best. After her experience with Phillip, I think she might be leery to meet other family members any time soon.

# Eleven

The last few days had been hectic, trying to get ready for today. Feeling exceptionally cold, I immediately regretted leaving the warmth of my covers. I put my slippers on and grabbed my robe before heading downstairs. Half asleep, I nearly missed seeing what was going on outside. *Mom needs to see this.* Shifting my direction, I headed straight for the third floor to get my mother. I started yelling before I even made it to her floor. I hollered, "Mom, you need to get up!"

In a drowsy voice, my mother asked, "Is everything okay?" Her body shivered as she left her bed.

I grabbed her robe from her chair and helped her put it on. Excitedly, I said, "You need to come quick. Where are your slippers?"

Mom pointed to her closet and said, "Why's it so cold in here?" Her teeth chattered.

I put her slippers down for her to put them on. Barely giving her time to catch her balance after the last one was on, I pulled her to the window. Excitedly, I said, "Look, Mom! It snowed! We're having our first white Christmas!"

My mother's eyes lit up. She seemed as excited as I was. In all the years we had come up during the holidays, I had never seen actual snow. We both started jumping around.

I grabbed her hand and pulled her toward her doorway. "Let's tell Phyllis," I insisted.

We both headed downstairs. Phyllis was in the dining room lighting a fire. Barely being able to hold back my excitement, I said, "It snowed, Phyllis!" She smiled back at my mother and me.

I ran toward the front door and grabbed Mom on my way outside. I took in a deep breath of the crisp morning air. The coolness filled my lungs. As I exhaled, I could see my breath. Mom and I stood on the porch and tried to catch snowflakes on our tongues. I reached down to grab the snow, and it was so soft and felt like a powder. My mother was not paying attention to me, so I balled the snow up to make my first snowball. My hands ached from the coldness, but I did not care. Confirmed, Mom was not aware of the imminent attack. Bam! I hit my unsuspecting mother in the back, who immediately returned fire. After a few direct hits from both parties, we both had a jolly laugh. We were having the best time. I couldn't remember the last time we had this much fun together. It was nice seeing her act like a kid.

We soon discovered pajamas and snow do not go well together. We both retreated to the warmth of the house. Pajamas were not cutting it. We needed warmer clothes. We ran into the dining room to get warmed by the fire. Our bodies shivered as they slowly defrosted. Phyllis told us we needed to get out of our wet clothes before we got sick. Mom and I did as she instructed.

When we came back down, Phyllis had the table set for breakfast. She made Blueberry Sweet Rolls with Lemon. We enjoyed breakfast and talking about how this was the most magical Christmas ever. As a custom, we opened our presents immediately following breakfast. Periodically, my eyes shifted to watch as the snow silently drifted down outside the window. I wanted so badly to go play in it.

We finished opening our gifts. I felt obligated to stay and spend time with Phyllis and Mom on such an important day. But deep down, I wanted to go out and try sledding or skiing. We sat in front of the fire discussing our favorite Christmas days and enjoyed the warmth of the fire. Phyllis seemed pleased with the books she received. She was figuring out which of her novels she wanted to read first. Mom was trying on her new shoes, and I set up the new touch screen computer I received. I had nearly finished when I received a text from Kevin asking me to come as soon as possible. He attached a picture for me to know where to go. *How was I going to leave on Christmas morning? How am I going to be able to leave?* When Phyllis got up and announced, she needed to get ready to head to her sister's house. This triggered Mom to look at her watch. She said she was not aware it was already nearly 10:30 am. She announced she had to get ready to go to Lance's house. Apparently, he had family in town he would like her to meet them. *Perfect!* I announced I was taking my things up to my room to try my new outfits on.

I made sure my outfits fit before removing the tags. Phyllis popped her head in my doorway to thank me again for my gift before heading out. I asked her if she wanted help to take things to her car, but she said she was all set. It wasn't much longer before my mother did the same thing. She asked me if I wanted to go, but I told her I was looking forward to my snow day.

Once I witnessed my mother's car leave the driveway, I looked closely at the picture before heading over to my full-length mirror. I took one last look at the picture to remember it before looking at the mirror and picturing the photograph in my head. The image appeared in the mirror. It was a room with a large armoire and a sitting area with a portion of the bed showing. Lainie was sitting on the loveseat. I stepped into the room and said, "Merry Christmas."

Kevin and his father were standing by a window. They turned and closed the curtains before saying Merry Christmas back.

William sat down and explained, "We closed the curtains because no one must see you here."

Curious, I asked, "Where's here?"

Lainie began explaining, "It's important you don't know. Besides, the book is being moved from this location to ensure its safety once you've left. We'll likely never meet here again." Lainie offered me a seat. She continued, "You must understand the importance of what's about to happen here. This document's a tool to help you understand the power behind the Bloom of Dreams. Lillie never had the power you now hold. It's also important you always protect the cradle just as you would the stone. If the book, well actually journal, is in danger, we'll let you know. At which time you must help to ensure its safety. The journal doesn't travel as you do, it merely holds your secrets and the secrets of those who had it before you. Others outside your trust circle must not know these secrets. I strongly encourage you to let no one besides those in this room know of the journal's existence. One day, we must entrust these secrets to others to become their protectors. Before that day comes, you must let us know who you have entrusted with your secret. We must let you know who will take over protecting the journal after us. Unfortunately, Lillie did not get to tell you about the stone or about us and the journal. However, she was aware of our selecting Kevin as our successor. We're not out of the picture though; we're here to show him how this works. Kevin is in charge now. We will only assist him and you, of course, if needed. More than likely, you'll only be able to see the book this one time, unless, of course, you discover new powers. Do you understand everything I've told you?"

As I thought about everything, I replied, "Yes, I understand. Please explain again why I'll only be able to see it once?"

William cleared his throat and explained, "It's not safe for the stone and the book to be together. We must keep them apart, which is why you mustn't have access to it."

I took in a deep breath and exhaled slowly to calm myself down. I thought about what kinds of things might be in the book and how this might cause me more danger than I had already encountered. There were many more people involved in the stone's protection than I had expected. *I wonder if there are more family members or treasure hunters that are looking for it?*

Kevin asked, "Are you ready to see it?"

Half afraid and half excited, I replied, "Yes."

Lainie stood up and asked me to lift my arms and spread my legs. This seemed extremely odd, but I did as she requested. She asked me to hand her my phone, which I did. She frisked me; I guess to make sure I had no other devices on me. Lainie checked me just as an officer would if they were looking for weapons.

"Please sit down at the desk and close your eyes," Kevin instructed as he motioned toward the desk.

*Close my eyes. Why?* I moved to the desk on the other side of the room and sat down. Before closing my eyes, I looked back at them, hoping I could trust them. I took a deep breath before closing my eyes. I could hear them moving in the room. They were near the armoire. It sounded like they opened it. It felt like several minutes before it sounded as if the armoire closed. I heard steps coming toward me. They could literally have slit my throat while I sat here with my eyes closed. However, I knew I was safe because the stone had not alerted me.

I could sense someone next to me. The smell of leather filled the air. I heard something being placed in front of me. I heard Kevin say, "You may open your eyes."

In front of me was a well-worn dark leather journal with a leather strap that wrapped several times around the book to hold it closed. The spine of the book had leather cords woven through it that bound the pages into the book. The thin leather straps formed what appeared to be overlapping Xs in two rows along the spine. One was

86

at the top of the spine and the other was at the bottom. Kevin handed me white gloves to wear before touching the book. The gloves felt like cotton and fit snugly. Kevin moved back to the other side of the room. I looked over at them before opening the journal.

I unwound the leather strap that was wrapped around the journal. I eased the strap out and gently pulled it off the book. As I opened it, I noticed the handmade paper with deckle edges. Everything appeared to be in English and the writing was its own art. It reminded me of the writing on the Declaration of Independence. I pulled the necklace away from my skin to see what language was written before me. It was in English. I let my necklace return to its resting place before I began reading.

The journal started off with a man named Benjamin talking about visiting a Seneca Village. It was comprised of two-thirds African Americans and one-third of Irish immigrants. The village was just outside of Manhattan. Their treatment within the city was poor. They established the village just outside the city. He met an African American shoeshine man named Anan. They became friends. Eventually, Anan told him about a ring he had brought with him from Africa. Anan wanted to know if he was interested in buying it because he wanted to buy some land and needed funds.

The ring had a unique stone set in silver. It had patterns of leaves making their way around the stone. The more he looked at it, the more he knew his wife would love the stone. He knew the ring would be too large and was a bit much for his wife, Fannie. However, he knew she would love the stone. Anan agreed on the purchase price. He could not afford a jeweler after what he had spent for the stone. He created a silver pendant with a wire for the stone to set in. While trying to remove the stone from the ring, he noticed the top portion of the ring easily separated from the ring. When detached, it made a pendant with the stone in the center. Allowing it to look more like a pendant with leaves around it. He admired the intricacy of how the pieces connected one with the other.

Fannie received the pendant with the metal wire as a Christmas gift and loved it. He showed her later the ring it came from and offered her the choice of which pendant she wanted to wear. She chose to put it back in the Bloom's Cradle but kept the one her husband had made.

The beauty of the stone fascinated Fannie. She wore it every day. Fannie soon discovered the many powers of the stone. She understood what the Indians were saying when they wanted to trade. They soon discovered the ring was not important. However, the piece the stone sat in provided the additional power. They had begun referring to the stone as the Bloom of Dreams because the stone looked much like a flower, and it was able to do things one could only do in their dreams. The original setting was to be known as the Bloom's Cradle.

It once warned her of a bear and her cubs approaching her child. She told the bear to back up and go back where it came from and, to her surprise, the bear and the cubs started backing up. The bears turned and headed away from them. She was not convinced the stone made them move. Later, she discovered she could get many other animals to do what she wanted.

Fannie learned of its healing powers one day when her cook accidentally cut her hand making dinner, as she cleaned the wound it healed. During a dance, she learned about how it allowed her to persuade people. She talked many handsome gentlemen into dancing with the most unattractive women at the dances. The women usually had no suiters interested.

On a voyage, she learned she could not only understand everyone speaking in a foreign language, but she could speak back to them. During a dinner party, Fannie became annoyed with her husband. She wanted him to stop boasting about his latest trip. He began hearing her talk to him, yet her mouth did not move. He heard her thoughts because she had wanted him to. *This is amazing. I can talk to animals and can telepathically tell people what I don't want others to hear.*

After further reading, I discovered, Benjamin lost his wife at an early age during the birth of their third child. He had the pendant placed back on the ring for himself. They decided soon after discovering the power of the Bloom and its cradle to keep the stone in the family and to keep the powers of it a secret. He created this journal as a tool for his ancestors to help them understand what it was capable of. He asked everyone to write any new discoveries in the journal to be passed down to the next generation. His last entry explained his son, Michael, becoming the protector of what his wife referred to as the Bloom of Dreams.

Michael discovered the ability to walk through walls, but he did not add any other discoveries to the journal. The next few entries only discuss who took possession of the stone until a woman named Madeline discovered she could transport herself through her compact mirror. She made this discovery when she was admiring a gentleman through the mirror. Madeline wanted to bump into him to get his attention. She teleported herself behind him while they were in a store. The shopkeeper went into the back to get the man something and he was at the counter looking at a catalog. She describes the mirror taking possession of her and then releasing her behind the man. Only she did not accidentally bump into him. She hurled at him and pushed him up against the counter and she found herself on the floor. The man helped her up, and the shopkeeper came running in to see what had happened. Madeline was very embarrassed. She practiced using the mirror. Madeline wanted to check in on her children and not disturb them when opening the door. She hoped to arrive invisibly, which she did. There was a note about the Granaldi family getting the ring. *That's how the Granaldi's got the ring!* When they recovered the stone, they could not locate the cradle, which means the Granaldis had separated the stone from the cradle. After the recovery, there were no significant findings. Just some notes about who passed it on to whom. The last line was about my grandmother receiving it. Once finished reading it, I looked up at Kevin.

He said, "I hope this was helpful."

"Yes, it was. Thank you for letting me read it," I said as I got up, but Kevin motioned for me to stay seated and handed me a pen.

"You must write about your grandmother's passing and you inheriting the Bloom of Dreams. Also, something brief about how you recovered the Bloom's Cradle. It is important we document everything," Kevin explained. He moved back to the other side of the room.

I thought for a minute about how I was about to phrase everything. Other protectors would read this, and I needed to be clear. As I wrote, I realized what it would have been like to sign something like the Declaration of Independence. My heart was racing, and I felt proud of what I was able to do. I began my entry:

Lillie Davis passed away unexpectedly and could not discuss the Bloom of Dreams with her granddaughter Brooke Garrison.

Brooke was willed the Bloom of Dreams and tasked with protecting it. Shortly after receiving it, she recovered the Bloom's Cradle from the Granaldis.

I turned to Kevin and asked him what he thought. He looked it over and said, "That's perfect. Now, if you discover any new abilities or when you pass it onto another, I will reunite you with the journal. Traditionally, your grandmother would've been here to write her last entry before you would've had the opportunity to read the journal."

I wished I had her here with me on such a special day. It had made this even more special than it already was.

"Brooke, thank you for coming. We are sorry we pulled you away on Christmas. We felt we were less likely to be followed today," William hugged me. "Kevin must move the book to a new secure location before it is discovered. We must ask you to leave now," William said as Lainie gave me a hug.

We wished one another a Merry Christmas and said our goodbyes before I headed back to my room.

# Twelve

Immediately, I jotted down every power I could remember reading in the journal. *Let's see; warning of danger, talking to animals, healing, persuasion, understanding and speaking other languages, telepathy, walking through walls, and teleportation.* I now knew the mirror was Madeline's, and I wondered why her mirror works and no other small mirrors. *Or do all work?* I had not tried using any other small mirror. Once I was sure I had forgotten nothing, I tried a few of the powers out.

I went to my bathroom and pulled out my eye shadow. It had a small mirror. Looking into the mirror, I had concentrated on the kitchen. Before I knew it, it sucked me in just like the compact mirror, and found myself in the kitchen. Apparently, any reflection would work. I just need to concentrate. *That does not mean I should leave my compact mirror at home. No, it's a perfect tool to have when there is nothing else to use.*

I saw the island counter and tried to walk through it. My first attempt did not work well. I ran my foot and my knee into the door of the cabinet. I told myself to stay focused before making another attempt. As I stepped forward, my mind told me to stop, but my body did not feel the counter as it passed through me. *Freaky. How is it I don't feel any different? It's as if I'm a ghost or something, only you could not see through me unless I was invisible. That gave me an idea.* The bar would be the perfect place to test another theory because I could watch myself in the mirror while I passed through it. I stood in front of the bar and concentrated. *Amazing!* I watched myself vanish as I became invisible. I did not even need to step through the mirror to become invisible. *This is fantastic!* I walked through the bar while I watched the mirror to see any difference in the bar or see myself. I saw nothing. *Wow, this is great!*

All I wanted to do was tell Greg, but disappointment came over me knowing I could say nothing. He would question how I learned so many skills in a day. I decided not to reveal my new skills unless I needed to use them in front of anyone. It also occurred to me; we had not come up with a name for our group. I sat down, trying to come up with a good name. There was a knock at the door. As the front door came into view, I noticed Greg and Karen wearing ski jackets.

"Merry Christmas," I said as I opened the door and gave Greg a kiss and Karen a hug before inviting them in.

Karen spirited, "We're heading to Mount Washington to do some sledding. Do ya want to join us?"

"Of course!" I said, excited about going sledding for the first time. "Let me go get some warmer clothes."

"Oh, we brought you my mom's snow boots to help keep your feet dry. Mom thinks they will fit you," Greg said.

I thanked them and asked Karen to help me find the right clothes for this type of activity. Karen told me we were going to Travis's house to sled. I had not seen him in a while. Greg and Travis had not seen each other much lately. Once I was ready to go, I texted my mom and Phyllis about my plans before jumping into Greg's truck.

On the way to Mount Washington, we discussed everything that had happened earlier in the day. However, I left out the part about my secret meeting with my cousins and my new discoveries. As I looked out the window, I found the view of the snow along the sides of the highway mesmerizing. I thought about the name of our group. Most of my ideas sounded silly. Some ideas were The Secret Whisperers, Brooke's Brigade, and Secrets of the Bloom. Then it hit me, The Bloom Keepers. *It's perfect!* We were the keepers or guardians of the Bloom of Dreams and its cradle.

Once we arrived at Travis's house, I noticed a big hill on the side of the property where everyone was sledding. Greg pulled a couple of plastic sleds out of the bed of his truck and handed one to his sister. "Sorry, I only have one for us."

We walked over to Travis and his family to say hello and wish them a Merry Christmas before Greg took me over to the hill. He laid the sled down and hopped on the front of it. "Hop on the back. I'll drive," he said.

As we headed down, the cold air hit my face, but it did not bother me. Perhaps because of the excitement of going down for the first time. It was wonderful. On the walk back up the hill, I told Greg about the name of the club. He loved it. Greg and I went down one more time together. He provided me with instructions on how to steer. The next time, I was going down alone. I had a blast. Greg let me go down several more times by myself while he talked with Travis. By the time I finished, I was cold and wet, but it was worth every minute. I joined Travis and Greg and thanked Travis for having us.

Travis seemed to notice I was shivering because he asked me to follow him into the house. He instructed me to sit in front of the fire while he got us hot chocolates. The fireplace looked outdated, and it appeared their furniture was out of style, but the home was clean and well taken care of. Karen joined me while Greg headed out for more sledding. Karen found it surprising this was the first time I had seen snow. She did not know what life in South Florida was like. When I told her, the only snow I had ever seen was handmade. She thought I was kidding. She asked what the beach was like. Raised in Florida, it had not occurred to me that many people had never been to a beach. We spent our time discussing the differences between Florida and Kentucky.

We were enjoying our conversation and did not realize how long we had been chatting. Greg came in, looking tired from sledding. He informed us we needed to head home. My clothes had dried some, but the cool air with the wet clothes chilled me to the bone. I could not recall a time in my life when I had been so cold. I warmed up a little when the heater in the truck kicked in.

When we arrived at Greg's house, Karen headed inside, and Greg walked me home. The house was a little chilly, so Greg started a fire. I went to the kitchen and made us hot chocolates. When I returned, Greg was standing in front of the fire. It looked as though he was drying his pants.

I smiled and said, "I've got hot chocolate."

He took the cup and put his hands around it. "I think I should've changed before heading over here," he said. His lip quivered.

"If you need to go, I understand," I assured him.

"No, I wanna give ya your Christmas present," he said, reaching inside his pocket. Greg held out a small box with a ribbon.

I slowly opened the box, wondering what was hidden inside. As I opened it, a beautiful silver ring surprised me.

Greg took the ring from the box. He looked me in the eye. I held my breath as I waited for him to say something.

"I love ya, Brooke. I couldn't imagine life without ya," Greg said before taking a deep breath. He continued, "This is a love infinity ring. It's my promise to love ya forever." He placed it on my ring finger.

*Wow!* I was all choked up. Tears of joy filled my eyes. "I love you too," I said. I gave him a kiss as tears fell down my face.

He pulled his face away from mine and asked, "Why are ya crying?" He wiped a tear away from my cheek.

I chuckled and explained, "I'm happy, silly. Never in my life could I've imagined someone as wonderful as you." We kissed again.

I wiped the tears from my cheeks and smiled at Greg. "I've got a gift for you, too," I said. I pulled a present from under the tree and handed it to him.

He took the tissue paper out of the bag and pulled out a framed picture of the two of us. He smiled and said, "Love it!"

"There's more," I explained.

He looked in the bag again and pulled out a framed Bruce Lee Photo. "Bruce Lee! This is perfect. Thank you," he said without taking his eyes off of it. He then placed it on the sofa and gave me a hug and a long kiss on my forehead.

God had truly blessed me. I could not imagine all the amazing things that had happened to me in such a short period. We were both still chilled. I grabbed a blanket, and we laid it in front of the fire. We sat there talking for a while about the magical Christmas we had.

Over the next few days, I had a lot of fun with my friends enjoying the snow and winter weather. I did not even think about trying out the other powers of the stone. I can't believe it was New Year's Eve. Mom was going out with Lance. Phyllis stayed home because she did not like being out on the road on New Year's Eve. She was usually in bed by 10:00 pm.

To enjoy our evening, we ordered some of our favorite snack foods. We would use paper plates and plastic cups for easy cleanup. As we set everything up, I realized I had done nothing like this since I moved here. It was exciting planning a party with Phyllis. We ordered hot chicken wings, spinach-artichoke dip with fire-roasted bread, fried pickles with buttermilk ranch, chips with guacamole, southwestern egg rolls, mini apple pies, mini cheesecakes, and churro bites with chocolate sauce.

Once the food arrived. We put the food that needed to be kept warm in chafing dishes. Phyllis showed me how to change the levels of the food to make the table look amazing.

I ran upstairs to finish getting dressed. My outfit was a long sleeve mini dress in dark silver. The dress appeared as though it wrapped around me. This was the most comfortable evening attire I owned, and the long sleeves kept my arms warm. My black heels complemented the outfit. I curled my hair and put my makeup on before anyone arrived.

The party started at 8:00 pm. Travis was the first to arrive with his girlfriend, Missy. Greg came just after him with his sister, Karen, and her friend, Lisa. Jacob and Juliet arrived with flowers for Phyllis and me. Phyllis did not want to invite anyone. She said she was looking forward to relaxing and enjoying the evening.

The evening was going to be interesting because I was going to practice using the power of persuasion. Part of me felt guilty trying this new power on people I cared about. But they were the perfect people to test it on because I knew their character. My plan was to persuade them to do things they would not normally do.

My first victim was Travis. It was my understanding his voice was astonishing. He had only sung at church on rare occasions. Greg said he never even heard him sing in this truck, no matter how badly someone begged. I made my way over to him and asked him to play Sweet Home Alabama. Travis responded, "I will play the piano if anyone else wants to sing."

Not knowing how this worked, I headed to the kitchen. If I had tried this in the room with everyone, it would draw some attention. I concentrated on Travis, telling him how talented he was, and assured him everyone would love to hear him sing. I continued this for a few minutes. Just as I had given up, I heard Sweet Home Alabama playing on the piano.

I joined everyone around the piano as he sang. Everyone seemed in awe of his talent. By the end of the song, everyone was singing with him and asking him to play something else, which he did. I could not understand why he was so shy about his singing because he had talent. This skill needed work. It was difficult to persuade someone.

Telepathy was the next on my list. Phyllis was the ideal person to do this with. I took a deep breath and concentrated on her. She was in one of the dining room chairs, watching Travis play his second song.

95

I asked, "Phyllis, can you hear me?" *Is she listening?* She started looking around the room. Again, I said, "Phyllis, can you hear me? How do you think the party is going?" Still no response. "Phyllis, if you can hear me, just answer back like you would if you were talking to yourself."

Phyllis looked over at me with a puzzled look. She asked, "Brooke, how are you doing this?"

I smiled at her and began eating a chip. While I ate, I said, "I'm sure it's the stone. Do you think everyone is having fun?"

"Yes, they are. Your friends are lovely," she said with a smile. It was strange having a conversation with someone when neither of us were moving our mouths.

Regrettably, Travis got up from the piano. Everyone seemed disappointed. I did not want to push further, so I turned on some music. I took hold of Greg's hand, and we started dancing. No one else seemed to want to. I began concentrating on persuading everyone to dance. *Why is it not working? Maybe I need to try each one separately.* I tried again, only this time, I concentrated on Juliet. It worked because she was trying to get Jacob to dance. Jacob needed some persuading. I began working on him. Finally, he began dancing with Juliet. I made my way around the room. Everyone but Phyllis was dancing. A slow song came on, and Greg pulled me closer to him. I was glad I did not need to persuade him to dance. As he held me, his touch comforted me. Everyone danced through several other songs.

Just before midnight, Greg asked me to grab my coat, and he led me outside. "I hope ya don't mind, but I wanted this moment for just us," he said. He turned some Harry Connick Jr. on his phone and asked me to dance. We danced until we heard everyone cheering inside. Greg looked me in the eye. Just before he kissed me, he said, "Brooke, this has been the best year because of ya. I love ya."

This kiss was by far the best he had ever given me. Perhaps it was the romance of the evening. It was different. Magical. It was the kiss from fairytales. I would forever remember that moment and that kiss.

After everyone left, Phyllis and I put the food away. Phyllis and I discussed how much fun everyone had as we headed to bed.

Something woke me at 7:40 am. It was a call coming from Kevin. Half asleep, I answered the call, "Kevin, is everything okay?"

With panic in his voice, he said, "No, the Granaldis took my parents!"

*What?* Barely being awake, I needed to confirm, "Did you say the Granaldis took your parents? What makes you think that?"

His voice crackled as he said, "They contacted me. They want the journal in exchange for their lives."

"Send me a picture of where you are. I will be there soon. I need to get dressed," I said before hanging up the phone.

I leapt out of bed and got dressed. I wanted to call Greg and ask him to come with me, but I knew I should try to do this myself. If he came, I would risk him finding out about the journal.

I checked my phone expecting a picture, but I received a text telling me he was at his home. Once I was ready to go, I grabbed a coat, gloves, and my compact mirror and headed to Kevin's house.

Kevin was pacing the floor when I arrived. He seemed to be in deep thought because he did not notice me arrive. "Kevin," I said in a calm voice, not to startle him.

He looked up and quickly came over to me and gave me a tight hug and said, "Thank you for coming so quickly." Once he let go of me, he stepped back. "They want the journal, Brooke. I can't let them kill my parents for it."

I assured him, "No one's going to die. Do you have the journal?"

Kevin took a deep breath before answering, "No, we need to get it." He picked up a picture from his counter and handed it to me.

The picture was of a bank of a creek with pine trees in the background. I took in everything I could from the image and asked Kevin to hold my left arm. Before grabbing my arm, he grabbed a coat, gloves, scarf, and hat. I noticed he was wearing snow boots when he grabbed my arm. I pulled out my compact mirror, and then turned to him and said, "If you've not done this before, prepare yourself. This is going to be weird."

He tightened his grip on my arm, but quickly released it. Kevin said, "Wait!" He dashed out of the room and returned with another hat and scarf. He handed them to me and said, "You're going to need these."

I grabbed the items and put them on. Once ready, we headed to the creek. When we arrived, the view differed from the picture. They had taken the picture during the summer, and it was December.

Snow blanketed the trees and ground. The edges of the creek had frozen.

Kevin looked around, possibly to get his bearings. He said, "We need to head this way."

We walked quite a while before I asked, "How much farther?"

"Not too much longer," he said, shivering.

I too was freezing. Kevin did not tell me we would be in this weather for this long. To say my shoes and socks were soaked, would be an understatement. I watched Kevin's feet, wishing I had a pair of snow boots. I made sure I stepped in his footprints to limit them from being sunk constantly in the snow. The hat and scarf were a blessing. The scarf kept the cold air off my face.

About 15 minutes later, we arrived at a cabin in the middle of the woods. Snow covered the roof of the structure. As we approached the cabin, I could tell it was old and in need of repair. The front porch ran the full length of the structure. As we stepped onto the porch, I could hear the wood creak under my feet. The building blocked the icy wind from us. Kevin opened the door, and I nearly ran him over to get out of the cold. He quickly closed the door.

The cabin was one room. On one end were two beds and a small table with two wooden chairs. In the middle of the room, stood a wood stove. Along the middle wall stood a rickety fireplace that seemed to be of no use. There were also a few empty shelves that appeared to be a type of counter and storage. There were just a couple of windows with sun-faded curtains. Small holes in them showed moths had been chomping away at them.

Kevin walked over to the bed and asked me to help him move it. We slid it toward the center of the room. He walked over to the space where the bed had been and knelt. With a small screwdriver from his pocket, he reached down and removed a piece of the flooring revealing a hidden compartment. It amazed me how well they disguised it. The compartment contained a small metal safe. It looked as though they mounted it inside the floor.

He asked me to turn away as he unlocked the safe. I turned back when I heard it open. He pulled what must be the journal out of the safe. They had wrapped it in a linen cloth. Kevin handed it to me before he closed the safe and replaced the floor. We put the bed back into its place.

"They're going to contact me with a location to bring the journal. We'll need to wait to hear from them," he said. He glanced at his phone.

I noticed Kevin had his phone, which was a bad idea. He was worried enough, so I did not mention it. "While we wait, I must go home and get in some dry clothes and shoes," I said as I grabbed the book and wrapped my arm around his to let him know he was coming with me.

# Thirteen

We arrived in my room, and I asked him to sit and to be quiet. I locked my door to ensure no one came in and found him. I swiftly got a new set of clothes and shoes and headed to my bathroom to change. My bare feet on the tile floor looked like prunes from being in my sopping wet sneakers.

Once dressed, I joined him in my room. "Please go hide in my closet. I will be right back with some food."

A quick glance around the kitchen for something to eat revealed the leftover lemon and blueberry rolls. I heated them up in the microwave and made some coffee to warm us up. I was afraid to attempt teleporting with hot drinks, so I took everything up to my room on a tray. Kevin seemed happy with his breakfast.

After cleaning our breakfast dishes, I took him into the sitting room to sit by the fire to warm up. Kevin did not know when they would call him back. We took this time to get to know one another better.

He had been to this house when he was younger. Kevin was glad we kept it. He had very fond memories of being here with my grandmother and his parents. As we sat there, it occurred to me I could try to talk to Lainie and William using telepathy. I explained to Kevin what I was going to try.

I said, "Lainie. William. Can either of you hear me?" I tried repeatedly, but nothing. I turned to Kevin and said, "Perhaps we are too far away from them."

"I don't know. The book's not specific about how to make it work," Kevin advised.

It had been hours since we arrived at my house. We still had not heard from the Granaldis. "Perhaps they're taking them to a location far from your home. We need to trust they'll not harm them. They know if they do, you'll never deliver the journal," I stated.

Kevin responded, "Perhaps we could bring a fake journal and keep the real one safe."

Although a good thought, I said, "What if Phillip's father has seen the journal, or at very least knows about the journal, which means surely, Phillip may know about it. What if Phillip is working with the Granaldis?"

"I suppose you're right," Kevin agreed.

There was a knock on the door. Greg had his back to the door. As I opened the door, he turned around with a small bouquet. I leaned in for a kiss as I took them from him. Greg followed me into the sitting room. Kevin stood up. "Kevin, I'd like you to meet my boyfriend, Greg Scrogham. Greg, this is my cousin Kevin Davis," I said.

Greg was a pleasant distraction while we waited for the Granaldis to contact Kevin. Greg and Kevin got along well. They both enjoyed sports and camping and spent quite a while talking about those two things. At lunchtime, I made us turkey sandwiches with some chips and sweet tea.

We had finished lunch when Kevin's phone rang. He excused himself from the table and took the call. He went out to the foyer a minute later. It sounded as though he was going through the desk. I quickly made my way to him. He frantically motioned for a pen. I opened the drawer and handed him a small pad of paper and a pen. He started scribbling, but I was not close enough to read it. Kevin tried to whisper to me, but barely got a word out when Greg walked into the hallway. We both looked at him with that deer in the headlight look. Neither of us knew what to say to him.

His eyes moved from me to Kevin and then back to me. Greg asked, "What's going on, Brooke?"

He knew me so well. We had been through so much together; I could not lie to him. I looked over at Kevin, wanting to keep our secret, but knowing Greg was only looking out for my safety. The guilt got to me. I blurted out, "Kevin's parents are missing, and he thought I could help."

Greg seemed to understand the situation. He asked, "Where'd they go missing? How do ya know they're missing? How can we help?"

Kevin looked as if he did not know what to say. I was honest. I responded, "The Granaldis took them. That was them on the phone."

"Why didn't ya call me? Ya know I'm here to help," Greg asked.

"I did not feel I was over my head. If I thought I was, I would have. But we know little," I said. The guilt of not telling Greg was getting to me. I wished I had told him sooner.

Kevin chimed in, "Well, we know where they want to meet, upstate New York. We're heading to Joncy Gorge Park in Angelica, NY. They're giving me seven hours to get there."

Greg asked, "How are ya supposed to get there in seven hours from here when airports are just opening back up from all that snow?"

Kevin looked at me, and Greg noticed.

Greg turned to me and said, "He knows, doesn't he?"

The best way to describe how I felt at that moment was like a mouse caught in a mousetrap. I looked at Kevin and then back at Greg. I explained, "Yes, Kevin and his parents are protectors of the Bloom of Dreams as well. They help monitor people who are aware of the stone. We let each other know if there's danger."

"I'm surprised you never mentioned them to me," Greg replied.

With a confused look, Kevin asked, "He knows about the Bloom?"

I realize how lies or lack of truthfulness could get you caught up in a web that would be difficult to get out of. I explained how helpful Greg had been in the past. Kevin listened as I explained how he had been training me. I elaborated on how instrumental he was in retrieving the cradle from the Granaldis. Kevin seemed to understand.

We formed our plan. Everyone agreed we should head to Angelica, New York. We needed to find Kevin's parents before the meeting in seven hours. I looked at my watch. We had until 10:00 pm to figure out where his parents were and what they had planned. Greg headed home to get some warmer clothes and some supplies we might need. Just before he left, I asked to borrow his mother's snow boots. He assured me he would bring them. Kevin and I grabbed some flashlights and layered up our clothes. We continued discussing the many things Greg had done to protect the Bloom of Dreams while we waited.

Once Greg returned, we looked up a place to arrive in the town. We noticed it was a rural area. We agreed they would probably keep them at a farmhouse or storage place nearby. There were only a few restaurants in the area. We headed to the American House and Hotel. We figured in such a small town; we might meet someone who could tell us about abandoned properties or properties for sale in the area.

We arrived invisibly behind some bushes between the hotel and the building next to it. It was the only place in the picture away from where customers would be. We crouched down behind the bushes to make ourselves visible.

Greg led us to the restaurant. We were going to enjoy a light dinner to not stand out. The hotel reminded me of a western saloon with a balcony upstairs. It was cute. When we entered the restaurant, it took me back in time. Everything was blue. There was blue carpet, blue vinyl chairs, and blue walls. A woman showed us to our table. Menus were handed to us. At the top of the menu, there was a brief history of the hotel. As we reviewed the menu, our server arrived and introduced herself. Maryanne stood about five foot six inches tall with dark curly hair and the cutest dimples.

I was not all that hungry, so I decided on the broccoli cheese soup. Greg decided on the beef tips and noodles, and Kevin ordered the prime rib. She thanked us for our order and said she would return with our drinks. The restaurant had a few people scattered throughout. I scanned the room to see if anyone was paying any attention to us. It appeared everyone was focused on either their phone or the conversations at their table.

When Maryanne returned with our drinks, we asked her about properties for sale or abandon in the area. Maryanne responded, "There are several for sale. Farmers have been struggling around here and have sold or lost their farms the last couple of years. There is one. I don't think they have sold yet it. It's the farm down on Peavy. Mr. Smith died, and Mrs. Smith needed help to get around because of a stroke, so she moved in with her daughter."

I interrupted her to ask more about the farm. I asked, "How far is the farm from here?"

We took the number. Kevin immediately called her up and inquired about the purchase of the farm. Once off the phone, Kevin appeared to be looking for something on his phone and informing us about the phone conversation said, "The owner said the farm was being rented out for a few weeks. She could only meet with us after the tenants left. Apparently, the property is rundown. She gave me the address so we could drive by there and check it out." He handed

104

me his phone with a picture of the farmhouse from the real estate agency's advertisement.

There were several pictures on the site which showed the deterioration of the farmhouse. Once we finished dinner, Greg and I headed over there. I explained to Kevin, he should stay at the hotel with the journal. It was not safe to bring it with us.

Greg asked what the journal was. Without going into a lot of detail, I explained it had secrets about the Bloom of Dreams.

After reviewing the picture, Greg and I determined where we should arrive. As soon as we arrived, I immediately missed the warmth of the restaurant. I tried to keep my teeth from chattering. We took a survey of the area. There were a couple of small buildings behind the house. The property was enormous and very secluded. We arrived invisibly to ensure no one would see us. Greg started moving toward the main house when I stopped him and asked him to wait a minute. I tried telepathy to reach Kevin's parents.

I concentrated and called out, "Lainie. William. It's Brooke. If you can hear me, we're nearby. Talk to me like you talk to yourself in your head. Tell me what it looks like where you're at."

"Brooke, you found us. They drugged us. I'm awake but groggy. William is out cold. He was putting up a fight. They got tired of dealing with him, so they drugged him again. We're in a round building with a high roof. There is a metal ladder that goes to the top. It is dark in here, but there was a little light coming in from the top of the building during the day," Lainie explained.

I whispered to Greg, "They're in the silo. Where is that?"

"If my bearings are right. It should be that way," he said, pointing to our left.

As we started heading over toward the other side of the property, Greg asked, "How do ya know they're there?"

I used telepathy to answer him.

Greg stopped in his tracks and said, "How did you did that?

"We need to keep moving, I'll explain it later. It's too cold out here," I insisted. I continued heading in the silo's direction.

We were nearly at the silo when we heard Anthony and Joseph talking. It sounded like Anthony said, "You better hope your son brings the journal because your lives mean nothing to us." We watched them exit the silo and head to a nearby vehicle. They were talking about heading to the American House and Hotel for dinner.

Once they were out of sight, we tried to open the door to the silo. We found it locked.

Greg said, "I'll climb in and get them."

"Wait," I said as I grabbed his arm. I concentrated on walking through the wall of the silo. I pulled Greg with me as I walked through. Greg was completely through the wall when I instructed, "Untie them. I'll be right back with Kevin." I grabbed my mirror and headed to save Kevin before the Granaldis found him with the journal.

I ran into the restaurant like a madwoman. I found Kevin chatting with Maryanne. "Excuse me, Kevin. I need to talk to you," I said, out of breath.

Maryanne excused herself and he asked what was going on. I quickly explained to him we needed to get him out of here. He threw some cash on the table and headed out to find a safe place to hide for our return to the silo. We returned to the bushes and squatted down before teleporting back to the silo.

When we arrived, Greg had given Lainie his jacket. William was somewhat awake and was wearing Greg's sweater. They huddled up together, trying to stay warm. "Let's get you out of here," I said. I took Greg and William with me first to Kevin's apartment. Greg tended to William as I returned to Kevin and Lainie. We quickly returned to Greg and William. Laine rushed to William's side.

"We can't stay here. They came to our apartment on the tenth floor when they took us," Lainie explained with panic in her voice.

"You're right. You can't stay here. Each of you needs to pack a bag. I have a place to take you until we can deal with them. We have plenty of time. Remember, they don't know you're gone yet. I'll be back to get you shortly. Greg, come with me," I instructed. I took Greg with me to see Leonardo and Isabella at the Villa Dianella in Florence, Italy.

We arrived in my room at the villa. My grandmother was smart to secure this place. It was a blessing she befriended Leonardo and Isabella. "We need to find Isabella or Leonardo," I advised Greg. We left the room in search of them. Leonardo was talking to a guest in the hallway. I got his attention and pulled him out of the earshot of his customers and explained the situation to him. He assured me they would take care of them.

"They'll be in my room shortly," I explained. Greg found us. He explained he informed Isabella about the situation. Greg told me to head back. He was going to explain more about what they would need. He also wanted to stay and help them get everything ready.

When I arrived, Kevin was zipping up a duffle bag he had placed on the sofa. I asked, "Are you ready to go?"

"Yes," he said. He looked at his phone.

"Get rid of your phone. They can track it," I advised.

Kevin turned it off and took out the sim card.

He put the sim card in his wallet and put the phone on the coffee table. There was a knock on the door. Kevin let his parents in. Lainie was pulling a suitcase and had a large bag and a purse in the other hand. William had two large suitcases and seemed to struggle with them. *Do they think they're moving?* "I'm not sure I can take all of this, at least not in one trip," I informed them.

I took Lainie over with her luggage. When I dropped her off, Greg had not returned to the room yet. I returned to William and Kevin. I had to take William and Kevin on separate trips. Once we were all in my room, I filled them in on Isabella and Leonardo. "They'll be here shortly with Greg to take you to your rooms. In the meantime, I think we should put the journal in a safe place," I said.

Kevin grabbed the journal and asked, "Where are we going?"

"Just trust me," I said as I took his arm. I brought him to the secret room behind the wine cellar. I opened the safe. "Leave the journal here. This is a safe place. If for any reason it needs to be moved, Leonardo can bring you here to get it," I assured him. I turned us invisible and looked out through the wall to make sure no one was in the room. I pulled him through the hidden door. To show him how secure the room was. Kevin was pleased.

We returned to William and Lainie and found Greg, Isabella, and Leonardo there. They brought them some food and drinks. It was a little cramped with so many people. Greg and I said our goodbyes and headed back home. We returned to my garage because I knew my mom would be home.

Exhausted, I expected us to say goodnight, but Greg wanted an explanation about how I learned to walk through walls and use telepathy. I looked at him, trying to come up with something to tell him without revealing the secret of the journal. I hated lying to him, but it was more important to protect him and the journal. "Kevin and his parents were aware of other skills, and they let me know about them. I tried them out on my own. It's not that I didn't want to tell you. There has not been an appropriate time to bring it up," I explained.

"I'm glad ya could find out more about the powers of the stone. I hope ya know ya can trust me," he said.

Now I felt guilty for keeping it a secret, but I think the fewer people aware of the journal, the safer it and they would be. We kissed each other goodnight before we headed to our homes.

When I walked in, Mom and Phyllis were chatting at the dining room table. They asked me if I had a good day and I told them I did. I said, "Goodnight." Grateful they did not ask more questions. I did not think I could dodge any difficult ones being so tired.

# Fourteen

It was time for the meeting of the Bloom Keepers. Greg and I filled everyone in on what had happened with my cousins prior to the meeting. "Greg and I have decided to keep the Bloom of Dreams safe; we must get the Granaldi family out of the picture. We need to figure out how to get them arrested, along with Phillip. It's important to discover something illegal they're involved with. We'll need firm evidence to prove their involvement, then we can expose them. We're going to head back to the Granaldi's home and try to see what we can make of the journal we found in Tony's room along with the logbook and contact journal we found in Anthony Granaldi III's safe. Jacob, we really need you to see if you can find anything on Phillip. There is nothing in his apartment and we only hope to find a lead on that flash drive," I said.

"Perhaps we can find a connection between the logbook, the contacts, the journal, and the flash drive," Juliet suggested.

"That's a great idea. We'll get the items. I'll try to translate them for Jacob to have a starting point," I informed them.

Jacob added, "There's a lot of information on that flash drive about properties. Maybe he had something to do with the rental of the property where you found your cousins."

"Perhaps, but we can't report that to the police. That would trigger them to ask us questions. Questions we shouldn't answer. We must find something we're not linked to," I said.

"There are also his bank accounts. Perhaps there's a link there with the Granaldis," Jacob added.

"Great, it sounds like we've got a lot of work to do. We'll meet again once I have translated a few things," I said as I got up.

Greg and I headed to the Granaldis to see if we could find evidence of criminal activity. We started with Tony's journal. The room was dark when we arrived. We went to the location of the journal, but it was missing. I told Greg they must've taken it with them when they left.

We went to the safe in Anthony's closet to look at the items he had. Looking at the clothes in the closet, it appeared they hadn't returned home yet. While I unlocked the safe with the key my grandmother had provided me, Greg checked the recording pen under the bed to see if it had anything on it. I pulled the logbook out and quickly glanced through it. It was a book of payments paid to companies and people. It also showed the income he had received. If we could find someone on the list that had accepted payment or was paid for something illegal, we would have proof. I reached back into the safe and pulled out the legal papers. Some were properties they owned, others were legal contracts between Anthony and other people. We would need to research these and read the entire document.

Greg returned and asked, "How's it going in here?"

"Good, we need to take these," I said, handing the logbook and the legal papers to him. I reached in and took the book with all the contacts and placed that on the pile I gave Greg. Anthony and Maria left their passports. Strange, they did not take them. *They're still in Italy. Unless they used fake passports.* We need to find them to find out for sure. We took everything from the safe except the passports. "I needed to get to work translating them, so we can return them as soon as possible. Let's head back," I said. Greg and I returned to my room. He could not help, so he headed home.

As I started translating, I found I wrote in the language I was reading. I had to stay focused on writing everything in English. When I started getting tired, I found focusing was difficult. I had to lift the stone to see how I was writing. I stayed up half the night translating the logbook and the contact book. Exhausted, I left the contracts to translate in the morning. I headed to bed at 3:15 am.

At 8:00 am, my mom woke me up and said, "We're going to be late if you don't hurry."

*Late? What would we be late for?* It hit me. My mother needed me to drive her to the airport because Phyllis had a doctor's appointment.

During the drive to the airport, Mom talked about everything she would do while in Florida with her friends. She explained she loved the winter weather but was looking forward to the warm weather. I was looking forward to coming and going without worrying about where she was. It was hard keeping my secret life from her. I would

110

miss her, but I would get a lot done when I did not need to be sneaking around.

After dropping her off, I thought about everything I translated the night before. I had a hard time remembering everything. I hoped Juliet and Jacob could find a connection. Once I was back home, I grabbed something to eat and headed back to my room to translate the rest of the papers.

One of the legal documents was about a non-profit Anthony set up for children. Somehow, I could not imagine Anthony Granaldi setting up a legitimate non-profit, let alone one in the United States, for children. *Why didn't he set one up in his own country to help the children there?*

The other contract was between Anthony Granaldi and his sons. This was the strangest thing I think I had ever read. It appeared there were criteria Tony and Joseph must abide by to receive their inheritance. Anthony required them to work for him and no one else. They had to live in their father's house no less than seventy percent of the time. They were required to be present for all holidays and birthdays unless Anthony Granaldi III told them otherwise. *What parent would demand these things from their adult children?*

Once I finished translating everything, I contacted Greg. I asked him if he wanted to go back with me to return the items. He told me he would be right over, so I headed downstairs with the documents. By the time I made it to the foyer, I noticed Greg opening the front gate. I put the papers on the foyer table and opened the door for him.

"Hey sweetie," I said as I leaned in for a kiss.

Greg wrapped his arms around my waist and gave me a gentle kiss on the lips. He looked down at me and said, "You look tired."

I explained my lack of sleep, followed by a summary of my findings on the legal documents. We gathered the papers and headed back to Anthony's closet.

Something caught my attention. I whispered, "Did you hear that? I thought I heard something." Greg shook his head. I reached through the safe and quickly put the papers back as we found them in the safe. "Let's check and see if anyone is here," I muttered.

As we exited the closet and entered the bathroom, I looked in the mirror to confirm we were invisible before continuing. It sounded like someone was yelling. It sounded as if it was coming from the family room.

Being incredibly quiet, we made our way over to that area of the house. Anthony was standing while Joseph and Tony were sitting next to each other on the sofa. He was yelling at them for not bringing back the journal or the book. Anthony paused for a moment and paced the floor. He turned his attention back to them and said, "You let a kid out whit you! Did I raise idiots? I'm too old to be dealing with this. Get that journal and the Bloom of Dreams. Do you understand me? Do I need to cut you off?" Neither of them said a word. He repeated himself, "Do I need to cut you off? Answer me!"

"No, pops. We'll get them," Tony promised him.

"Get out of here and don't come back until you have at least one of those items," Anthony shouted. He walked toward the dining room. I grabbed Greg and took us to their foyer, which was next to the formal dining area. Anthony stormed into the room and started yelling at his wife about how incompetent their sons were. Tony's wife got up and took her child upstairs. I'm guessing she knows when to exit a room. Grabbing Greg, I took us upstairs to Tony's room. Tony's wife did not come into the room. She must be in her daughter's room down the hall. I saw the journal and quickly grabbed it We headed home.

Opening the book, I realized it was a new journal. It was only half full. As I read, I decided only to write information I thought might be important. Most of what I was reading was about how Tony wished he could leave the house or about his father being too evil to ever die. *Ah-ha! Finally, something useful.* Tony wrote about some jobs he had done for his father. Swiftly jotting down every detail. My hand was cramping when I finally finished! We returned the journal, hoping no one discovered it was missing.

Once we got back, I texted Jacob and Juliet to see if they could meet to go over everything from the safe. Juliet texted back and said they could not meet for a few hours because they were downtown with her parents. Greg and I headed downstairs and got something to eat and sat in front of the fire in the sitting room. That was the last thing I remembered until the doorbell suddenly awoke me. I nearly fell off the sofa when I woke up.

Greg smiled down at me. I was sleeping on him. He asked, "Did you have a nice nap?"

Trying to get myself up, I stretched slowly before answering the door. Juliet and Jacob had arrived. Upon seeing them, I immediately found myself awake. Without even a hello, I started filling them in on the contents of the safe and the journal. I gave them the papers, and they said they would research everything to see if there was anything we could use.

Juliet asked if she could borrow a sweater from me. I took her upstairs to my room. She confessed she did not really need a sweater. She wanted to tell me how well things were going with her and Jacob.

"He's such a gentleman. Even my parents love him," she declared with enthusiasm.

I was so happy for her. We sat down and talked about what they had been up to and somehow; we started talking about what we did with Nadine and Eddie. Juliet told me she wanted to have a little fun before heading back to the guys. I pulled out the address I had copied from Eddie's wallet. We looked it up and found the satellite picture of their home. We quickly transported there and when we could see in the window, we popped into the house, making sure they would not see us. The house was old and run down. Eddie had his head under the kitchen sink and Nadine was standing next to him with her hand on the faucet.

"It's still not working, Eddie," she said, turning the faucet on and off.

"Look, I'm trying here. I'm no plumber," Eddie responded.

Nadine rolled her eyes and said, "That's for sure."

Juliet scared them and picked up a screwdriver from the toolbox on the counter and said, "Don't think we've forgotten about you."

Nadine looked up and saw the floating screwdriver and in a shaky voice said, "Uh, Eddie... Eddie, the ghost is back." She kicked him as he was trying to get out from under the sink.

Thump. Eddie hit his head on the sink. As he was about to get up, but suddenly froze.

Juliet had the screwdriver right next to his wife's neck.

"Don't make it angry, Nay," he said fearfully.

I did all I could to keep from laughing. I knocked a plastic glass off the counter and added to their paranoia by saying in a deep voice, "We need to know how Phillip contacted you."

Eddie slowly stood up, and Nadine got behind him, moving away from the screwdriver. "It said we. There is more than one of them," she muttered.

Trying to sound tough, Eddie said, "We've done work for him before, and he wanted us to get the necklace for him."

Juliet moved the screwdriver back to Nadine's throat and pushed it with a little pressure. Juliet asked, "What work?"

"We've stolen a few things for him over the years and roughed up a few people," Eddie answered. His voice sounded nervous.

Eddie turned toward Nadine, "Okay, okay, we stole some diamonds from a lady, uh named... Nay, what was her name?"

"Albisu, I don't remember her first name," Nadine blurted out.

I looked over at Juliet and, using telepathy, told her, "We're done. Drop the screwdriver." Which she did. Once they thought we left, they started hugging each other. That's when we left.

When we returned to my room, we had a good laugh about it before heading downstairs. We both forgot to bring a sweater with us.

When we came down, Greg and Jacob seemed to be cross-referencing the names in the journal with the contact names to see if they could find a connection. Greg was writing the log page next to the name on the contact sheets. Once they completed the one they were working on, they both looked up at the same time. Excitedly, Greg said, "We don't know what it means, but a few of the names are on both lists. Perhaps you two can catch up with us. Check and see if Tony's journal has any of these names in it."

Juliet turned to me and asked, "Did you put this in a word doc so we can search it?"

I answered, "We're hacking into their computers. They could hack us as well. I thought it would be safer to just write it down the old-fashioned way."

Jacob sat up and started stretching. He commented, "That was smart, Brooke."

Juliet said, "Drumroll please, Brooke."

I moved my hands as though I was playing the drums and made a sad attempt at making a drumroll noise. Juliet smiled and made a weird face at my lack of drum rolling skills before she told them what we had just done to Nadine and Eddie.

When they thought she was done, they started commenting on our cleverness.

"You have not heard the best part yet," I said before motioning to Juliet to tell them.

"They confessed to us. They've done numerous jobs for Phillip and even stole diamonds from someone with the last name Albisu," she informed them.

"That sounds familiar," Jacob said, before he began pounding on the keyboard of his laptop. He did not look up for a few minutes. We all started looking at one another, wondering if we were meant to remain in silence while he concentrated.

He looked up with a look of satisfaction on his face. Jacob announced, "Alessandra Albisu of New York City is one of his clients." He started typing again. His fingers were pounding on the keys. He shouted, "Hah ha." He continued reading his screen.

As though I was talking to a child, I said, "Would you like to share with the rest of the class?"

He backed away from his computer, realizing his mistake of not letting us in on his discovery. He leaned back, put his arms behind his head, and took a deep breath. Jacob explained, "Apparently, eight months ago Alessandra Albisu had her diamond jewelry stolen, which was valued at $2,300,000."

We all looked at each other with our mouths open. Jacob continued, "Phillip has a file with his passwords on, but it looks like the company files are encrypted." Jacob took another deep breath. He announced, "This is going to take time, but if we can prove he paid Nadine and Eddie, we might be able to pin him to the crime." Jacob closed his computer and collected the papers I had supplied. He turned to Juliet, "Would you mind getting started on these, while I work on getting access to his bank accounts?" He turned his attention to Greg and me. Jacob explained they were heading out to get working on it immediately.

# Fifteen

Greg and I had a plan that would help pin Phillip, Nadine, and Eddie to the diamond heist. During our research, we discovered Alessandra Albisu worked with students studying communication at New York University. I was going to pretend to be a student working on a communication project regarding how to get investors to invest in real-estate.

I asked my friend Mechelle, who had once lived in New York City, if she knew anyone attending New York University. Lucky me, she did. Her cousin Keith was in his second year there. She was able to obtain the name of a female student named Kelly LeWinter that was studying communications at the university. I didn't want to have Mechelle or her cousin to get suspicious of why I need the number. I called Kelly and asked questions as if I had been considering transferring to her university to study communication. I only needed her name in case Alessandra called the school to confirm Kelly was a student.

Jacob made a fake school identification card for me and gave me the phone number to Alessandra's company. I reached out to her assistant to see if I could interview her for a project I was working on. What she did not know, was our mission to have the people who stole from her put in prison.

Jacob suggested I go incognito. I was not sure what he meant. Apparently, he watched a lot of crime shows. Jacob explained a person could change their look using makeup. He contacted a friend of his who was going to cosmetology school about giving me a completely new look for the interview. His friend assured him she could make me look like a totally different person.

Juliet and I were hanging out in my room when my phone rang. It was Alessandra Albisu's assistant Eric. He explained she would like to meet with me. He asked if I would be available tomorrow at 2:00 pm to meet with her at her office. I assured him I would be there.

Juliet could barely hold back her excitement while I was on the phone. As soon as I was off the phone, she said, "It's like you're a real spy going on a mission."

I thought about what she said. *I'm like a spy.* I replied, "I guess you're right."

Juliet called Jacob and told him we needed his friend to do her magic on me tomorrow morning. Anxiously waiting, we hoped he would call right back to confirm she could make it, but he did not, so we decided to try to see how successful we could be at giving each other makeovers.

Juliet was finishing me up when Jacob called. I could not hear what he was saying to her, and she was not providing me with any clues while she talked with him. She just smiled and nodded her head. Finally, she said, "Great thanks." She put her phone down on the counter and continued working on my makeup.

I backed away from her and said, "Juliet, what did he say?"

She started taking the makeup brush toward my face again and looked at me turning her head to the left and to the right as if she was trying to decide where her next brush stroke should go on a painting. In a weird French accent she said, "I think we may not need her; you look fabulous darling."

I got up and looked at myself in the full-length mirror. I was amazed at the image before me. Not having words, I said, "Wow!"

"You look marvelous, darling," she proclaimed, in her weird accent.

I looked again not sure what to say. It hit me. I realized what she was going for. "This is perfect! Well, perfect if I was transported back in time to the 80's," I announced.

We both burst out laughing when she looked at herself in the mirror. Juliet looked like she should be standing on a street corner.

"I hope this girl is more talented than us," Juliet commented. "Oh, she will be here at 10:00 am. Jacob said she does not live too far from here," she continued. We took a picture of ourselves to remember this moment before cleaning ourselves up.

I wondered what this person was going to make me look like. I tried to picture myself arriving for my interview. The image was not clear. In a serious voice, I asked, "What should I wear for the interview?"

Juliet pulled her phone out and started typing. "She is an investment advisor for a mutual fund company," she said before handing me her phone.

Before me was a picture of Alessandra. She presented herself as a classy well-dressed lady, which tells me I should be the same. We did not find anything appropriate in my closet. We headed up to my mother's closet to see what we could find.

After flipping through half of her wardrobe, Juliet found a light grey skirt with thin black lines. I informed her I had a black turtleneck sweater that looked great with it along with my black boots and my black leather jacket. We brought the skirt back to my room.

My mother had not worn the skirt in a long time. It might not have fit her anymore. We went downstairs and grabbed one of Phyllis's notepads. Pulling out my computer, I researched the building and nearby area to figure out where I would need to arrive. I decided to arrive invisible, find a lady's room stall to become visible. Now, I just needed to distract myself until my make over tomorrow. Juliet and I spent the rest of the day watching movies.

When I woke up, I immediately remembered what my day had in store for me. I leaped from my bed. I was excited. I was anxious and needed to calm my nerves, so I went for a run. The ground was wet from the melting snow and recent rain. When I got back, I ate breakfast before taking a shower. I needed to be ready when Juliet and the makeup artist arrived. I was busy drying my hair when Phyllis knocked on my door. She let me know there was a young lady here to see me.

I provided an explanation to her as we made our way back to the first floor and advised Phyllis to send anyone else up that arrived. As she came into view, I saw a beautiful girl with soft curls in her light brown hair. She had a natural beauty about herself. Even without wearing makeup, she still looked amazing with her flawless skin. She was holding two large cases and seemed young. We introduced ourselves before I took her up to my room.

Her name was Kylee. She commented on how impressed she was by our home. I asked her what she needed me to do to help set up an area for her to work. She looked around my room and asked for a folding chair. I ran down to the garage to get one. I returned and placed it on my bathroom floor by the counter and sat down. A chill came over me from the cold metal. She asked me what type of look I wanted.

"I'm interviewing someone but need to look vastly different. I need to look like a well-educated professional and classy college student," I explained.

She nodded and opened her cases. *Why's she not asking me more? Should I say more?*

Kylee pulled out a brush and started working on my hair. Once my hair was brushed out, she handed me a mirror. I adjusted the mirror to allow me to see a bit of what she was doing.

"I'm going to show you a professional hair style you can do in 3 minutes. This style's great for weddings or interviews. Even better it'll look great all day," Kylee said before she began showing me the first step. She instructed me to pay attention because she wanted me to repeat what she showed me. I watched her bring stands of hair up and made it like a loose braid. She repeated the process. She informed me to take over. I continued until I got to the nape of my neck. She put a ponytail at the bottom. "Now you just twist the hair and wrap it around in an interesting way and pin it," she explained. Kylee sprayed my hair to ensure it would stay.

I got up and looked at the back of my hair with the mirror she gave me. I said, "That was so easy, and it looks perfect. Thank you."

She smiled and motioned for me to sit back down. Kylee started applying foundation to my face. I heard a knock at the door. It was Jacob and Juliet. There was not enough room for them to stay in the bathroom, so they said they were going to hang out in my room until I was done.

Kylee worked quickly and seemed to be very knowledgeable. I asked her how long she had been doing this. She informed me her mother was a makeup artist and she had begun teaching her the secrets of makeup artistry when she was a little girl. When she was done, she handed me a mirror and asked me what I thought.

I looked at my reflection and did not recognize the person looking back at me. I looked like a model in a magazine. *Wow!* "Where were you when I went to prom? I look fantastic! I belong on Palm Beach or in Manhattan," I said before giving her a hug. I joked, "So, I'll need you to come by every morning?"

I heard Greg's voice in the other room. I took one last look at myself with my outfit, and it was perfect. I felt confident and ready for the interview. I hollered to the other room, "Drumroll please." As soon as I heard their attempt at a drumroll, I strutted into my room.

They all looked in shock when I walked in. Greg had his mouth open. I was in shock. *They don't like it.* I asked, "Is it bad?"

Greg looked at me and shook his head. He muttered, "No, not at all. You just look so different. Even a look a little older with that outfit and wow."

"Greg's right, you look amazing. You just don't look like you. The contouring makes your face look so different," Juliet explained.

"What she said," Jacob chimed in.

Once Kylee left, we started discussing what information I needed from Alessandra. Before I knew it, I needed to head to New York City.

I arrived next to a potted plant outside the building and waited for someone to go into the building. As I waited, I remembered, I could now walk-through walls. I entered and immediately noticed the windows provided a lot of natural light in the entrance. They decorated it with a modern minimalist design using gray, blue, and hints of brown. I looked around for the bathroom. It was just past the front desk.

I entered and waited for the one lady washing her hands to leave before revealing myself. I headed back out to the front desk to check-in and find out where I should go.

The man behind the desk was on the phone, so I patiently waited for him to end his call. Once he completed it, he looked at me funny. In a New York accent, he said, "I'm sorry, I didn't see you come in."

Getting warm, I took my coat off and explained I was here to see Alessandra Albisu. He quickly picked up the phone and relayed to the person on the other end I had arrival. The man asked, "What's your name?"

I informed him.

He provided my name to the person on the phone. "Very good," he responded before hanging up the phone. "You'll take the elevator to the seventeenth floor. Alessandra Albisu's assistant Eric will wait at the receptionist's desk for you," he instructed. He motioned towards the direction of the elevator.

I made my way to the seventeenth floor. The elevator surprised me at its speed. I had never been in a building this tall before and it was a little intimidating.

I exited the elevator to discover this floor seemed a bit cozier than the entrance to the building. There was lots of wood trim. It reminded me of a cozy study. I noticed the receptionist was chatting with a tall Hispanic man in his twenties. They both looked up and seemed to look me over when a smile came across the young man's face. "You must be Kelly," he said as he extended his arm to shake my hand. "I'm Eric. Ms. Albisu's assistant," he advised.

Eric guided me into her office. He asked me to sit and informed me Alessandra would arrive shortly. Her office was a large room with lots of woodwork. At the far end of the room, a large arched doorway led to a balcony. Her desk was between the sitting area and the balcony. The right side of the L-shaped desk contained several computer monitors. The sitting area had a small beige sofa with a delicate flower pattern that showed sophistication. There were two armchairs.

Before sitting, I thought about where she might sit. The armchairs were a little higher than the sofa and one would force better posture. The chairs were far enough apart that I could interview her, and it would not be uncomfortable. I decided on the armchair closest to the sofa.

When Alessandra walked in, I quickly stood up to greet her. Eric entered with her. He was informing her of her missed calls and before she acknowledged me, she said, "Please call Charles and my children and tell them I'll meet them at 7:30 at The Capital Grille. I've already made a reservation." She moved her attention to me. Alessandra looked me over. With a smile, she said, "You must be Kelly."

"Yes, it is a pleasure to meet you, Ms. Albisu," I said as I reached out to shake her hand. She sat down, as did I. I took a deep breath and slowly exhaled to calm my nerves before beginning. "For my communication project, I'm focusing on the art of persuading people to purchase things they might not normally purchase. You're an investment manager," I said. *She knows that.* I tried not to sound like an idiot. I continued, "You must find creative ways to get investors to purchase your funds rather than other products. What do you find works best to influence people to invest in your product?"

122

She began providing a bunch of statistical data about her portfolio. I continued my questioning about mutual funds before shifting questioning to real estate. I asked, "I want to know how someone may have persuaded you to make a large purchase. Have you purchased any new property lately?"

"Yes. About seven months ago, my husband Charles and I purchased a new place," she informed me.

*Now I am getting somewhere.* I proceeded to inquire about the details of the purchase. Alessandra provided me with her real-estate agent's name, which confirmed to me they were working together. I inquired further, "Are there any regrets about this purchase?"

"Yes, I've a very annoying neighbor. She thinks I have time to provide free investment advice. I think she must know my schedule because she's always in the elevator with me," she explained. It looked as though she wanted to tell me something else.

I asked, "Is there anything I should be cautious about?"

"Always be aware of the risks involving an investment and make sure you have precautions in place before moving your valuables," she advised. Alessandra seemed agitated.

Hoping she would tell me more about Phillip, I asked, "I understand your frustration with your neighbor. Would you mind providing more details about moving your valuables?"

"I informed my real-estate agent I needed a safe in the new apartment. The one we purchased didn't have one. Phillip claimed to have many reliable contacts. He gave me the name of someone who could assist me with the purchase and installation of a new safe. I trusted him. Unfortunately, it didn't work out. They told me they would not install it until after I moved in. They never showed or returned any of my calls. I moved in without having a safe. I made the mistake of not putting my fine jewelry into a safe deposit box, thinking the chances of it being stolen were slim. They stole everything about a week after we moved. All my jewelry was gone. Make sure you protect your assets," she advised.

"That's terrible. Were they extremely valuable?" I enquired.

"Very. A few pieces were family heirlooms," Alessandra said as she lowered her eyes.

I did not want to push her too much. I continued questioning, "Are there any leads to finding out who did this?"

"Unfortunately, there's not much to go on. The police think people came into the building pretending to be maintenance workers. Fortunately, insurance covered the loss, but I had some lovely pieces my husband had purchased for me which I miss. I had to hire an alternate company to install a safe. I can't believe Phillip recommended them," she stated.

I stood up and shook her hand. I said, "Thank you for answering my questions. May I contact you if I've any further questions?"

"Certainly," she said. She motioned for me to exit her office.

Upon exiting, I asked her assistant where the nearest restroom was. From there, I headed home.

When I returned, my room was empty. I walked out of my room and heard voices coming from down the hall. I headed in the noise's direction. It sounded like everyone had moved to the library. On the sofa, Jacob and Juliet snuggled, and Greg was leaning up against the desk. They appeared to be talking about the latest Marvel movie, but they stopped immediately when they saw me come through the door.

Greg blurted out, "Well, how did it go?"

"It went well. She confirmed Phillip was her real-estate agent. He even provided her with the contact information of the company she had hired to install a safe. The home did not have one, despite her telling him that was something she wanted her new home to have. Alessandra said the person he referred, never came to install the safe. She had to hire another company."

Jacob took his arm from around Juliet and sat up. He said, "That's important information. We now just need to find the documents to prove she was his client. If we can prove Phillip's connection to that company, we might have enough evidence to put Phillip, Eddie, and Nadine in jail. I need to figure out the company he referred her to?"

"I knew that wouldn't be an easy task. We also need to find something on the Granaldis we can use against them," I reminded them.

# Sixteen

Jacob needed to get into Alessandra's computer in the middle of the night. We snuck into her office, and Jacob worked his magic. While I waited for him, I went through her desk to see if I could find anything but found nothing. I went to her assistant's desk. Look *at this, a business card for Safe Safes.* If only I could take a picture, but we were smart and left our phones at home. As I read the card, I noticed there was not a company email address. It was a Gmail account. This can't be a legitimate company. I grabbed a sticky note and pen and wrote the information down. I realized Jacob was taking longer than normal and headed back into Alessandra's office.

He was still tapping away on her computer. I asked, "Is everything okay?"

"Yes, I'm nearly done. She has good security, but it's not able to stop me. Give me a minute," he advised. Not once did he stop working.

I looked around the office and found a picture of Alessandra and a man. It must be her husband, Charles. She was in a gown, and he was wearing a tuxedo. Upon closer look, she was wearing expensive diamond jewelry. I took a mental picture in case we need to know what her jewelry looked like. *A Polaroid camera would be a handy thing to have.* I wondered if someday I would ever have an office this nice.

My daydream vanished when Jacob started turning the computer off and wiped everything to make sure he did not leave prints behind. Without a word to one another, we headed back to his house.

The next morning before the Bloom Keepers meeting, I dedicated my time to researching Safe Safes online. At the meeting, we discussed everything. I started, "I found a card for Safe Safes at Alessandra's office. We need to confirm this is the place Phillip suggested she use. I've already researched the company. I found out it was not a legitimate corporation. Jacob…" I said before handing him a piece of paper with the Gmail address from the business card. "We need to see who this email account belongs to," I said.

Jacob started clicking away on his computer. "I knew that company sounded familiar. I've got emails between Phillip and

Alessandra about the Safe Safes. Phillip told her it was the only company he would recommend. I also have several emails from Alessandra about the company not being able to install the safe in a timely manner. She used some choice words to describe how truly upset she was about being robbed and, according to her insurance company, the thieves got away with $2.3 million."

Jacob leaned back in his chair, "Alessandra told him he should pay more attention to what his customers wanted. If he had, her new home would have had a safe and her jewelry would be still in it. Alessandra says he should learn to distinguish between reputable companies and disreputable ones. According to her, they disconnected the phone number for Safe Safes. At least we're getting somewhere. We need to connect Eddie and Nadine to the crime," he said, filling us in on his findings. Jacob sat back in his chair and added, "Oh, Juliet and I have been creating a spreadsheet for tracking everything. We logged everything from the logbook, contact book, and journal. It's saved on a flash drive."

"We're nearly done with it, but the spreadsheet does not contain anyone's name. Jacob assigned everyone a number," Juliet explained. She handed me the pages with the key. "See, we have numbers next to the names on these sheets. That way, no one will know what this is," she concluded.

Jacob followed up with, "There are a few names that appear on several of the documents."

"We need to make those people a priority. If you need help with it, let us know. We only have a few days before our classes start back up. We need to get this done before then," I instructed.

We all agreed, and Juliet and Jacob left to get everything done before we met again, which they hoped would be sometime tomorrow.

Greg and I had wanted to drop in on my cousins in Italy to see how they were doing. It was nearly time for dinner to be served, so we agreed to dress appropriately before heading over. Greg and I arrived in my personal room. We headed down to locate William, Lainie, and Kevin. We made our way out to the dining room and there were several people there, but I did not see them.

Because it was dinner time, we knew Isabella and Leonardo would show up soon. We sat down at a table for six. A server came by and asked for our drink order. About a minute later, I saw Isabella come into the dining room. I waved at her to get her attention. She came right over. The noise from the other diners made it difficult to hear. We chatted for a few minutes. Isabella informed me my cousins should be down shortly. She moved them to other rooms. She also informed me they had not seen or heard from the Granaldis in quite a while.

That was splendid news because it meant my cousins were still safe here. When my cousins showed up, I could tell they were happy to see me. I caught them up on what had been going on and they wanted to help. I told them it was too risky for them to be doing anything right now. We were working on a way to make it safe for them to go home. The large group interrupted our conversation. They were celebrating a birthday of a middle-aged man at their table. We discussed what they had been up to since we last saw them and worked on getting to know one another better. After dinner, Greg and I headed back to my room at the villa to teleport back. It was 2:15 am our time. Exhausted, I gave Greg a kiss good night before heading home.

The next morning, I looked for anything that might show a connection between any of these people. What I found was a police report regarding the stolen jewelry. *Found it!* In the report, there was a statement from Alessandra. She stated a man and woman she did not recognize were exiting the building when she was entering. It described them as a thin woman of average height with black curly hair and a blonde man of medium build, about six feet tall. They were both wearing black leather jackets, gloves, black jeans, and sneakers. That certainly sounds like Nadine and Eddie.

I printed the document to show to the Bloom Keepers. I continued searching for more information, only now I was looking into the real-estate sale to see if there was any connection with Phillip. During my search, I received a group text from Juliet to the Bloom Keepers. We need to meet. Everyone was available, so we met at my house. Phyllis sent everyone up to the library when they arrived.

The meeting of the Bloom Keepers was underway. We agreed Jacob should go first since he requested the meeting. "Juliet and I have been remarkably busy trying to find connections between the items found in Anthony Granaldi's safe, which consists of the logbook, book of contacts, two contracts, and Tony Granaldi's journal. We went even farther than that by including the information from the computers I have been searching and monitoring. Well, we've found some connections," Jacob informed us.

Juliet looked eager for us to hear their discoveries. Jacob cleared his throat. He continued, "There's a connection with the logbook and contacts. It looks like Mr. Granaldi received a painting by Joseph Mallord called Seascape, Folkstone. This painting is from 1845 valued at over $80 million. He received it from Marco Russo. The log shows it being sold to Jonathan Laurent. We researched these people and discovered Marco Russo has done time for counterfeiting paintings. Jonathan Laurent comes from old money. He has an appreciation of fine art. The logbook shows payment to Marco Russo. Additionally, a payment made to Daniel Pierre, who has a history of taking expensive things that do not belong to him and selling them."

Juliet added, "Tony's journal talks about a meeting between him and Daniel about six months ago, which was immediately followed by a meeting with Marco. The next day. He talks about making deliveries to a Jonathan and a Daniel."

"It sounds like Daniel stole the painting and gave it to Tony, who gave it to Marco to make a copy of," Greg stated, before being interrupted by Juliet.

"Exactly. He gave one to Daniel to place back in the location they stole it from, and the other went to Jonathan," Juliet interjected.

I commented, "The question is, who has the original?"

"Brooke and I will see what we can find. I'm sure Jonathan would love to know if he purchased a stolen painting or paid a fortune for a fake. We'll look into questioning the others also," Greg suggested.

I inquired, "Anything else?"

"Yes, I found emails I think are between Phillip and Nadine. Phillip was asking if she could help with a rare stone, he was trying to get. They arranged a meeting to discuss it further. That was probably when he hired Eddie and Nadine to get the stone. That was nearly a month ago. This is all we have for now," Jacob updated us. Greg thanked them for the update.

"Alessandra provided a statement to the police about two people exiting her building the evening of the robbery. She described Nadine and Eddie, which I don't believe is a coincidence," I said as I passed the police report to Jacob. He looked it over and passed it to Juliet.

Juliet proclaimed, "Good find Brooke!"

"Well, if there's nothing else, I wanted to let you know my mother's going to be returning tomorrow. As you know, we must be extra careful what we discuss in this house when she's here. Also, with the new semester starting, we're going to have a hard time getting things done and finding time to meet," I explained.

Juliet suggested, "We could meet in one of the library meeting rooms. The room will need to be reserved. Does everyone use the school app?" Everyone did. We provided her our school schedule for her to schedule our meetings with the group. "I'll email you the days and times once I have figured it out," she advised us.

"It sounds like our task now is to find either Daniel Pierre, Marco Russo, or Jonathan Laurent. I think we should meet when we have something to report. Each of us will let Brooke know if we find something that needs to be addressed immediately. She can convey the message to Greg," Jacob suggested.

"Sounds good," Greg confirmed.

Once everyone left, Greg pulled me to him and wrapped his arms around me. "How about you and I go out for a nice dinner tonight?" he suggested.

I smiled and gently kissed his lips. I responded, "I think that sounds lovely, Gregory."

We kissed again before he pulled away and said, "Now understand, a nice dinner doesn't mean expensive. Ya know I'm a college student, right?" We both laughed before he kissed me and headed home. We both needed to get ready.

I could not believe I had such an amazing guy. It was a good thing I did not deck him when I first met him. I started thinking about Juliet and Jacob. They made a great couple, too. It was amazing how much he knew about computers. I was glad I could trust them to help me and to keep my secret. The more I thought about them and the friendship I had with Juliet, it made me feel guilty I had not contacted Mechelle in a while.

I called her, and we caught up while I put my makeup on. She was glad I called. Mechelle wanted me to come down for spring break. Unfortunately, our spring breaks did not fall on the same weekend this year. I told her I would try to see about coming down for a long weekend. She even told me to bring Greg. I asked her to confirm her parents would be okay with us both staying at their house. She told me she would let me know.

Greg arrived at 6:00 pm as planned and took me to Outback for dinner. We had just received our meals when Jacob texted me.

**JACOB:** Got info for Jonathan. Parental units R out.

**BROOKE:** I will call when we finish dinner.

Saddened by the interruption, I looked at Greg and filled him in on the text. I said, "I look forward to a day when you and I can just hang out and enjoy one another."

"Me too, but you must admit this stuff gets your adrenaline pumping," Greg declared.

"I know, right," I agreed. We both laughed. After dinner, we headed back to my house and teleported to Jacob's home. Our curiosity was getting to us.

I thought it best to appear in Jacob's room because there was not enough room in his closet for both Greg and me. This time, my arrival did not startle him because he did not have his headset on.

He whipped his chair in our direction and rolled to the side to allow us to see his monitor. "I found this article in The Art Newspaper about Jonathan Laurent's collection," Jacob explained. He showed us pictures of the artwork in his home.

"This is great! Thank you. Now we need to figure out how we're going to approach him," I said. Ideas started swirling in my head. I suggested we leave him a message somehow and tell him we needed to meet. Not understanding where this house was or if he was even there during the holidays, we could find a public place to meet. This would allow everyone to feel secure. We agreed and before I knew it, we were off to his home.

I made sure we arrived out of the way and out of sight. The room was amazing, with arched dark wood-framed windows, one on each side of the fireplace and the other two on both sides of a door which had the same design. There were two different sitting areas, one with a couch and two chairs near the fireplace and the other had four chairs around a circular glass coffee table. A large chandelier hung centered in the room. Above the fireplace and above a cabinet, which was centered along the wall opposite the door that led to a patio, were beautiful pieces of art. Flanked along the sides of the cabinet were smaller paintings. It was the middle of the night and if he was home; he was likely sleeping. Greg and I quietly made our way through the house until we found some mail with the address on it. We were in Rome. I popped back to Jacob and asked him to find a park near the address on the letter. Once he had one, I went back and returned the mail to its place. Greg found a pen and some paper for me to write a note to Jonathan about when we should meet. I wrote the note in Italian.

I've valuable information. Let's meet, Trevi Fountain at 11:00 am. I'll find you.

My gloves were a little tight. It was uncomfortable writing the note with them on. I found his bedroom and put the note on his cell phone, which was on a desk to the left of the bed. He was sound asleep. I woke him up to make sure he saw the note. He just rolled over. I wanted to turn the light on, but it was difficult to find a light switch. He needs to wake up and read the note. The room was dark, which made it hard to see, but I finally found a light switch. "Click." I turned it on. The room was beautiful and masculine. The headboard was a piece of art. There was a small shelf that ran along the back of the bed and the wood that ran up the wall had a pattern that looked like a giant tic-tac-toe board. The lines were a darker wood than the squares. The lights were mounted on the second row of the headboard just to the left and right of the sides of the bed. He started stirring, and when the light hit his eyes, he tried to cover them with a pillow. Jonathan seemed confused when the light turned on because he sat up half asleep and started looking around the room. He quickly got up and grabbed his phone and the note. He began dialing a number but stopped and looked at the note. Jonathan put his phone down and looked around the room. Then he opened the note. Again, looking around the room, he started heading downstairs. I moved to the room Greg was in and quickly got him out of there because he did not know Jonathan was heading in his direction. Upon arriving back in my bedroom, I explained the need to leave the house.

Greg then informed me, "I am going with you tomorrow. I want to make sure you're safe."

"I figured you would." I smiled. "We need to leave here about 4:45 am."

We spent the rest of the night watching a movie with Phyllis.

Greg texted me at 4:30 am when he arrived at the back door. I let him in. We each had a cup of coffee. I put on my coat, boots, gloves, and scarf to prepare myself for the thirty-seven degrees at the fountain. I grabbed my camera because we needed to look like tourists. We could not take our phones out for fear they were tracking us.

When we arrived, there were a few tourists at the Trevi Fountain. Greg and I started acting like a couple on vacation. We pretended to take pictures of ourselves at the fountain. What I did not consider was Jonathan being bundled up like Greg and me.

"We need to look for someone by themselves," I instructed Greg.

I saw a man walking by on the phone, but he seemed focused on his phone call, not looking for someone looking for him. Greg and I snuggled up next to each other to keep warmer. I noticed a man standing alone, looking around. I let Greg know. We moved closer to see if it was him.

"Pull your scarf up so he can't see your face well," I suggested when I knew it was him. It did not appear he thought we were the contact he would look for. I pulled my sunglasses from my pocket and put them on to hide my eyes. Greg stayed back while I went over to Jonathan. Before making contact, I made sure my scarf was covering my face. "Thank you for coming Jonathan," I said.

He jumped a bit. Jonathan demanded, "Who are you and what's this about?" He said this as if he was in control of the situation.

I took control. "Who I am is not important. What is important is the information I have regarding the Seascape, Folkstone, you recently purchased," I advised. I had his attention.

"I'm listening," he replied.

I tipped him off by saying, "I have reason to believe you possess a stolen painting or a forgery. The question is, do you have the original or a copy? The legal owner of the painting had it stolen without knowing. They created a forgery. We do not know which one is the original."

Surprised by my comment, he asked, "How do you know this?"

"I have evidence and I want the people responsible for this crime to be put away, but to do that, I need to know if you have the original or the copy," I explained.

Jonathan asked, "Why don't you just submit your evidence to the police?"

"We need to stay anonymous. I'll supply the police with the evidence, but not until I have all the facts. I don't want you, an innocent man, to become a suspect," I replied.

"Thank you for that. How do I contact you once I find out? Oh, and how did you get into my house?" he questioned.

I said, "Let's just say I have certain skills; I will come to you in a week. Will that be enough time for you to have an expert examine the painting?"

"I will make sure it is done by then," he promised.

I walked back over to Greg, and we headed away from Jonathan. Once we were out of his line of sight, we moved behind a tree and, like that, we were back in the warmth of my kitchen. Seconds later, Phyllis walked in. We startled her.

She asked, "Why are you up so early?"

I filled her in on what was going on. She was pleased to know both the Granaldis, and Phillip might end up in prison.

# Seventeen

School started, and it was nearly time for the Bloom Keepers first meeting in the library, but first I needed to talk with Jonathan about the painting. As soon as class was over, I headed home. It was 2:40 pm in Kentucky, which meant it was 6:40 pm in Rome. He was not expecting me, but I waited for him at his home. I arrived invisible; in case he was home. It would not be good for him to see me suddenly appear. I arrived in his living room wearing a winter hat I had my hair tucked into, dark sunglasses, and my winter coat and boots to make it appear I had been coming from the outdoors. Jonathan was sitting in a chair talking on the phone about a meeting he had attended. I went into the kitchen to make myself visible before returning to the living room.

As soon as Jonathan realized my presence, he got off the phone abruptly and stood up. He inquired, "How did you get in here?"

I firmly replied, "That's not important. What is important is knowing if you have the original or a fake. Have you discovered which one you possess?"

He commented on my age, "You seem very young to be involved in such a sinister plot to defraud me," Jonathan said as he stepped closer to me.

Straightening my posture, I said sternly, "Mr. Laurent, I can assure you my involvement is merely to bring those involved to justice. You were a victim, and I plan to prove it. Do you have the information I'm requesting?"

Joseph looked me over. He replied, "If what you say is true, I should thank you because I have purchased a forgery."

"It may not sound like it, but that's good news," I announced. The warmth of the jacket starting to get to me.

Jonathan appeared surprised by my announcement. He asked, "How's that good news?"

I explained my theory. "If you had the original, it would be difficult to prove you were not behind the crime. Being you have a forgery; it will be easier to prove they conned you. Especially if you have a receipt for the purchase of the painting. Please tell me you do," I explained.

"Yes, of course," he said, as he walked over to a briefcase. He pulled out several papers and flipped through them before handing me a copy of the bill of sale.

I questioned, "Did you realize you purchased a painting valued at over $80 million for only $15 million?"

Jonathan answered, "Of course. The original owner of the painting passed away, and I figured the new owner did not know the value of the art. I thought it was a brilliant investment." He looked at me puzzled before continuing, "The owner did not die, did they?"

I held up the receipt and asked, "No. Would you mind making me a copy of this?"

"Of course," he responded before taking the document back and heading out of the room. Upon his return, Jonathan supplied me with the copy.

As I looked closer at the copy, I realized Daniel Pierre did not sign it. I inquired, "I'm not sure who Jacque Frances is? How did you know him?"

Jonathan explained, "He contacted me because I'm a collector. I'm contacted frequently."

I asked, "Would you mind supplying me with his contact information?" He grabbed a sticky note and pen from his briefcase and wrote the information he had stored on his phone. "I'll be back if I've more questions. May I use your restroom?"

"It's just down the hall," he said, pointing in the bathroom's direction.

The door was open, which made it easier to locate. I turned back to him and smiled before closing the door. There was a window in the bathroom, which I opened to lead him to believe this was how I exited his home. I left the door unlocked and quickly made my way back home.

I texted the Bloom Keepers to notify them we needed to meet. Juliet texted back to tell me she reserved a room at the library for 10:30 am tomorrow. I did not want to wait that long. We needed to figure out who Jacque Frances was and what his connection was to Daniel Pierre. I texted them to meet at my house after dinner. We all agreed to meet at 7:30 pm. I ran downstairs to fill Phyllis in on everyone coming over. During our conversation, I noticed she did not seem to act like herself. I inquired, "Are you okay?"

She looked at me with what looked like she had pain in her eyes. "Not really. I feel off today. My neck is stiff, and I have a bit of a headache," she explained.

I wanted to help, so I put one hand on the back of her neck and the other on her forehead. *I hope I'm doing this right.* I looked at Phyllis and she had a weird look on her face.

Phyllis asked, "What are you doing?"

I said, "I'm trying to heal you with the stone. Is anything happening?"

"If you're asking me, if this is making me feel better, it's not," Phyllis informed me.

Removing my hands from her. I thought about how it worked the last time. *Think Brooke! I know. I asked the stone to heal Greg's finger.* "Let me try again," I said, positioning my hands back in the same spots. I asked the stone to take away her pain. The stone and my hands began heating up. When the stone returned to its normal temperature, I removed my hands.

Phyllis looked confused and relieved. "I think it worked," she said, moving her neck about. Phyllis continued, "Yes, it worked. I feel better. Thank you."

I smiled at her and gave her a hug. I do not believe she had any idea how much she meant to me. Until dinner, I worked on my homework. Mom texted me to come down for dinner. As I headed downstairs, I heard a man's voice. *Was Lance here? Mom's home.* I ran down the stairs, hoping to find my mother with him.

When I saw the table, I noticed Lance sitting in my chair. It was important to me my mother be happy, but it was at that moment I realized his presence was going to change things for not just my mother but for me as well. I was just getting used to things here and now more change. I said, "Hi Lance. Do you know where my mother is?"

He smiled at me with those incredibly white teeth and tried to start a conversation with me by saying, "She'll be here in a minute. How was your day, Brooke?"

Not meaning to be rude. I responded, "Fine." I had my mind racing with things at that moment; wondering who Jacque Frances was, how I was going to survive the chemistry class when it already seemed overwhelming, and what else in my life was going to change because of this man.

My mother walked in and gave me a hug, "I missed you Peanut." She made her way to her chair. She asked, "Brooke, tell us what you did today?"

Great, an open-ended question. Now I was required to provide details. Knowing I needed to leave out anything about the Bloom Keepers and my quick trip to Rome after class to see Jonathan did not leave me much to tell. I informed them, "I had my chemistry class today, which is a tough class. I don't know anyone in the class to study with. Due to a lack of motivation, I didn't work out this morning. The rain did not help to motivate me."

"Unfortunately, I can't help you with chemistry," Lance said.

Phyllis came in with bowls of soup for everyone. I noticed there was not a table setting for her to join us. Loudly, I asked, "Phyllis, why are you not joining us for dinner?" I wanted to ensure everyone understood what I had asked. My mother needed to know; I did not approve.

Phyllis looked at me and then at my mother. She seemed unsure of how she should respond.

My mother spoke up, "Phyllis, please join us." After Phyllis nodded and headed back to the kitchen, my mother looked over at me and smiled.

Phyllis returned with a place setting before returning to the kitchen. I excused myself and went to find out why she had not sat down with us.

I was barely in the kitchen when Phyllis turned to me. She said, "You know very well why I was not sitting in there."

"Yes, but you're a part of the family. If he wants to be a part of it, he needs to know how important you are to us." I retorted back. I looked around the kitchen and asked, "Now what can I do to help you, so you can enjoy your meal?"'

"Go on back and be nice. I'm almost done here. I'll be joining you in a minute. If you would like, you may take my drink in," she said, pointing to a glass of iced tea on the counter.

I placed the tea at Phyllis's place setting before returning to my seat. Lance asked me about my workout routine and made additional small talk throughout the meal. It pleased me he tried to get to know Phyllis as well. He did not seem to be bothered by Phyllis joining us for dinner. My icy heart softened a bit about him. This made me happy. I did not know why I was so hard on him, but I needed to give him a chance. Dinner took a little longer than normal and we were just being served dessert when someone rang the bell. Phyllis was serving the red velvet cake, motioned for me to stay at the table, and headed to answer the door. She returned with Greg, who quickly found a seat and had a slice of cake. He and Lance had a few things to talk about. Lance enjoyed fishing, and they compared their favorite fishing spots.

When we finished eating, Greg and I helped Phyllis clear the table. Phyllis told us she would take care of everything. "Head up to the library. I'll send Juliet and Jacob up when they arrive," she advised. Before we left, she handed Greg a tray with four hot chocolates with mini marshmallows for our meeting.

Just as we made our way to the landing of the stairs, the bell rang. I let Jacob and Juliet in. The breeze that crept in while the door was open made the already cool foyer even colder. We headed upstairs, but not before I hollered at Phyllis to let her know I let them in.

Before I started the meeting, I closed the double doors to the library to help prevent anyone from eavesdropping. Greg worked on building a small fire to warm the room. It was wonderful, having so many chimneys.

"I called this meeting because we need to discuss Jonathan's purchase of the stolen artwork," I said. As my bottom landed on the leather sofa, a chill ran through me. "He provided me a bill of sale, which was signed by a Jacque Frances. I don't know who he is or how he obtained the painting, but we need to figure out how Daniel Pierre and Jacque Frances know one another. We need you to do your magic again, Jacob," I said as I looked over to confirm he was okay with this. Something seemed off with him. Concerned, I asked, "Jacob, is everything okay?"

Jacob provided reasons for his behavior. "It's just. Well, I'm hoping I'm covering my tracks well enough. The last thing I want is to end up in prison for this," he explained.

Greg asked, "We understand. If this is too much to ask of ya, we'll find another way. Is there something we can do to help prevent things from being tracked back to ya?"

"I'm afraid. They can track me. If I could use another computer, that would be great. I would need access to the computer to ensure the police have no way to trace anything back to me," he informed us.

"That sounds reasonable," I replied.

"How're we going to afford a computer for him?" Greg asked. He moved to the desk to find his usual position of leaning against the front of it.

"I'll take care of it. Jacob, write everything you need on the computer, and I'll see what I can do for you. Oh, would you also write what your current computer has? Thanks." I instructed him.

"I guess I'm up for the challenge then," Jacob said before clearing his throat. "I was able to find the contract between Alessandra and Phillip for the purchase of her condo," he added. Jacob handed a copy of the document to Juliet. He continued, "I also found several emails to Phillip sent by Nadine's phone about meeting times and locations." Another document was passed to Juliet.

Juliet reviewed the documents before passing them to Greg and me to review. I looked over the documents. I remarked, "Fabulous work!"

Greg spoke up, "Brooke and I have not made it back to the Granaldi's house yet to see if we can find anything to help us there, but I'm sure we'll be working on that soon."

I nodded to let him know I agreed with him. I turned to Juliet and asked, "Do you have all the documents we have collected so far?"

She assured me she did and pulled them out of her backpack. I looked over the items. "I'm going to get copies of these to ensure there are no fingerprints on them. I'll have the originals shredded. When we deliver these to the authorities, we want nothing leading them back to us," I informed them.

We were all startled by a knock on the library door. Greg took the pages from me and shoved them in the desk before I answered, "Come in."

As mom moved out of Lances way, she told me, "Lance is about to leave, and he wanted to say goodnight." She introduced them to Lance before closing the doors.

"I think that's enough for tonight," I said. Greg handed me the documents. "I'll be right back," I said. I pulled out my mirror and headed to the Villa Dianella.

In my search for Leonardo or Isabella, I ran into Kevin. After greeting one another, he asked, "Any idea when we'll be able to go home?" he asked.

I replied, "I'm working on it, which is why I'm here. Do you know where I can find either Leonardo or Isabella?"

Kevin said, "I think Isabella is taking someone on a tour and Leonardo was with a guest at the bar the last time I saw him."

I thanked him before heading to the bar. Leonardo was talking to a thin, older man with very white hair. I did not want to interrupt them, so I tried to get his attention to let him know I needed him. Eventually I managed to catch his eye. He ended his conversation and joined me.

"We need to speak somewhere more private," I instructed.

He led me to his room. I explained, "I need two computers with these specifications." I handed him the list and pointed to the first computer listed. "This one must be untraceable, and I need these quickly. I'm not sure how I'm going to pay for these, but they're important," I said with concern.

Leonardo put my hand in his, just as my grandmother did when she told me about her many adventures. "Brooke, your grandmother has arranged for you. There are plenty of funds available to you for these things. She kept an extensive amount of money out of her estate. Money is not and will never be an issue for you," he advised.

"I'm sorry, I know you told me that, but I had forgotten," I said, feeling stupid.

"I also need these documents copied, and the originals destroyed. I will submit the copies as evidence. It is extremely important there be no way of trace it back to anyone. The paper can't even be traced. No fingerprints, no DNA. Place the copies in a sealed bag in my secret place. I will get them later. I'm sorry, I know it's a lot to ask of you," I explained.

"Not a problem. I've got a few connections that helped me do things like this from working with Lillie a time or two," he assured me. He gave me a hug before explaining he needed to get back to his customers. I headed back to the library.

When I returned, everyone jumped. "Sorry, I didn't mean to startle you. Jacob, I'm getting you two computers. One will be a new computer for your personal uses and the other will be for Bloom Keepers. Once you have them set up. Remove all data from your current computer and we will destroy it. The Bloom Keeper computer will be untraceable, and the other will be just like the one you have," I said, realizing, other than schoolwork and maybe gaming, I do not know what he used his computer for.

With a confused look on his face, Jacob asked, "Really? How do you manage that in the 20 minutes?"

"There are some things you're better off not knowing about. What I mean to say is, for your safety and for the safety of the stone, it's better to keep you out of the loop on some things. Even Greg does not know everything," I said, realizing I stuck my foot in my mouth, but it was too late now. It was out there. I looked over at Greg and received a face that said, "What don't I know about?"

I think they picked up on my error in mentioning Greg did not know everything because Jacob and Juliet headed home. "Well, we've got class tomorrow. We'll let ourselves out," Juliet said as she grabbed her things.

Once they left the library, Greg shut the door and turned to me. He said, "I hope ya know ya can trust me, but just make sure ya aren't keeping anything from me that would put you in danger."

"I do trust you. I'm not keeping anything from you. They don't need to know about Kevin and his family. It could put them in danger," I assured him.

"Well, I've got homework," he said. He leaned in and gave me a quick peck before heading down the stairs.

I knew it hurt him, but I hoped he knew I was being honest. The protection of the journal was most important, which meant they do not need to know about Kevin. I had this necklace for six months and already three people knew about it, and I was incredibly lucky I could trust them. This information in the wrong hands would be catastrophic. I headed to my room to get ready for bed. As I took off my makeup, I could not stop thinking about how hurt Greg appeared before he left. Why does it hurt so badly when you hurt someone you love?

# Eighteen

The next morning, I texted Greg to see if he wanted to go to Parkour after class, but he texted, "Can't". No explanation, he must be really hurt. I went for a run before class to relieve some of my stress. As I stretched, I found myself looking towards Greg's house, hoping to run into him, but he was not home. I really thought he would understand. This behavior seemed out of character for him.

I decided I would not let it bother me. I tried to focus on my breathing and the coolness of the air as I inhaled the brisk air during my run. The run helped me get my mind straight. After showering, I headed to class.

The professor was reviewing our assignment when the stone heated. I slowly looked around the room to see what danger was lurking but found nothing to sound an alarm in me. A female student came in and sat in an available chair at the back of the room. I found myself not even listening to the professor.

I decided to go to the restroom to see if the stone would cool down. That would tell me if it was someone in my class or someone outside the room. As I exited the classroom, I noted a student sitting in the hallway on the floor reading a book. His backpack was sitting next to him. I walked down the hallway to the restroom.

When I entered, the stones temperature had not changed. I took a deep breath as I tried to figure out what was happening. In the mirror, I looked at the stone. *What are you trying to warn me about?* I used the restroom before heading back to class. Just as I was about to flush the toilet, I heard someone come in. I waited to see what they were going to do. The stone was getting warmer. The person never entered a stall. I took a deep breath before exiting my stall. As the stall door opened, I could not see the person. When I had exited the stall, I saw the girl from my class leaning up against a wall chewing gum. I washed my hands, making sure I kept her within view. I grabbed a paper towel and started heading toward the door. She stepped out in front of the door to block my path.

With what sounded like an Italian accent, she said, "Where do you think you're going?"

"Excuse me?" I retorted. *Who does she think she is?*

"You're not going anywhere with that necklace," she snapped.

"I'd like to see you try to take it off of me," I challenged her.

She stepped forward and shoved me. I asked, "Is that all you got?"

She attempted to punch me, but I dodged to the left to avoid her fist. The girl tried to kick me, and I jumped back to avoid the impact. "You know you're going to have to touch me to get to the necklace," I sarcastically commented on her fighting techniques.

The anger built up in her face. She charged at me. I quickly spun around to the right, avoiding her. As I came around, I punched her in the stomach. She went face-first to the ground and slid a little along the bathroom floor. Holding my stance, I asked, "Who sent you?"

She made her way back to her feet and tried coming at me again, only this time I stepped to the side, but left my arm in her path. She ran into it, and as she did, I pushed with all my force into her jaw. This caused her to fall to the ground. "I don't want to hurt you, but I will if you don't stop this," I informed her.

"I will get that necklace," she stated just before she got up and came after me. This time, I grabbed her head and pulled it down to my knee. When she fell to the floor. This time, she looked defeated.

The bathroom door then flung open. The kid reading the book in the hall entered the bathroom and started heading straight for me. He threw a punch at me, which I dodged. While he was distracting me, the girl struck me in the back. I twirled around and kicked her in the head. I directed my attention to the young man. With all my force, I spun around and kicked him. I knocked him off balance. Once he fell to the ground, I was able to get his head locked between my legs and kept squeezing. The girl was lying on the floor, barely moving, and he was calming down. I asked him, "Who sent you?" When I did not get an answer, I squeezed my grip on his neck tighter. I asked forcefully, "I asked, who sent you?"

He started slapping my leg lightly as if to say he wanted to tell me but couldn't. I released a little of the pressure on his neck to allow him to tell me.

In a soft, hoarse voice, he said, "Uncle Anthony."

Needing clarification, I asked, "Anthony Granaldi?"

"Yes," he informed me.

"Please give my regards to your uncle and inform him you were not up to the task. Now, if you wish to make it through the day, I suggest you head back to Italy. I will not go so easy on you the next time we meet," I said, releasing my grip on his neck. He fell to the ground. I got up and straightened my clothes before leaving the lady's room. I tried to keep my composure as I made my way back to my class. It was difficult. I could not believe what had occurred. At the same time, I felt proud of myself. I could use the skills Greg taught me to fight those two off.

I was expecting to see them when I left my class, but they were nowhere in sight. Perhaps they took my advice. I texted everyone to see if they could meet today.

**JULIET:**         Everyone is available. Library 4:00 pm.

I texted Greg privately to see if we could meet before heading over to the library. He did not answer. I glanced at the picture of his schedule to confirm he was in class. His class ended at 3:00 pm. I headed to the food court to get something to eat and to work on my homework until he was available.

At 3:06 pm, I received a text from him. I told him where I was. He said he would meet me at the food court. When he arrived, he got his food before joining me. He put his food on the table and leaned over and gave me a kiss before settling into his seat.

"I need to apologize," he said before taking a sip of his soda. "I was way out of line last night. You're right. The safety of ya and the stone are the most important things. I'm sorry."

"Thank you. I'm sorry too. I don't want to keep secrets from you, but I may need to from time to time. Several people are protectors of the stone. I haven't met them all yet. You never asked about the book Kevin had. I appreciate that. It's best you don't know. I promised them to keep it a secret," I explained.

"I understand," he stated again. Greg kissed me again and said, "I love ya." He dipped a French fry in some ketchup and offered me a bite.

"I'm glad we addressed what happened last night. But that's not why I wanted to speak with you. I need to tell you about what happened to me today," I said. He stopped eating and gave me his

145

full attention. I filled him in on the details about the incident in the restroom. It surprised him, but what shocked him the most was finding out they were relatives of Anthony Granaldi. We discussed what needed to be done. We needed another trip to the Granaldi's home. Evidence collection needed to be a priority. They would keep trying to get the stone until they were stopped.

It was so nice having the tension between us gone. We were enjoying our time together and nearly forgot about the 4:00 pm meeting. We quickly cleaned up the table and ran to the library to make sure we arrived on time.

Jacob and Juliet were waiting in the library's lobby when we arrived. Juliet and I walked over to the lady at the counter to find out about the room. As Juliet provided information about the reservation, I noticed the girl's name tag. Lorie looked at her computer to confirm our reservation and gave us a room number. We motioned for the guys to follow us.

Once the door to the room shut, Greg started explaining what I told him about being attacked, but Juliet abruptly interrupted him. "I'm sorry to interrupt, but you're very loud, and these walls are thin. We need to speak softly to avoid being overheard by anyone," she explained.

"Good to know," Greg commented before continuing in a softer voice. He finished filling them in. He asked, "Did I miss anything Brooke?"

"No, I believe that was everything," I assured him.

Juliet commented, "I wish I could've seen you show them whose boss. Are you okay?"

"Yes, I'm fine. I must admit I'm proud of myself for dodging their attempts to strike me," I said, trying not to be boastful.

Greg informed them, "Brooke and I are going to the Granaldi's after class today to see if we can find anything on them. Any ideas on what we should look for?"

"Tony's journal mentioned something about a hidden safe in the garage. Apparently, he found it when he was working on his motorcycle. He seemed mad his father never told him about it. I believe he said, "that man and his secrets". It sounds like he only let Tony and Joseph know things he needs their help with," Juliet informed us.

"Greg, we need to make that area a priority," I instructed.

"I agree," Greg confirmed.

"I need to head out. I'm meeting my study group at 5:00 pm and I need to grab a snack before we meet," Jacob said as he stood up.

"I've got an apple if that will help," I offered, pulling it from my backpack.

He grabbed the apple. "That's great, thanks. I don't want to be late for my first meeting with them. We're working on a project together," Jacob said before leaning over to Juliet for a kiss. As he opened the door to exit the room, he turned to Greg and me and said, "Good luck."

There was nothing more to discuss, so Greg and I headed home to prepare for our trip to the Granaldi's garage. Greg and I made sure we were wearing our ski hats and gloves to prevent us from leaving any DNA. As I looked into my full-length mirror into their garage, it appeared the main car they used was not there. This was good news for us. We made sure we were invisible as we stepped into the garage. We went to work immediately. Greg took one side of the garage, and I took the other.

Along the side of the garage was a well-organized wooden workbench. This was the fanciest workbench I had ever seen. No area was to be left unchecked. We moved everything not pinned down to look for secret compartments.

As I moved down the wall, there were cabinets containing coveralls, tools, towels, cleaning supplies, oil, and other fluids for vehicles, but no safe or secret room. Greg and I were to meet in the middle of the back wall. I turned to see where Greg was on his side. We were both nearly at the back wall. *Don't rush. You need to check everything. This isn't a competition.* I had to keep reminding myself to stay focused.

I stood back, looking at the wooden shelves. They looked as though they belonged inside of the home, not in a garage. *Why would someone go to such an expense for a garage?* Working my way from the corner of the room toward the center still finding nothing out of the ordinary. I caught Greg looking over at me and he motioned his hands as if to say he had found nothing. Mimicking him with the same motion, I let him know I had found nothing on my side either. *Lord, please let us find the secret room.*

It occurred to me; I could ask the stone to reveal it to me. I began concentrating on it being revealed, but nothing happened. *Well, it was worth a try.* I looked to see where Greg was, and he had made little progress. I looked to see how much more needed to be checked. *What is that?* I rubbed my eyes, not believing what I was seeing. I looked at the back wall again and there was a strange glow coming from the shelves. In a soft voice, I asked Greg, "Do you see that?" I pointed to the shelf.

Greg seemed puzzled by the question and said, "The shelf, yes, Brooke, I see it. What about it?"

"The light around the shelves," I explained.

Looking even more confused, he asked, "What are you talking about?"

Quietly, but swiftly, I moved to the glowing shelf. I began investigating the shelves where the glowing light seemed to come from. "There is a light in this area. I think the stone's trying to show me where to look," I explained.

"Well, I don't see anything, but I'll help ya look," he said, trying to help me. I searched for a secret lever.

I accidentally knocked a small box to the ground. I put my hand on the shelf it fell from to make sure I returned it to its original location. As I bent down to grab it with my other hand, I found the box was nearly out of reach. I clung on to the shelf and stretched my body out to get the box. When I did this, the shelf pulled away from the wall. The shelves I was holding on to and the shelves next to it connected and as I pulled on the shelves. The backs of both shelves moved toward each other. *What? This is a secret door.* The shelves connected to a track hidden under the decorative part of the top of the shelf and another track was located under the shelves. Behind the folding door was a small room.

Greg and I stepped into the room and closed the secret door behind us to ensure the room was not open in the event someone came into the garage. Inside the room was a small table with two chairs, a wall with surveillance cameras, and a large safe at the far end of the room. There were two beds, one along the wall in front of the door and the other attached to the wall but folded up against it. It was like those on a train or in an RV. The lower bed had storage under it. Greg opened it up. The compartment was filled with bottles of water, canned foods, and protein bars. There was also a first aid kit, some batteries, and a flashlight.

"This is a safe room," Greg explained.

"I think you're right," I agreed. *Why would he keep this room a secret from his children?* I glanced at the monitors. The only surveillance was of the areas around the garage and the main entrances of their home. There was nothing inside the house.

I made my way over to the safe, which appeared to be large enough to walk into. I turned to Greg and said, "I need that flashlight."

He handed it to me, and I tried to turn it on, but it was not working. Greg took it from me and banged on it a few times before the light started working.

I thanked him. Concentrating on the safe, I stuck my head in the safe. But I still saw nothing. Not even the light. I pulled my head back out and looked at Greg with a puzzled look.

He asked, "What's wrong?"

I was not sure what was wrong. "I stuck my head in and moved the flashlight in front of my face, but I saw nothing," I explained.

"Brooke, it's a safe. A very large, thick safe. I'm sure the walls are thick. Try moving in farther," he instructed.

I did as Greg asked. Only this time, I saw the safe was huge. I found a light on the ceiling with a pull string. I turned it on. The light glow from the bulb revealed guns mounted on the walls, an enormous pile of money, numerous passports for Anthony and his wife, a folder with some papers and some artwork. I stepped the rest of the way in. As I looked around, I realized there was enough room for both Greg and me, but it would be a tight fit. There was not much air in there. I grabbed a large folder with papers and exited the safe.

"It's so weird watching you walk through things," Greg said as he grabbed the large folder from me and took it to the small table where we made ourselves comfortable. Greg took the papers from the folder and handed me the first packet of stapled papers to read. He told me he would make sure we returned them to the spot they came from. Greg explained he could not read them. He believed they were in Italian.

As I reviewed the documents, I found contracts between Anthony and many of the people from the contact book we found in the safe in his room. Several of the contracts had terminated, and a date was written across them. I looked at Greg, who was clearly waiting for a response from me. "We need to remember Charles Garrett,

149

December 13, 2000, and Terry Lee November 20, 1998," I muttered. I read a few more before returning them to Greg. He placed them back in the correct order. He handed the entire pile back to me to put back in the safe.

This time I grabbed two canvases that were on a shelf and brought them to the table. I carefully unrolled one, and Greg did the other. The paintings were very similar, each oil painting had a pillar with an urn at the top. The pillars were nearly double the size of the people in the painting. One painting had a few people walking by the pillar and the other had two couples, one on each side of the pillar. We rolled them back up, and I returned them to the safe.

As soon as I returned to Greg, I grabbed his hand and took him to my library, where I quickly grabbed a pen and paper. "One name was Terry Lee, and the date was November 1998. I can't remember the day and the other person's name was Charles, something I am pretty sure it was 2000," I stated while I wrote the information down.

Greg said, "Charles Garrett and I am sure it was December 13th because my Grandmother Samantha's birthday is on the 13th. I think Terrys was the 20th or 30th. Sorry, I should bring a pen and paper with me to write these things down."

"It's okay. I didn't want to forget either, which is why I didn't read everything aloud to you, because one of us shouldn't have information overload. We can always go back and look if we need to," I commented.

I handed the pen and paper to Greg and asked him to write what I told him. Concentrating, I said, "We found contracts between Anthony Granaldi III and a variety of other people. The contracts included money laundering, stolen property, hits on people, basically a slew of illegal activity. We've got him, Greg. Although I don't think we can connect Tony and Joseph to any of these things. Perhaps the police can," I said excitedly. The thought of his incarceration excited me. He deserved what was coming his way.

Greg asked, "What's the significance of the names and dates?"

"There's a contract for each of them with the word Terminated and a date next to it. I figure we could research them to see if these people died on those dates. This could be more evidence to use against Mr. Granaldi if we found out they died on those dates," I explained.

Greg added, "And the paintings, they're probably stolen."

150

"Exactly!" I said, smiling with pride at our discovery. I wrapped my arms around his neck and gave him a big kiss. "We make a great team," I informed him.

I let Greg know I would be right back and went to my room to get my laptop. We sat on the couch in the library with the laptop on the coffee table and began trying to discover anything we could about Charles Garrett and Terry Lee, but mainly trying to discover when they died. After a few minutes, Greg used his phone to see if he could find anything, so I moved to the desk to be more comfortable. "How about you look for Charles Garrett and I'll search for Terry Lee," I suggested.

"Sounds good," Greg stated, without looking up from his phone.

"Hey Greg, I was able to find an obituary for Terry Lee and it states he only had a son named Brent who survived him," I said. I continued searching. "Greg, come here; I found an interview his son gave to the press.

Greg came over and stood behind me to view the video. As I clicked on the video, a balding man was talking to a reporter. "This was no accident. Someone murdered my father. My father just put new brakes on his vehicle about two weeks before his accident and he is meticulous about ensuring they're installed properly. His brakes went out, which means someone tampered with them. My dad had been working on cars his entire life and knew things needed to be installed properly."

The reporter stated, "There you have it. Terry Lee's son Brent believes his dad was murdered. If you know anything about this, please contact the authorities."

"I found this about Charles Garrett," Greg said as he opened a new window on my computer and pulled up a website, which contained information about him. "It says here, Charles Garrett had been in prison for money laundering. If you scroll down, it goes on to say," Greg paused as he tried to find the area, he wanted me to see. He continued, "He died on December 13, 2020, from a gunshot wound. The case was never solved."

"Perhaps we just solved it," I said gleefully.

As we continued discussing how proud we were for locating the evidence and how we discovered a new ability of finding secret doors. It occurred to me I needed to let Kevin know about this and to check on the status of the computers.

# Nineteen

Greg and I found Isabella at the front desk checking a couple into the Villa. Once the couple left, I inquired about the items Leonardo was trying to get for me. She led us to her room and had us wait while she went through her closet. After hearing her shuffling things around, she returned with a leather satchel.

She placed it on the table and opened it. Isabella said, "There are two laptops in here." She pulled one computer out. Isabella continued, "This one can't be traced. It's a satellite computer and will always have internet access." She pushed it back into the satchel. "The other computer is in here. The papers you needed copied are in your safe room. If you don't need anything else, I need to get back to my guests," she said. We thanked her. Isabella gave each of us a peck on the cheek before leaving.

Greg and I returned to my bedroom and stowed the items in my closet until we could get them to Jacob. In the distance I heard my mother calling for me, so I hollered back, "I'm in my room."

She questioned, "I was just here and didn't see you. What're you guys doing?".

*Think quick Brooke!* I saw a photo album she hadd made me of my father and me. I responded, "We were on the balcony looking at the photo album you made me with all the pictures of dad and me together. I wanted to show it to Greg."

"That's nice. I didn't think to look out there for you. It's dinnertime. Greg, would you like to stay for dinner? Phyllis made meatloaf and mashed potatoes," she replied.

"I can't tonight but thank you," he said before saying his goodbyes to us and heading home.

I told my mother I would be right down. I put a suitcase in front of the computers to hide it in case my mother needed something from my closet. I headed to dinner.

During dinner, Mom asked me about my day. I told her about my classes and having lunch with Greg, but what I really wanted to tell her was the truth. The truth about the necklace, our family, her mother, my amazing sleuthing skills, and how I had defended myself against some of the worst people, but I couldn't put her at risk. She told me about her day. The more I thought about my secret and how it would affect her, it comforted me to know I was keeping her safe.

After dinner, I texted Jacob and told him I needed to stop by. He texted me to tell me I could pop in, which had become our code for "my closet awaits you". As I stepped into his closet, I was greeted with a bigger mess than usual. I knocked on the door to let him know I was there. As he opened the door, I wobbled on the clothes at the bottom of the closet and fell to the floor. Fortunately, I protected the computers, but not my face. I went face-first into the carpet. "There's nowhere to stand in there," I said, annoyed by his disorganization. I lifted myself up off the floor.

"I'm sorry. Juliet told me she was on her way over and I just threw everything in the closet in a rush to pick everything up before she arrived," He explained.

"Here are the computers. Once you get everything copied over from the other one, the old computer will need to be destroyed," I instructed.

He smiled and informed me, "It's ready for destruction. I've been working on it the past few days. When you said you were coming over; I finished the job. I've everything I need on a flash drive ready to be installed on the new one."

I opened the leather satchel and explained the differences between the computers. I asked him if he wanted his old computer destroyed. He did.

I returned home to work on homework I had been ignoring. Once finished, I grabbed Jacob's computer and headed to the Villa. I ran into William, Lainie, and Kevin while I looked for Leonard. William asked, "Any news yet?"

"Yes, it shouldn't be much longer," I assured them. "We've a few details to work out, but I'll take you back home when it's safe."

Lainie said, "It was sweet of you to bring us here. This has been much like a vacation for us. We've enjoyed getting to know Leonardo and Isabella, but we're ready to head home."

I responded, "I understand. I really must find Leonardo. Have you seen him?"

"He has usually turned in by this hour," Kevin informed me.

I made my way to Leonardo and Isabella's room and knocked on the door. Leonardo opened the door and it appeared he came straight from his bed. His hair was a mess, and he was in his pajamas. He seemed to be half asleep until the sight of me seemed to awaken him. He did not say a word, he just pulled me into his room.

"I need you to make sure this has no fingerprints or anything to trace it back to anyone and it must be destroyed," I instructed.

"I'll take care of it, Brooke," Leonardo said before taking the computer and heading toward his bedroom. I headed home to create a list of the evidence and options on what to do with it before turning in for the night.

The next morning, before heading to work, Mom informed me, she and Lance were meeting for dinner. I asked if she minded if I had my friends over for dinner.

"That's fine. Just order a pizza and let Phyllis have the night off," she instructed before heading out the door.

I headed to the kitchen for breakfast and found Phyllis at the stove making an omelet. I gave her a kiss on the cheek and asked, "Is that for me?"

"Yes. I ate with your mother," she said as she pushed some toast down for me.

I made myself some coffee and explained to her my plans for the evening. She said everything would be ready for my friends at 6:00 pm. I texted the Bloom Keepers and asked them to come for dinner. On Fridays my schedule was free. I spent the day working out, creating my list of evidence, and getting my assignments for my classes done before they arrived. I slowly heard from everyone, confirming they would be in attendance.

It was nearly time to head downstairs when I found an article about two Maxfield Parrish paintings stolen in 2002 from a gallery in Hollywood, California, valued at more than $4 million. I scrolled down and discovered these were the paintings Anthony had in his safe. I printed the article and put it with my notes.

I headed down to help Phyllis set the table. As I made my way to the kitchen, the aroma of blueberry pie filled the air. "You're supposed to be taking the night off," I informed her.

"Oh, I am. I bake because it brings me pleasure, and it tastes so good," Phyllis said with a giggle.

I informed her everyone was coming and asked her to join us for dinner. As I was filling the glasses with ice, Greg knocked on the back door before entering. He went straight to Phyllis and kissed her on the cheek.

"Phyllis, I guess I let the cat out of the bag about us," he joked before giving me a kiss.

We sat in the dining room chatting until we heard the doorbell. I grabbed my credit card from my pocket and made my way to the door, where I found Juliet, Jacob, and the delivery guy. Jacob took the pizzas while I paid the man. After receiving my receipt, I quickly closed the door to prevent any cooler air from entering.

We headed to the dining room and sat down. We prayed and everyone snagged their piece of the pie. As I watched everyone enjoying their pizza, I thought about this small group. It was amazing what brought us together. It was fate. Greg dropped a slice with everything on it on my plate, interrupting my thoughts. "Thank you," I said.

Once done with my second slice, I excused myself from the table. I darted to my room for my notes and quickly returned to the table. Mostly, everyone finished eating by the time I returned. "I'd like to call to order the Bloom Keepers meeting," I announced. Jacob, Phyllis, and Juliet seemed confused. Juliet and Jacob looked at Phyllis. Phyllis's attention was on me. She also appeared to be confused.

That was when I realized they did not know Phyllis knew about the stone and Phyllis was not aware of the creation of Bloom Keepers.

"My grandmother entrusted me with her most prized possession, the Bloom of Dreams. She also entrusted her secret to her best friend, Phyllis, who has guided me on my mission to protect the secret of the Bloom of Dreams and to keep it safe," I informed everyone.

I could see the relief on my friend's faces. "Phyllis, I'd like to invite you to be a member of the Bloom Keepers. We work together as a team to keep the secret of the Bloom of Dreams and to protect the stone," I continued.

Phyllis smiled and said, "The Bloom Keepers. Lillie would've loved this. She would be proud of you right now, Brooke."

I could see her eye had watered. "Everyone, please raise your right hand and repeat these words," I said as everyone stood up and raised their right hand. "As a member of the Bloom Keepers, I promise to protect the Bloom of Dreams, its secrets, and the Bloom Keepers members at all times. I will work toward stopping evil and protecting the good. Discussion of Bloom Keepers' business will only occur in secure areas and only with other members of the group." I shook each of their hands and thanked them for everything they had done. "If everyone's done, let's clean the table. We have a lot to discuss," I instructed.

"I'll clean everything up," Phyllis stated.

"Not tonight, Phyllis. As the newest member of the group, you don't need to do anything. We've got this," I said. I picked up our plates and made my way to the kitchen.

Once the table was clean, we officially began the meeting. "As you know, Greg and I went to the Granaldi's home last night in search of a hidden safe. We discovered the safe room hidden in the garage, which had a large safe inside of it. The safe contained guns, ammo, documents, and artwork. After some research, we discovered the following," I said, pulling out my notes with the listing of items. I continued, "There were two Maxfield Parrish paintings, which were stolen in 2002 from a gallery in Hollywood, California, valued at more than $4 million. There were contracts between Anthony Granaldi III and a variety of people, which provided proof of an extensive list of crimes. Two of the documents had terminated, written in large letters across the top of the documents along with a date. After some research, we discovered the dates were the dates of death for the person he was in contact with. They shot one man and the other's brakes suddenly went out. The family believed he was murdered. With these items and the information, we have on Phillip, we have enough evidence to put these men away for a long time. Have I forgotten anything?"

Jacob stated, "You asked me to find a connection between Jacque Frances and Daniel Pierre, which I did. They arrested Daniel Pierre in 1997. The article stated Jacque Frances is an alias of his."

"Really?" I thought about everything for a moment.

"I can't believe it; we've done it, guys. We're going to help put these people away for a long time," Greg said before turning to Jacob for a high five.

Phyllis turned to me and said, "I'm so proud of you. I know Lillie's gleaming with pride at what you have accomplished." She looked at everyone at the table. "I truly believe God has his hand in this. Only he could have brought such an amazing group of young people together. Just remember, before you provide anyone the evidence you have collected, make sure nothing will lead them back to you," Phyllis said. She excused herself and headed toward the kitchen.

"Phyllis is right. Jacob, I will take you back to each of the computers to undo anything you've done. Greg, we need to get all our cameras and recorders removed as well," I advised.

Juliet spoke, "We need to destroy all notes and copies of documents as well. Brooke, we need to make clean copies of all the evidence before destroying our originals. They can't trace physical evidence back to us," Juliet opened her bag and handed them to me.

I looked over them to make sure everything was there. Phyllis returned with blueberry pie for everyone. We compared notes to determine what we still needed to do before we supplied the authorities with the evidence.

"We also need a letter detailing everything to help lead the authorities in the direction they should go. It should be short and to the point. We will need Jacob's computer to create it," Juliet added.

"One of us should go to the New York City District Attorney with the information related to Phillip and the other should go to... Well, I don't know who we should send Anthony's evidence to," Greg added.

Jacob grabbed the computer and began clicking on the keys, "It should go to the Polizia or Police Station in Florence. I've a picture. I'll see if I can find some pictures of the interior for you, Brooke."

"Perhaps we should come up with an image to stamp in the corner of the letter. That way, if we prove to the police, we're trustworthy, when they see our image, they will know it is from us. It could be something as simple as a drawing of the flower on the stone. Although they will not know the name of our group; we'll create a type of partnership with the police. It would be our trademark," Jacob suggested.

"As much as we don't want someone being able to trace things back to the Bloom Keepers, this could be helpful if they ever caught us. They might go easier on us if they know we work to assist them by making sure they have evidence they need," Greg provided us with something to think about.

I thought about it. I advised, "There's a lot to consider. How about we all think about this and vote the next time we meet?" I looked around the room to see what everyone thought about my suggestion. It was as if no one heard me. I asked, "Does everyone agree with that?" There were a lot of nods. "I'd like everyone to provide me with suggestions for our note as well. Please bring them to the next meeting. In the meantime, I will work with Jacob and Greg about removing evidence. They can tie nothing back to us," I said.

Jacob and Juliet informed us they were going to head out. We said our goodbyes. Greg took my hand and lead me to the sofa in the sitting room. We made ourselves comfortable in front of the fire. Greg and I had little time to enjoy one another for a while. We snuggled up together. As much as we tried to not discuss Bloom Keepers business, we seemed to keep circling back to it. After a brief discussion, we decided to head back to the Granaldi's tomorrow. We agreed to head to Parkour for a good workout first. We were getting lazy because neither of us wanted to be out in the cold.

# Twenty

The next morning, I was up and ready to go at 8:30 am. Greg joined us for breakfast, which was oatmeal and fresh fruit. I was not that big a fan of oatmeal, but Greg loved it. Mom wanted to know what our plans were for the day. Greg explained we were planning to go to Parkour, and we were meeting up with friends afterward. She and Phyllis went shopping and had planned on having lunch out since we were busy. It made things easier when mom was out of the house.

As we walked into Parkour, I ran into Gloria. I do not think I had ever seen her with her hair straightened, but it seemed shinier somehow. She offered us a discount, which I appreciated. Perhaps she felt bad for me. I thanked her again for helping me when I broke my hand. That was only a few months ago. I had changed so much since then.

As we stretched, I noticed they had changed the course a bit. This made me even more excited about getting started. I ran out and started jumping from one platform to another. Swinging from bar to bar, eventually landing on a stand. I dove over platforms and slid under the platform. Amazingly, I completed the flip and landed on my feet on another raised platform. I do not know if I was just getting better or if the stone was helping me. I knew it felt good to workout. When we were leaving, I thanked Gloria again.

She stopped us from leaving. Gloria said, "I saw ya'll out there. You're both exceptionally good. We've a group that meets at random places in the city. We just run wild for an hour or so. If ya'll are interested, I'll add you to our distribution list. A text will be sent a few hours before we meet. What do ya say? Wanna try it?"

Greg and I looked at each other and smiled. Greg said, "We'd love to. What could be better than doin' this at no charge and getting practical experience out in the city?"

I felt like I was on an adrenaline high, but my stomach wanted lunch. We knew we had a lot to do, so we ran to Wendy's and grabbed lunch to eat back at my house.

While we ate, we created a short list of everything we needed to do at the Granaldis. Greg went home to get cleaned up, and I headed upstairs to do the same. I texted him when I was ready to tell him he could come on over. In the meantime, I called Jacob to see if he could be available to head over to the Granaldis when we finished, but only if the coast were clear. He told me to call him when I was ready for him.

I got dressed and put my hair in a bun. I dressed the part and wore all black clothes, my black sneakers, black ski mask, and only needed to put on my latex gloves to make my outfit complete. Greg announced he was heading up the stairs while I was tying my shoes. Surprisingly, he wore all black, as well. Even though no one would see us, it was kinda fun dressing up for the part. We both laughed when we saw each other.

I handed him a pair of latex gloves and put a pair in my pocket for Jacob, before putting a pair on myself. I looked at Greg and smiled. As I exhaled from the deep breath, I had taken to calm my nerves, we stepped into the mirror.

We arrived in the Granaldis sauna. Greg quickly went to work removing the camera. He even brought some wood putty to fill in the hole. I placed the camera and his tools in his backpack as he finished with them.

"This one's all set," he informed me.

I opened my mirror and brought us to the top of the stairwell that led to Anthony's closet. I looked in the mirror to see if I could see anyone, but it was too dark to tell. I grabbed Greg's arm and poked my head through the door. I did not hear or see anything, so I continued pulling him into the closet through the door.

"That's the strangest thing," he whispered.

Motioning to Greg to stay where he was, I made my way through the bathroom to the master bedroom and was happy to report there was no one in the room. "Hurry up with this one. I'll keep watch in the other room," I advised him. I left him and went to get the recording pen from under the bed.

I heard footsteps coming down the hall, so I moved over to the wall along the hallway. I concentrated on putting my head through it. Once my eyes made it past the wall, I could see a maid waiting on the elevator. They had come back home. I felt a light tap on my lower

162

back, followed by my arm being grabbed. He pulled me back through the wall into the bedroom.

Greg whispered, "Is everything okay?"

"Yes, I think they may be back at the house. I saw a maid at the elevator," I answered.

"I just have the camera aimed at the computer to remove," he said before walking over to it.

I decided to check out who was in the house. I stepped through the wall and made my way toward the kitchen. There was another maid in the kitchen, putting groceries away. She had a movie playing on the television and seemed to pay little attention to the movie. Even less to the groceries. She nearly dropped a bottle of milk on the floor. She did not realize it was not completely on the refrigerator shelf. The butler and the maid who had been waiting for the elevator were nowhere in sight. I pulled out my mirror and returned to Greg. "I think just the maids are here and they're not acting like the Granaldis are home," I whispered.

Greg put his tools and equipment in his backpack. "We just need Jacob to clean up his mess," he advised me.

I took his arm and brought him to the safe room in the Villa.

Greg looked confused. He asked, "Why are we here?"

"We don't need this equipment in either of our homes. Leave it here," I instructed.

Once he finished emptying the equipment onto the table, we returned to my house. I collected my phone from my dresser and quickly called Jacob to let him know I would be there in a few minutes. I told Greg I would call him when I got back.

"I can go back with you," he informed me.

"No need. There's no one there but the maids," I stated as I stepped into my mirror, not waiting for his response.

Jacob was ready to go when I arrived. We went straight to Anthony's bedroom. I stuck my head out into the hallway to confirm no one was heading our way. The coast was clear. Jacob quickly started clicking away on the keys. I could not believe how fast the guy could type. I was fast, but I would make a ton of errors if I even attempted to type as fast as him.

He seemed to make himself at home because he slouched in the chair just as he did when he was at his own desk. After about fifteen minutes, he took a deep breath and let it out before whispering, "Nearly done."

I was glad to hear it. Grateful he was on my team, but his work bored me. I focused on how badly I need a manicure.

Bam! The door then flung open, and Anthony marched in. Jacob sat up in the chair and froze, not knowing what to do. Anthony was heading straight for his computer and quickly pulled the chair back to sit down. Fortunately, Jacob moved swiftly in the opposite direction and found himself on the floor. I used telepathy to ask, "Did you finish?"

"Nearly done. I need another minute," he pleaded.

Anthony opened the desk drawer and grabbed a pad and paper and jotted a note. He did not seem to pay any attention to the computer screen being on or the screen Jacob was working on. He left as abruptly as he arrived.

"Quick, finish here. I'm going to see what is going on," I instructed him using telepathy.

He answered back, "Don't leave me here alone."

"You'll be fine," I answered. Without looking back, I exited the room through the wall. I looked toward the far end of the hall but did not see him. A door slammed behind me. I spun around and realized he was in the library. I opened my mirror to see where I should enter the room without being discovered. Anthony, Tony, and Joseph were in the room. I realized I needed to enter from the other side of the room to avoid being detected. I put the image of the reading nook in my head to be sent to it.

Anthony was yelling at the boys about their incompetence. He said, "The two of you are notorious for not getting things done. We can't mess this up, it's too important!"

Tony said, "We got this Pops, right Joey?" He slapped Joseph on the back.

"Take this note to Dante. Tell him Jacque must pull this job on the 17th between 8:00 pm and 9:30 pm," Anthony instructed. He headed toward the door, but he halted. He continued, "By the way, we've got dinner plans on the 17th at 8:00 pm and you both will attend along with your wives at Ora d' Aria." Spinning on his heels, Anthony exited the room.

I immediately returned to Jacob. He was pressing himself against the wall, appearing to become one with it. Using telepathy, I asked,

"Are you done?" He nodded. I quickly grabbed his arm and brought him back to his room.

"Wow, that was close," he said as he fell into his chair. "It amazed me I could get out of that desk so quickly," he informed me.

Not paying much attention to Jacob. I focused on what had just happened. *What did Anthony write to Jacque?* "I need to go back," I advised.

Jacob asked, "Why?"

"I need to know what Anthony wrote on the note," I stated. As I pulled out my mirror, Jacob pushed my hand down. He reached into his pocket and pulled out a piece of paper that appeared to be from Anthony's pad. "I need the note, Jacob," I explained.

Not saying a word, Jacob grabbed a pencil from his desk and turned it on its side, and scribbled side to side. This revealed a message. He read it aloud, "17-8-10-E-Natali-Riders on the Beach. What could that mean?"

Jacob jumped to his desk and began clicking away on the Bloom Keepers computer keyboard. "Aha, E. Natali must be Ernesto Natali. He is a private art collector, and he owns a painting named Rider's on the Beach. A Paul Gauguin painted it in 1902 and they value it from $80,000,000 to $140,000,000," he stated. Clicking away some more. He added, "Not a clue what 17-8-10 means."

*Why do those numbers sound familiar? Think Brooke!* "I've got it! Anthony and his boys are having dinner with someone on the 17th at 8:00 pm. It must mean Jacque had to steal it between 8:00 pm and 10:00 pm. I got it. They're having dinner with...," I paused. Reviewing the computer screen to confirm the name. "Ernesto Natali," I said. I turned to give Jacob a high five. He finally noticed my hand hanging there waiting for him and slapped it. I asked, "Have I told you how fantastic you are?"

"The 17th is only a week away, Brooke. We don't have a lot of time," Jacob said as he turned away from his computer.

"You're right. We still need to go to Phillips and take care of his computer. Do you want to do it now?" I said as I pulled out the mirror.

"Na, how about tomorrow? Tonight, was exciting, but I'm mentally exhausted," he said as he returned to his bed.

He was right. I nodded and headed home.

I woke up invigorated. It was warmer than usual at this time of the year, so I took advantage of the beautiful weather and went for a longer run than usual, which nearly made me late for church. Mom, Phyllis, and I had lunch out before returning home. I ran up to my room and locked my door before heading to Phillips's condominium. He was nowhere in sight. I returned home and immediately contacted Jacob. I asked, "He's not there. Can you go now?"

"I need fifteen minutes to get dressed and grab something to eat," he blurted before hanging up on me.

As I waited, I used telepathy to let Phyllis know I was leaving. I asked her to cover for me. When I arrived in Jacob's closet, I could hear him talking to his mother. I needed to be as quiet as possible, which was difficult in the small, disorganized closet. I heard his mother tell him he needed to clean his room. *That's for sure. Let's start with this closet.* Jacob told her he had a lot of homework to finish and asked not to be disturbed. He promised to clean it when he finished his work. I heard a door close. The next thing I knew, I was again falling forward as Jacob opened the closet door.

"I'm sorry, Brooke," he said, catching me mid-fall.

I stood up. I whispered, "You ready to go?"

"Yes, let's get this over with," he said as he grabbed my arm.

While Jacob worked on Phillip's computer, I took the photograph of my Great Grandmother. I retrieved it from his closet. Making sure I put the box and its contents back the way I found them. I know I should leave it, but I did not have a photograph of her. She had died when I was very young. Besides, *you will not need this where you're going.* I slipped the photograph into my pocket.

I returned to Jacob. He focused and did not notice me enter. Before I knew it, he had completed his work. I returned him to his room.

When I arrived in the comfort of my room, I unlocked my door and began working on my homework. As much as I tried to stay focused on studying, I kept thinking about the note I needed to draft about the evidence for the police. *Focus, Brooke.* I finally could get my mind off the letter and on to my assignments. Before I knew it, my mother called me and told me dinner was ready.

Phyllis had prepared beef stew and cornbread for dinner. The smell was amazing. We were blessed to have her with us. We sat down and said grace before enjoying the savory dish. Phyllis told us she and her sister were planning a trip to Florida next month. They were going to be gone for a week. If anyone deserved a vacation, it was her. Mom told us about how well things had been going at work.

After dinner, we continued our conversation in the sitting room by a fire. I had spent little time with either of them lately and enjoyed our chat and the crackle of the fire. It did not last too long, though. Juliet texted me.

**JULIET:**          I have a draft.

**BROOKE:**          Great!

From that moment on, I could not concentrate on the discussion. I excused myself and headed to my room to begin my draft. I grabbed my computer and my notes and headed to the library to sit at the desk. As I stared at the blank word document, I tried to think about what should be included in the letters.

For the Granaldis, we needed to include the location of the hidden safe, to mention the contract Anthony Granaldi had with Charles Garrett and Terry Lee. *We must also mention the termination date on the contract's correlates with the date of death for each of the men. So much to remember.* The stolen Maxfield Parrish paintings were in his safe. I created my draft in word but copied it onto a pad to bring to the meeting. I deleted the draft before exiting my computer.

Before starting the letter related to Phillip, I headed downstairs for a drink and a snack. My mother was at the desk working on her bills. I asked, "I'm grabbing a snack. Do you want something?"

My mother looked up, "What did you have in mind?"

"Not sure," I answered.

Mom got up, and we both headed to the kitchen. We found Phyllis at the counter. Mom said, "We're getting a snack. Do you care to join us?" Mom opened the refrigerator.

"There's not much in there. I'm composing a grocery list as we speak," Phyllis said, as she put her pen down and got up to head to the pantry. She had an amazing way of making something out of nothing. "I've got it," she said. Phyllis placed a bag of marshmallows, a chocolate bar, and some graham crackers on the counter. She filled the kettle with water and put it on to heat. "Brooke, please grab the hot chocolate." Which I immediately did, while she grabbed three mugs and a plate. She built three s'mores on the plate and placed them in the microwave for a few seconds. The marshmallows and the chocolate had begun to melt. Once the hot chocolates were ready, we sat at the counter and devoured the sweet pieces of perfection.

These were the fond memories I would always cherish. My grandmother would love this. I had been so engrossed in my responsibilities with the stone; I had missed out on some of those moments. This motivated me to get back upstairs so I could complete the task of having them arrested for their crimes. I needed this done so I could return to the safety of a normal life without walking in fear because of the Granaldis or Phillip.

I reviewed the information we had on him before composing a draft. We had a contract between Phillip and Alessandra, texts between them as well as text between Phillip, Eddie, and Nadine. We could prove the company, Safe Safes, did not exist. *Wait, we still need to prove he received compensation for the stolen jewelry. How could we have forgotten such an important detail?* I quickly texted Greg.

**BROOKE:**       We need to talk immediately!

Greg called and sounded half asleep. He asked, "Brooke, are ya okay?"

Anxiously, I asked, "I'm fine, but can you meet me now or can I come to you?"

"Can it wait till tomorrow? I am in bed," he asked. Greg sounded as though he could easily fall back to sleep.

I looked at the time and it was 12:18 am. "Yes, sorry. I didn't realize the time," I apologized. My adrenaline was flowing through me. I decided to pay a visit to Nadine and Eddie to find out what happened to the jewelry and see if I could trace it back to Phillip.

When I arrived in their bedroom, they were sound asleep. I began flicking the lights on and off until I knew they were awake. Nadine woke first and started nudging Eddie. She said, "Eddie, wake up!" He did not move. She pushed him harder.

*Come on Eddie, we need to talk.* I looked around the room to see what else I could do to get him up. A glass of water was on his nightstand. I picked up the glass and held it above his head.

Nadine hollered, "Uh Eddie, get up!"

Eddie asked, "Dang, Nay. What's up?" He squinted as he looked at her. She pointed to the glass hovering over his head.

Just as he looked up, I began pouring the glass of water on his head. Once empty, I dropped the glass next to him. He quickly sat up. Trying to disguise my voice by making it sound deeper, "Where are Alessandra's jewels?"

Nadine blurted, "Phillip told us to hold on to them until he could find a buyer for them. When he finds one, we will bring them to him."

"He needs them. Bring them to his home Thursday," I demanded. Before providing a time, I had to think about my school schedule to ensure I would be available to let them into his condo. "Arrive at 10:00 am. The door will be unlocked. Place the jewelry under the bed in the guestroom. Do not be late! If you fail, I'll haunt you for the rest of your lives. Complete this task and you're likely to never hear from me again," I instructed.

"We'll be there," Nadine promised.

Just before leaving, I grabbed the blanket and yanked it off them. I gleamed with pride. *They're so much fun to torment.*

# Twenty-One

The next morning, I texted Juliet because the Bloom Keepers needed to meet as soon as possible. Everyone was available to meet for lunch, but we could not get a room at the library. We agreed to meet in the courtyard. With the cooler weather, there would be fewer people. I explained our error in collecting evidence and what I had done to assure the jewels would be at Phillip's home. "We need to have the letters ready by Wednesday. I can drop them off as soon as I'm done letting Nadine and Eddie into Phillip's condo," I explained.

I gave my draft of the two letters to Juliet to review. She gave me hers. We compared the two to determine what the final should say. "Juliet, would you mind typing these up? I trust whatever you come up with will be fine. Make sure you don't touch the paper before or after it's printed. Place them in a plastic bag. I'll get them from you when they're done," I requested. She agreed. We quickly ate before heading back to class.

Throughout the day I ran the list of evidence through my head, ensuring we had not forgotten anything. Once my classes concluded, I went to Parkour to get my mind off everything. Gloria greeted me with a warm smile. "Hi, Brooke. I'm glad you're there. There's a rumor, we might get a text this weekend. I hope to see you there," Gloria said.

"Really? Greg and I are looking forward to it. I hope we can make it," I said, handing her my card.

"If not, there will be others. They don't come in from the same number all the time," she advised. She handed me my receipt and told me, "Have fun."

There were very few people there. This allowed me time to focus on myself. I frequently studied others as they went through the course. After stretching, I tried a few new things. I went through many obstacles on the course. My skills were improving each day. The practical skills I was learning would help me escape a situation or even catch a person. Pleased with myself for choosing to work out here. I was ready to take on Phillip and the Granaldis. When I

171

grabbed my phone and purse from the locker, I noticed I missed a couple of texts from Greg.

**GREG:** Hey babe. What's up?

**GREG:** Just checking up on you. I figured you couldn't get our assignment off your mind.

I knew he was not talking about a class assignment because we did not have classes together. I called him. After our greetings, I said, "It's been difficult. I got a workout in. I'm just leaving Parkour."

"I'm heading over to Austin's house. He needs help to repair the chicken coup. His dad's sugar was off and backed into it with the tractor," he informed me.

Austin is a great guy but every time I hear his name I am reminded of Greg and I being on his farm. "Is he going to be, okay?" I said as I opened my car door.

Greg said, "He's fine. Austin wants his dad to rest. We're going to fix it, so Bill does not have to be reminded of the damage he caused. He's embarrassed. Do ya want to hang out tonight?"

"Of course. Have fun with Austin and let me know when you're heading over," I said as I buckled myself up.

Just as I pulled into my neighborhood, Juliet called to let me know she was ready for me to come over. I explained I was driving home and needed to shower. She told me she would deliver them to me.

Phyllis was on the phone when I entered the kitchen. Trying not to disturb her, I grabbed a glass of water and an apple and headed up to my room for a shower. I was getting dressed when I heard a text come in.

**JULIET:** I'm here.

**BROOKE:** Come on up.

I opened my door and greeted her as she made her way down the hall to my room. "I hope you don't mind me coming over. My parents are driving me crazy, and I needed to get away," she muttered.

"No problem," I said as I brushed my hair.

She plopped herself in a chair. She said, "Apparently, my mother's not happy about her mother-in-law coming to stay with us for two weeks. She can usually handle my grandmother for about three days before she loses her mind." She handed me a plastic zip-lock bag with two letters inside.

I asked, "Are ya sure there are no fingerprints on these?" I read the letters through the plastic Juliet had slid them in back-to-back to allow me to read them without touching them.

"Positive," she said proudly.

"Thanks for putting them this way," I said before reviewing the second letter.

"I figured if something was wrong, we would need to change it," Juliet informed me.

I continued reading before offering my critique. "Absolutely perfect! Well done Juliet and the bloom in the corner is perfect," I commented.

We spent the next hour chatting about Greg, Jacob, and the accomplishments of the Bloom Keepers before she had to head back to the battlefield at her home. I put some makeup on and prepared myself for some time with Greg. I did not hear from him until after dinner. Which worked out well because I could enjoy more quality time with Phyllis and my mom. Phyllis told us more about what she planned to do in Florida. They were planning on going to St. Augustine.

When Greg arrived, we caught up on things before settling down to enjoy a movie and a bowl of popcorn in the library. It was nice getting to spend time with just him. We enjoyed being together. Greg had become my best friend. We finished our evening off with a good-night kiss under the moonlight.

The days felt long as I waited for Thursday morning to come. As I was finishing my last class for the day, I received a text from an unknown number.

**UNKNOWN:** The Jam will begin in two hours at Waterfront Park.

As soon as class was dismissed, I texted Greg to see if he could go. He did not immediately text back. I headed to the cafeteria for a light snack and a bottle of water. Greg called while I was eating my snack. I told him I was at the cafeteria, where he joined me a few minutes later.

Greg sat down and pulled an apple and a bottle of water from his backpack. We discussed the Jam. I said, "I'm so excited about it. Aren't you?"

"I've done this as I walked around, but just jumping over things here and there. Nothing like what they do in these groups," Greg informed me. He took a bite from his apple.

In the corner of my eye, I noticed Jacob and Juliet in line. I hollered at them, but it seemed the noise of the cafeteria made it difficult for them to hear me. Greg put his two fingers in his mouth and whistled. The sound made its way to everyone in the cafeteria. Once we had their attention, we motioned for them to join us. Greg moved over to my side of the table to allow them to sit next to one another.

Jacob let Juliet slide into the booth first. Juliet had a hot chocolate and Jacob a soda and a bag of Doritos. Jacob asked, "Aren't you both done with your classes for the day?"

Greg responded, "Ya, but we're heading downtown for a Parkour Jam. Do ya guys want to join us?"

"Oh no. I am nowhere near ready for that," Jacob announced as he threw his hands up and dramatically shook his head. "No way, no how," he advised us.

We all laughed.

Juliet patted his hand. She added, "I'm with Jacob. We've been working out, but we're still in no shape to attempt anything like that. I would like to join you for Parkour one day. If you don't mind?"

"I'd love that," I said. I looked over at Jacob and asked, "Perhaps we could introduce Jacob to it as well."

Greg interrupted the conversation by saying, "We need to get going if we're to be on time."

"Sorry guys, but that's my cue to leave," I said as I followed behind Greg, exiting the booth.

When we arrived, I was a little concerned because there were plenty of parking spaces. I thought we might be in the wrong place or the only ones to showing up. As we made our way to the primary area of the waterfront, we found a small group chatting. I noticed Gloria. She was in the middle of a conversation with a blond-haired man with glasses. Once there was a pause in her conversation, I tapped her on the shoulder. Gloria swung around and smiled. She quickly grabbed me and pulled me in for a hug. "I'm so glad you made it. Greg, you're here too. That's wonderful," she said before introducing us to her friend Chuck. "This is his first time, too," she explained.

A tall man interrupted our conversation. He asked if everyone was ready to head out. There were a few nods. He took off, and the group took off behind him. We followed behind those with experience. Gloria hung back with Chuck, Greg, and me.

We headed down toward the water. I looked ahead and saw the stairs. I picked up my speed to clear the jump down three gigantic steps. We made our way down the waterfront, avoiding pedestrians. Everyone jumped on or over many things as we made our way to the Louisville Belle. Then everyone reversed course and headed back. Chuck struggled a bit. I looked at Greg. Using telepathy, I told him we should stay and give Chuck moral support. He agreed.

"You're doing great," Greg said, slowing his pace down more.

"I need to stop," Chuck said, nearly out of breath. He stopped and looked like he was about to throw up.

Gloria and I stopped as well to catch our breath. Gloria looked over to check on Chuck. She asked, "Do you think he's going to be okay?"

I looked over. The green in his face seemed to lighten a bit. "He'll be fine. We may need to give him a minute," I assured her.

Gloria looked over and said, "Perhaps you're right. What do you think about the event? Will you do this again?"

Not wanting to offend her, I thought about how I could politely explain my opinion. "It was a good workout, but I must admit I expected more," I said honestly.

She smiled, "Oh, you want the hard-core jams. It's rare for them to have those in the winter. It's just too cold. Be patient, those are just around the corner." Gloria interlocked her arm in mine, and we walked over to check on Chuck.

Chuck seemed embarrassed. Directing his question to Gloria, he asked, "Do you mind if we walk for a bit?"

"No problem," she said with a smile. Gloria grabbed his hand.

It appeared this might be a new relationship. They need to be alone to get to know one another. I asked them, "Do you guys' mind if we continue on?"

"No. I'll see you soon," Gloria said with a smile.

Greg and I made our way back to the starting point where everyone was resting. We said our goodbyes and thanked them before heading home.

"I would describe this as a pleasurable distraction," I said as I got into the truck.

"I agree. I'm looking forward to the hard-core Jams Gloria mentioned," Greg said as he leaned in for a kiss. "Thanks for getting us signed up for this," he added.

I buckled up and started thinking about how wonderful the decision to move to Louisville was. My life was amazing. In such a short time, my life had changed for the better. I had not been here a year yet and I was a different person.

I joined Greg and his family for dinner but left soon after eating. I had neglected my homework long enough, and I had a lot to do tomorrow. Mentally, I needed to prepare for the delivery of the letters to the police departments.

# Twenty-Two

I woke up early with the intent of an early workout. Working out cleared my head, which I needed, to focus on my tasks for the day. I needed to be at Phillips before 10:00 am to unlock the door for Nadine and Eddie. I only had two classes. The first one was at 1:00 pm. I finished the assignment due today before heading down for breakfast. Phyllis was sitting on the sofa reading a novel. She looked for a moment and said, "There are blueberry muffins on the counter." Her gaze moved back to her book.

I went in and made myself a cup of coffee and grabbed a muffin before settling onto the bar stool. I pulled out my phone and began texting Mechelle. It had been too long since our last conversation. She texted me to tell me she had an early class and could not talk. *Lord, thank you for this food and please be with me today.* Trying to keep myself from overthinking everything, I tried to distract myself with social media as I enjoyed the muffin and warm coffee.

I cleaned up my mess before heading up to shower. As I got dressed, it hit me. We were nearly at the end of this story. The Granaldi's and Phillip could be locked away soon. I grabbed a set of latex gloves before heading over to Phillip's home. I wanted to arrive early in the event he was at home. It would give me time to stop Nadine and Eddie from going up to his home.

Upon arriving, the eerie sound of silence greeted me. It was strange being in his home alone. I took a quick stroll to confirm he was not at home before unlocking the door. I looked in my mirror to confirm I was invisible before sticking my head out the door to see if they were heading in my direction. They were nowhere in sight. *What time is it?* Without my phone, I needed a clock. I headed to the kitchen to check the clock on the stove. It was 9:54 am. I heard a door open and close quickly. I silently made my way toward the door and saw Nadine and Eddie in the foyer.

"Man, Phillip's got some coin. Look at this place," Eddie said.

177

"I'd say. Let's split up and find the room," Nadine instructed. Eddie headed toward Phillip's room. Nadine headed toward the spare room. I followed her.

She looked around and opened the closet and glanced inside before closing it. Nadine pulled a bag from her jacket pocket and shoved it under the bed. She practically sprinted back to Eddie. "It's done. Let's get out of here," Nadine said in a loud whisper.

Once they left the condominium, I locked the door and returned to my room. I changed my latex gloves and looked at the picture Jacob provided me of the New York District Attorney's office. I concentrated on appearing in his office by the corner window.

He was at his desk when I arrived. I stood there waiting for a chance to drop the letter off. I saw his business cards. *Steve Mishoe.* It had been nearly thirty minutes when a man entered the doorway and said, "Hey, Steve. Chief Rios is here. We're meeting in the conference room." Steve grabbed some papers from his desk and left his office.

*Lord, let this work.* I pulled the letter from the zip-lock bag and placed it along with the backup documents on the District Attorney's chair. I waited for Mr. Mishoe to return.

Nearly ten minutes had gone by when he returned to his office. He shuffled through a pile of paper on his desk. He appeared to be looking for something. *Look at your chair.* He grabbed another pile and went through it. Whatever he was looking for, he had not found it. He started looking around his desk. His eyes locked in on his chair. Steve walked over to his chair and picked up the pile of papers and read them. He hollered out the door for a person named Jackie. A short lady with wavy hair and brown eyes emerged.

She stood in the doorway and asked, "What's up?"

He inquired, "Who was in my office while I was gone?"

Looking confused, she responded, "No one. I have been at my desk the entire time. Why?"

"Get Detective Roberts down here," he demanded.

"What's going on?" she asked.

Annoyed, he said, "Just do it! Now!" He returned his eyes to the papers.

I knew he was taking it seriously. I smiled. *We got you, Phillip. One down, one to go.*

I returned home to grab the other papers and to get a good look at the photo of the Police Station in Florence. It looked like it might be a photo of the main lobby. This was going to be much more difficult because I did not know where to put the letter.

I took a deep breath and concentrated on being invisible before stepping into my full-length mirror. Several people surrounded me. I began eavesdropping on conversations to determine who was in charge. I was grateful the stone allowed me to understand everyone. A few officers walked toward a backroom. I followed them.

This room had many desks and a few officers. There appeared to be some administrative staff as well. The two officers I was following split up. One started talking with another officer about a drunkard throwing up on his shoe and in the back of his vehicle. *Gross.* The officer he was speaking to, started laughing at his coworker. Seeming to be annoyed, he retreated to a desk and began working on paperwork.

I looked around the room to determine who was in charge, but it appeared they were all equals. Moving down another hallway toward the back of the building, I discovered several offices. I dodged people as I made my way to what appeared to be a secretary with a desk in front of an office. The door to her right had a plaque that read, "Chief Bianchi".

I moved toward the door and popped my head through it to see if anyone was inside. Fortunately, the room was empty. I quickly made my way to his desk. I placed the letter and the backup documents regarding the Granaldis on the chair. I returned to the secretary's desk, to see if I could discover the whereabouts of Chief Bianchi. I found her speaking with an attractive officer. They appeared to be flirting with one another. After nearly 15 minutes of them complimenting one another, she sent him away. She claimed she was expecting the Chief.

I stood there for approximately 20 minutes more before I noticed the secretary seemed to change her posture as a gentleman in uniform approached. Once he was nearly at her desk, she opened the office door and let him inside. She had a pad and pen in hand as she followed him in and closed the door behind her. I walked through the door to see his reaction to the letter. He had not moved toward his chair and was telling her how annoyed he was with the results of a meeting. His secretary was taking notes as he instructed her to get an Officer Gentile to his office.

He continued telling her what else he needed as he made his way around his large wooden desk. The Chief noticed the papers in the chair and abruptly stopped speaking. He picked them up and began looking over them. He turned to the woman and asked, "Did you put this here?"

She moved next to him and reviewed the documents. She replied, "No. I've never seen these. It is in English. What does it say?"

"My English is rusty. Get me Sartori so she can translate it and get an evidence bag and some gloves," he ordered. He placed the papers back in his chair and checked the windows. He looked like he was checking it to make sure it was locked. His secretary returned after a few minutes and returned with a pair of gloves. "Office Sartori is going to bring an evidence bag with her," she advised him.

About ten minutes later, a female officer walked in with an evidence bag and some latex rubber gloves. She looked around the office and asked, "What's up, Chief?"

The chief put his rubber gloves on. He picked up the papers and walked them to the officer.

The officer, who was a rather small woman in stature, grabbed the papers. The Chief asked, "Tell me Sartori, what does it say?"

Officer Sartori began reading the detailed letter regarding Anthony Granaldi and his son's illegal activities aloud. She summarized the backup documents. Once finished, she looked up at the Chief. She asked, "Sir, this is about Anthony Granaldi. The Anthony Granaldi. This is not good, sir. Who sent this to you?"

Without answering her question, the Chief instructed, "Open the bag." The officer did as she was instructed. The Chief slid the papers in the bag and grabbed it from the officer. He sealed it. "I don't know, but if this is true, it will be the largest case of my career. Yours too," he said, taking a deep breath. He sat in his chair and rubbed his chin. The chief leaned back and appeared to be thinking.

The officer appeared to be reading the letter again. "Sir, there is a flower in the letter's corner. I'll have someone see if there is anything in the database about it," Officer Sartori said. She appeared to be waiting for a response.

"Because Mr. Granaldi has so much influence in Florence, we need to be careful who we trust," the Chief said. He paused and seemed to think again. The Chief took off his gloves and threw them in his trash. He picked up his phone and said to the person on the other end of the line, "Get me, Detective DeSantis, immediately."

The Chief looked up. He said, "I want you to check the database for the flower but make a copy. I don't want anyone other than you, me and Detective DeSantis seeing the evidence yet or even discussing this case with anyone. Granaldi might have people on our payroll. Perhaps that's why he has been so generous to the city." He picked up his pen and started tapping it on his desk. "I need you to stay late tonight. We need to find out as much as we can while there's less staff here. We need to fingerprint my office and see if there is any other evidence from the person who left these documents in my chair. I will help you."

Determining this was being handled well, I returned home to grab my backpack and head to class.

Just before entering the classroom, I texted the Bloom Keepers asking for a meeting. I sat in the room listening to my professor. As the minutes passed, I daydreamed about what was going on at both police stations. My instructor's voice sounded much like the teacher in a Charlie Brown cartoon. *Wah wah wah wah.* My desire to return to the Police Station and the District Attorney's office was distracting me. *Brooke, get your mind on your class.* I tried the best I could to stay focused. As soon as the class was over, I checked to see if anyone had responded, but no one had.

I made my way across campus to my other class. I scanned the grounds, looking for members of the Bloom Keepers. As a last resort before class started, I tried using telepathy. After several attempts, there was still no response. *They must be too far away.*

My second class did not start off much differently. I was not paying attention to the instructor and was merely watching the clock. That was, until the instructor put us into groups of five students. Each group would be given a different question. Everyone had to answer the question honestly. Without judgment, we had to listen to the answers and write a two-page paper on the exercise. The instructor handed our questions to a guy in our group wearing cowboy boots and a t-shirt.

He sat up in his chair and read the questions to himself before reading it to the group. He said, "Hey, I'm James. The question is, under what circumstances would you steal?" Everyone looked at each other to see who would answer first.

This question hit home. It did not appear anyone wanted to be the first to answer. I said, "This is an interesting question. People steal for a need or for greed. Some people steal and don't even realize they did it. See if you use a pen at the bank or a store to sign something and do not return it, you're stealing. For me, if someone had taken something cherished or valuable from me or a family member, I would steal it back to return it to its original owner."

James smiled and said, "I'd do that, too."

A thin girl with black curly hair looked over at me. She asked, "What's your name?

Feeling my cheeks get flushed, I said, "So sorry, I'm Brooke."

She smiled at me. She said, "Well, I'm Elaine. If it were a life-or-death situation and someone had something that would save a person's life. I would steal it to save another." Everyone seemed to agree that would be a good reason.

The large guy to her right had a mustache and turned to Elaine. He commented, "That's a noble reason, Elaine. I'm Howard. It's hard to say. I plan on being a police officer and it'll be my job to enforce the laws. I suppose I might do it to save a person, too."

The quiet African American girl added, "I'm Aaliyah. I've known some that steal for necessity. I suppose if I were poor, I would steal food or clothing to survive."

The remaining member of our group was a thin white man wearing ripped jeans and a t-shirt. He looked at each of us. "I'd steal from millionaires. They've plenty and should share it. I'd share it with those that needed it. Man, I'd be a modern-day Robin Hood," he informed us.

Looking annoyed, Howard asked, "What's your name, Robin Hood?"

"Sorry man, Tommy," he said as he looked as though he was about to fall asleep.

"Although I haven't intentionally stolen, I may have unintentionally snagged a few pens along the way. I listened to everyone's reasons and realized someone could easily sway me to steal even though stealing goes against everything I stand for. This really makes you think," Elaine elaborated before leaning back in her chair.

We continued discussing our answers until class let out. This made me think about the things I had done since becoming the protector of the Bloom of Dreams. I knew many of the things I had done would put me and others in prison, but to do what was right, sometimes the rules must be bent. Bending the rules was not something I liked to do. I think I needed to make sure the rules were bent only when necessary. I do not know how we could accomplish what we had if we had not done things, we knew were wrong.

As I exited the class, James stopped me. He asked, "Do ya think ya could read over my paper and give me ya opinion before I turn it in?"

"Only if you don't mind doing the same for me," I said with a chuckle. We exchanged email addresses and went our separate ways.

**JULIET:**     No rooms available at the library.

I went straight home to see if there was anything about the letters on the news or on the internet. No one was home. I ran up to the library and turned the news on. I grabbed my computer and started looking on the internet for news in New York City or Florence. I found nothing on either. *Why are they not arresting them?* I continued searching but knew in my heart nothing had been done yet. Mom sent Phyllis and me a text.

**MOM:**     I need to work late. I will not be home for dinner.

That was splendid news. I texted everyone to come over for pizza at 6:00 pm. I thought I heard something downstairs. Rather than run down, I opened the mirror and began looking in the rooms. I found Phyllis bringing in groceries. I quickly teleported myself to the kitchen to help her.

I startled Phyllis when I appeared. "Child, you scared me half to death," she said, trying to catch her breath.

"I'm sorry. I just wanted to get here quickly to help you," I explained.

"There's more in the car," she said as she began unpacking the items, she had brought in.

Without a jacket, I made my way to the trunk and collected the last couple of bags and headed back to the kitchen. The wind was up, which made the cold air feel worse. "It's so cold out there," I said, shivering.

As I was helping unpack, I remembered, "Just a reminder, mom will not be here for dinner, but the Bloom Keepers will be here at 6:00 pm. I'm getting pizza for all of us. You need to join us, being a member and all," I said with a smile. I added, "No, this is not an option." I giggled.

"Okay. I think they might want something other than pizza next time. I'm sure you have a lot to share with everyone and I want to hear about everything. Now get out of here. I've got work to do," Phyllis said.

As much as I wanted to tell her, I was going to save it for the meeting. I had work to finish. I went to my room to work on my psychology paper. As I began writing, I realized this was a fun assignment. The words seemed to flow out of me onto the paper. I had mine completed before James sent me his. It pleased me it did not take me that long to finish the first draft. After reviewing it one more time, I emailed my draft to James.

I would review his paper after the meeting. I headed out of my room and heard the television on in the library. Phyllis was curled up with a blanket, watching the news. I asked, "Anything good on?"

"Not really. There's an accident on the freeway holding up traffic," she informed me. She made room for me next to her under her blanket.

I curled up next to her and asked if she minded turning on the national news. I listened to the news as I scrolled through my phone to see if I could find anything about the evidence. It was nearly 6:00 pm when Phyllis asked, "Did you order the pizzas?"

I was so engrossed in finding the story; I had forgotten about them. I quickly got online and ordered a few pies. We headed downstairs to set the table. Everyone arrived on time and while we waited for the pizzas, I started the meeting. I informed them of all the events of the day. Everyone agreed to notify the group if anything about the cases was announced. After everyone left, I sent James my notes on edits to his paper and headed to bed. It had been a long day. I put my phone on silent, hoping to sleep in. The stress of the day wore me out and I dozed off soon after my head hit the pillow.

# Twenty-Three

I laid under a tree in a meadow watching a rainbow finch singing on a branch above me. There was a gentle breeze in the air that caressed my skin. I closed my eyes for a moment from the sun and heard the light buzzing of a bee. I did not see a bee, but the buzzing continued. *Where is the sound coming from?* I reached toward the sound. Suddenly awakened, I realized the sound was my phone vibrating on my nightstand. I rolled over, trying to ignore it. *I don't want to get up. Whoever you are, go away.* I tried to return to the peaceful meadow but woke up. That was when it hit me. I needed to check the news. I grabbed my phone and sprung out of bed. I had missed a call from Jacob. *Coffee. I needed coffee.* Heading toward the door... *No bathroom, then coffee.*

The coffee pot was off when I arrived, but there was a little left in the pot. I looked at the clock. It was nearly 10:00 am. I made myself a cup and while it warmed in the microwave; I called Jacob back. "Sorry I missed your call. I slept in."

He stated, "I have seen nothing on the news in Florence yet. Have you?"

"No, I need coffee before I can do anything," I said, trying to sound like a robot. I pulled my mug out of the microwave and added cream and sugar. "I'll let you know if I hear anything," I informed him.

I slowly made my way to the sofa in the sitting room, trying not to spill my coffee. I made myself comfortable before starting my search for news about Phillip or the Granaldi's. Still nothing. My desire to see how the cases were going, but I told myself to stay out of it. I cleared my mind by going for a run. As I enjoyed the crisp morning air, I tried to focus on the sounds of nature. I heard birds chirping, but the sounds of cars passing by quickly drowned them out. All the encounters I had with the Granaldis made me a stronger person. Blessed I survived the dangerous situations I had been in. Unharmed too. I had made it home and realized I had not seen Phyllis. I texted her to see what she was up to but heard nothing back from her. After showering, I headed downstairs to see if Phyllis was home yet, but she wasn't. Bored, I needed something to take my mind off the lack of news about the evidence.

I checked to see if James had sent me anything about my paper. He had. I read his email and reread my paper. He made some good points. Pleased with the changes, I submitted it through the online portal. I started another assignment. I was about two-thirds done with my assignment when an alert came across my phone. "Real Estate Mogul Arrested for Jewelry Heist." Immediately, I clicked on the alert, which brought me to a live news feed. "After obtaining a warrant, police arrested Phillip Davis today after detectives found $2,000,000 in stolen jewelry in his home."

*We did it. We really did it!* After jumping around my room like a crazy person. I forwarded the story to the other members of the Bloom Keepers. We had done it. I began jumping up and down again. I turned up the music on my phone and began dancing throughout the house. As I celebrated, I never heard Phyllis arrive. I leaped in the air when she tapped me on the arm and surprised me.

"Phyllis," I said cheerfully. My mind was racing, trying to get the words out. I jumped up and down as if I was on a pogo stick. "Phyllis. I've got good news," I said as I danced around the hallway.

"Well, spit it out, child," she said, annoyed by my behavior.

I handed her my phone and asked her to watch the video. I could barely compose my excitement at what she was watching.

She looked at me with such pride and said, "Wow! You did it!" We both began dancing and jumping around. "Your grandmother would be so proud of you, Brooke," Phyllis said, with tears developing in her eyes. She hugged me and told me she was proud of me, too.

We wanted to celebrate. I called mom and asked if we could take her to lunch. We met her at the Goose Creek Diner because it was close to her office. After the server took our order, I handed my mother my earbuds and asked her to listen to a video. She placed them in her ears and began watching. I anxiously waited for her reaction.

Mom covered her mouth in astonishment as she watched. She looked over at me and back at the video. Loudly she asked, "Is this true?"

I nodded with a big smile.

Mom was quiet for a moment. She seemed to be in deep thought. She turned to me and pointed to the Bloom of Dreams. "Phillip must think this necklace is valuable," she said.

"You're probably right," I said, knowing it was priceless. I knew I could not share the reasons he really wanted it, but I was glad we could rest easier at night knowing he was behind bars.

When Phyllis and I returned home from lunch, I surprised her with a quick visit to Italy. We exited my private room and headed toward the dining room. There were several groups playing cards, but we did not recognize anyone and continued our search. A large group, including several staff members, were watching the news in the lounge. I stepped in and noticed Leonardo, Isabella, and Kevin were among the group. I sat down next to Kevin and asked, "What's going on?"

He seemed surprised by my arrival. He asked, "Did you hear?"

Confused, I asked, "Hear what?" Isabella shushed me and Kevin pointed at the television.

"Police aren't providing many details but here is what we know; one or more members of the Granaldi family are being investigated. The police are currently searching Anthony Granaldi III's estate." The screen changed to a picture of numerous police vehicles at the front entrance of their home. Several officers were standing outside. The news broadcaster began speaking again, "Although police have not confirmed this, our resources stated, someone provided the police with an anonymous letter with details of their crimes. These crimes include grand theft and murder."

I wanted to scream from the rooftop. *We did it.* I covered my mouth in astonishment. We continued watching the news for a while but discovered nothing new. I looked around the room for William and Lainie. They were not here. "Kevin, please get your parents and meet me in my room in thirty minutes," I asked.

I headed over to Leonardo and Isabella and asked them to join me there as well in thirty minutes. I turned to Phyllis, who had been talking to Isabella, and asked her to follow me to my room.

As soon as we entered, I locked the door. "I'm going to get the Bloom Keepers here for a quick meeting. I would like you to be here when they arrive," I said.

"Not a problem," Phyllis said, as she made herself comfortable at the table.

I went back to my room and grabbed my phone and texted the group.

| | |
|---|---|
| **BROOKE:** | 911!! Need to pick you up. ASAP. |
| **GREG:** | Are you home? I can come right over. |
| **BROOKE:** | I will be in a few minutes. |
| **JACOB:** | We're in my car. |
| **JACOB:** | Juliet and me. |

I quickly popped into Jacob's backseat and said, "Hey guys!"
Juliet said, "Brooke? Hey, what's up?"

I looked around and noticed Jacob was parking at a shopping center. There was no one around. I quickly reached over the seat and grabbed both their hands and looked into the rear-view mirror and brought them to my private room in Italy. Without providing them an explanation, I left to get Greg.

I arrived in the downstairs hallway, next to the piano. I went to the kitchen to grab a bottle of water and waited for Greg. I had barely got the cap off when I heard him at the back door. I pulled him inside and locked the door. "Hang on," I spurted before opening the compact mirror and returning to join the others.

When we arrived, Juliet grabbed my arm. She asked, "What's going on?"

I took another gulp of my water. Took a deep breath before slowly exhaling. "Well, first off, welcome to Italy," I announced.

Jacob's face was that of shock. Frozen in his spot, only his eyes moving back and forth between Greg and me. His mouth was open wide.

Juliet looked around the room excitedly. "Seriously! We're in Italy," she said. She ran to the window, nearly tripping over Phyllis' foot to look outside.

I could feel how excited she was because I was about to burst with excitement myself. Trying to be a suitable host, I asked, "Would anyone like a drink or something?" I picked up the phone to call the front desk. Isabella answered. "Isabella, please send up 10 bottles of water. Oh, and you can come now." She assured me I would have the drinks shortly.

While we waited, I told them about the Villa Dianella and how Isabella and Leonardo had assisted my grandmother and me. Once they arrived, with Kevin and his family, I began, "I call the meeting of the Bloom Keepers to order." Everyone fell silent.

"Today, we've gathered here to bring those tasked with protecting the Bloom of Dreams together. We would like everyone tasked with its protection to become a member of the Bloom Keepers. The current membership includes Greg, Juliet, Jacob, and Phyllis. Phyllis has been protecting this stone with my grandmother Lillie for most of my grandmother's adult life. She has been on many adventures and can provide a great deal of knowledge about those after the stone," I said motioning for her to join me.

"She helped me learn how the use the power of the stone. Next are Greg, Jacob, and Juliet. Each of these members' lives was in danger because of being at the wrong place at the wrong time. At first, I was nervous about revealing my secret, but I had to reveal it to each of them to protect their lives," I said motioning for them to join me.

I continued, "It turned out to be a blessing. Jacob is extraordinary with his knowledge of computers and has helped us obtain evidence and information valuable to the safety of the Bloom of Dreams. Juliet is a sleuth when it comes to finding information. Her research has aided in the collection of evidence. Juliet also has some self-defense skills. She has mastered Kapu Ku'ialue, an ancient Hawaiian martial art. She is attempting to teach these skills to Greg, Jacob, and myself."

I walked over to Greg and put my arm around him and pulled him close. "Greg has had probably the biggest challenge. He's been teaching me karate and parkour. That's not where his skills end. Greg has rescued me many times and has been on nearly every escapade with me. Soon after receiving the stone, he began helping me protect the stone. He has kept me and the Bloom of Dreams safe," I said as I leaned over and gave Greg a quick peck.

"Now, for the newest members, we created the Bloom Keepers. We have vowed to protect the Bloom of Dreams, its secrets, and its members safe. None of us are to discuss Bloom Keepers information with outsiders. Unless, of course, it's life or death for someone

189

outside the group," I informed them. Knowing I cannot disclose the journal and my cousin's responsibility in keeping it safe, I continued, "My cousins William, Lainie, and Kevin. Our family has entrusted you with the protection of the stone as well. You've not only provided me with valuable information, but you have helped other members of our family. For that, I thank you," I said as Lainie blew me a kiss.

"Leonardo and Isabella, you both have become family. My grandmother has entrusted you with so much. You've also risked a great deal to keep her and me safe. I don't know how we could ever repay you. Your generosity is much appreciated. If there's anything I can do to help you, please let me know," I said, nearly in tears.

"Each person in this room has a certain skill set and a vast amount of knowledge that has helped us to protect the stone from my cousin Phillip and the Granaldi family. They're dangerous people. Thank you for everything. I believe Phyllis and I are currently the only ones in this room aware of what your hard work has done," I said, turning to Greg. I said to Greg, "Drum roll, please."

Greg pretended to play the drums and made his version of a drum roll with his mouth.

I concluded, "We've done it! Phillip and several Granaldi family members are under arrest!" I looked around at all the faces. They went from shocked to elated. "We don't have all the details yet, but the news stations are covering it. Leonardo and Isabella, do you think the chef could throw something together for our celebration?"

"Of course," Isabella said as they made their way toward the door. "Let's go help them get this party started," William said as he led the group down the hall toward the lounge.

Phyllis grabbed my arm and advised me, "We need to let your mother know when we will be home. She'll worry."

I said, "I'll go back and leave her a note." I informed Greg I would be right back.

I went back to my room in the Villa to teleport back to the pantry. Using Phyllis's pad on the counter, I wrote mom a note. Explaining Phyllis and I would not be home for dinner.

I popped into my room to grab my phone to text her the same message. I put my phone on the charger and returned to the lounge at the villa.

Just as everyone came into view, I stopped and took in the moment. I wanted to remember this forever. We, this group of people with little training, just took down a bunch of criminals. *Grandma, I hope I made you proud. Who am I kidding? I know she would be proud.*

I returned to my room before heading out to join the group. For hours, everyone got to know one another better. Everyone made sure not to disclose anything that might make the other guests curious about us. It would be easy for them to overhear our conversations. We just had a wonderful time. Isabella even put music on and several of us danced.

I did not want to take away from the fun of the evening, but there was still more work to be done. Kevin smiled as he watched everyone. I said to him, "You can finally go home."

"Yes, thank you for that," he said as he gave me a side hug. "Your friends are great." We looked over and saw Jacob's attempt to spin Juliet around on the dance floor.

I leaned over to him and whispered, "We need to make an addition to the log."

He pulled back and moved to look me head-on, and asked, "Really?"

"Yes, should we get your parents for this?" I asked as I glanced over at them, enjoying the party.

"No, they've turned this over to me now," he advised.

I pulled him away from the group, and we returned to my room. I grabbed his hand and took him to the secret room. It was exceptionally cold. I turned the light on, grabbed a pen, and took the journal from the safe. Beginning my journal entry by talking about the new skills I had acquired. Concluding with a brief comment about our adventure to protect the stone from Phillip Davis and the Granaldi family. It was doubtful we had heard the last of them. I looked over at Kevin, who was shivering on the bed. I asked, "Do you want me to take you somewhere to hide the journal?"

"No. It's safe here for now. Besides, it gives me a reason to return here," he said with a smile. I placed the journal back in the safe.

When we returned to the party, Greg was dancing with Phyllis. Everyone celebrated for about another hour. It was getting late here.

Lainie came over to Greg and I and said, "Thank you for bringing us here." She placed her hand on my cheek, "Lillie would be so proud of you."

Her comment brought a tear to my eye. I would love to hear my grandmother say those words to me. I missed her so much.

"It's late. Would you mind bringing us back home tomorrow? We still need to pack," Lainie asked.

"Of course," I said before she walked over to William. They left the party. I went over to the group and informed them we needed to head back to my private room. I could see the disappointment on their faces.

# Twenty-Four

Over the next few weeks, we discovered details about the cases, which included the charges each of them faced. It appeared Phillip and the Granaldis would be out of our hair for a long time. I was concerned about other Granaldi family members trying to get revenge, but for now, I was just going to enjoy my friends and work on my studies.

It was finally spring break. Greg and I headed to Florida to see Mechelle for a three-day weekend. She believed we were flying in and would pick us up at the airport. We checked the flights before arriving and made sure we arrived when the flight from Louisville landed.

I had been to the restroom at the airport many times and could bring Greg and I, along with our luggage, to the handicap stall. There was another woman there when we arrived. I waited for the coast to be clear to get him out of the stall. We quickly exited the restroom. A man sitting across from the bathroom noticed us and seemed surprised we both exited the lady's room. I paid little attention to him and continued to the area Mechelle was going to pick us up at. It was so nice not needing to pay for a ticket. As we made our way toward the door, I could feel the Florida sun penetrating through the windows into the airport. I stopped to text Mechelle.

**BROOKE:** Let me know when you're here. We are just inside the door at the arrivals entrance.

Mechelle called me immediately after I sent the text. She said, "I'm late. There is an accident on I-95. I will let you know when I reach the airport. This could take a while."

I filled Greg in on the situation. Knowing it could be a while, we found a bench near a baggage carousel. Passengers hovered like vultures looking for their belongings. I noticed the man that witnessed us exiting the restroom on the other side of the room. I found it odd he did not seem interested in looking for his luggage. It appeared he was staring at Greg and me. *Creepy.* I was now watching the man watching me. *This is crazy, Brooke. He's not an evil man, he's just a man that saw Greg and I exit a ladies room together. He probably thinks something occurred that didn't.* I snuggled up next to Greg and began talking to him about the many things I wanted him to see and do on our brief visit. I knew there would not be a lot of time for everything, but I hoped we could do some of the things on the list.

**MECHELLE:** I should be there soon.

Nearly everyone had retrieved their luggage and had left the area. Yet, that man was still there. I could not tell if he had a suitcase with him. Perhaps he was waiting on a ride as well. It had been about five minutes since Mechelle texted when we heard from her.

**MECHELLE:** I'm here. See you in a second.

"Come on Greg, she's here," I said, getting up and grabbing my suitcase. We made our way through the doors and into the Florida heat. I took a moment to enjoy the warmth, but my enjoyment ended quickly when the man from the bathroom bumped into me. As I turned toward him. I noticed him looking straight at my necklace. Nervous, I asked, "Did you see that, Greg?"

Confused, he asked, "See what?"

I watched the man get into a taxi. Seconds later, Mechelle pulled up and popped her trunk. Greg grabbed my bag and put the suitcases in her trunk, while I jumped in the front seat. I quickly greeted her but felt compelled to watch the taxi as it passed us. *Brooke, you need to relax.*

Greg got in the backseat. I introduced them as Mechelle pulled away from the curb. Mechelle started telling us about everything she wanted to do with us over the weekend. She wanted to have a cocktail party for us, but most of our friends were out of town or already had plans.

Confused, Greg asked, "Cocktails?"

Mechelle explained there was no alcohol. It was just sodas and appetizers for us and a few friends. I noticed a taxi on side of the road as we approached the intersection to leave the airport. When we passed it, I realized the person in the back seat was the man outside the restroom.

Mechelle turned her blinker on and moved to the right turning lane. I turned around and noticed the taxi pulling onto the road and moving into our lane. *Brooke, you're worried about nothing.* Mechelle talked about her classes and her assignments. She got off I-95 at the Southern Boulevard ramp and headed west toward Wellington. I glanced behind us and noticed the taxi was still heading in our direction. I needed to determine if he was following us. "Mechelle, pull into a gas station," I requested.

"Sure, there's one just before we get off at 441," she informed me.

Using telepathy, I started explaining the situation to Greg. He tried assuring me nothing was going on, but I was not so sure. She pulled up to a pump and said, "I might as well fill up." She got out to get gas.

I opened the door and noticed the taxi on the other side of the station. "Greg, look over there." I pointed in the taxi's direction.

"I must admit that's strange, but I can't see who is in the taxi from here," Greg said as he leaned back in his seat.

"I'm going to see if I can get a better view from inside the store," I said, getting out of the vehicle. Greg got out too. I looked back, and he took over at the pump. From the store, I still could not see the person well enough. The taxi looked like it was leaving, so I headed back to Mechelle's car. *I think I have lost my mind. Brooke, no one is following you. The stone has not warned you of any danger.* I had my guard up for so long, I forgot what it was like to just be me. It's decided, from this moment, I would just enjoy my time here in Florida with friends and hopefully a trip to the beach.

# Discover other titles by D.A. Dwinell

# Guardian of the Stone Series

Bloom of Dreams – Book 1
The Bloom's Cradle – Book 2
The Bloom Keepers – Book 3
Path of the Guardian – Book 4
Bloom of Secrets (Coming soon)

Connect with D.A. Dwinell
If you want the latest news on D.A. Dwinell
or are interested in connecting on social
media, please visit the following site:
www.facebook.com/DADwinell

www.ingramcontent.com/pod-product-compliance
Lightning Source LLC
Chambersburg PA
CBHW020620180626
46810CB00007B/2871